SOMETHING REAL

WENDY SMITH
ARIADNE WAYNE

Edited by
LAUREN CLARKE

Cover Design by
MOSS BOOK

All rights reserved. No part of this book may be reproduced or transmitted in any form, including electronic or mechanical, without written permission from the publisher, except in the case of brief quotations embodied in critical articles or reviews.

This is a work of fiction. Names, characters, businesses, places, events, and incidents are either the products of the author's imagination or used in a fictitious manner. Any resemblance to actual persons, living or dead, or actual events is purely coincidental. Ariadne Wayne is in no way affiliated with any brands, songs, musicians or artists mentioned in this book.

© Wendy Smith 2015

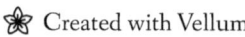 Created with Vellum

1

HE WAS HOT.

Dark hair and blue eyes, with those long eyelashes I could die for. A man in uniform? Who could resist that, right?

Except, he'd asked a question that made my head swim, my blood racing away to who knows where, leaving me unable to answer.

"Do you know where your children are?"

I gulped, my throat tightening at the question. "They ... they should be inside the house with Evan."

"Evan is ...?" He cocked his head. I'd just pulled into my driveway to find the police car parked by the garage. This wasn't good, whatever it was.

"Umm, my husband. Their father. Please, what's this about? What's happened?"

Panic grew inside me, my hands tightening into fists in response. I strained to catch a breath as the fear grew.

"I'm Officer Ben Parsons, Mrs Grant. We had a call from the school, and then from the day-care about Jack and Thomas. No one picked them up, and they couldn't get hold of you. They call us as a last resort. Who was supposed to collect them?"

Tears welled in my eyes, I didn't know whether out of fear for my children, or Evan.

"Evan was. He didn't let me know he couldn't pick them up, or I would have been there. I just changed jobs, I didn't even think about updating my contact details."

"No mobile?"

I nodded. "Yes, but the battery's dead. I didn't realise until I went to text my husband to say I'd be home late tonight."

He nodded, walking back to the car and opening the rear door. Jack came out first, followed by Thomas, and I dropped my shopping bags as they ran to me. A can rolled out of the bag and, under the car as I bent, hugging them tight, closing my eyes as I held my babies.

"I'm so sorry, officer. I thought Evan would have called me at work if he needed anything."

I picked up the bags, pushing the contents back into them. Tears were rolling down my cheeks in relief at my boys being okay. Hopefully Evan was too.

I stood, and Ben took the bags from my arms. "Let me take that. I'll come in and we'll have a chat with your husband."

Numb, I nodded as I led him to the door. I tried the handle first, but it was locked. *Weird.* Fishing the key out of my handbag, I slid it into the lock and turned. With a click the door opened and I stepped aside to let Ben go through first.

He looked around as I guided him toward the kitchen. "Doesn't look like your husband's here. How about I check around the hospitals, see if he's turned up at one of them?"

I poked my head in the bedroom door, checking if Evan had fallen asleep or something stupid like that. He hadn't done it before, but among all the other useless things he'd done, it was always a possibility.

The wardrobe door was open, as were all his drawers.

All his clothes were gone. My throat tightened at the realisation of what had happened.

"Bastard," I exclaimed, entering the room.

Ben followed me, seeing the state of the furniture. "That explains things," he said. He poked around in the wardrobe, as I scanned the room. Everything of Evan's was gone.

I looked up at him, sighing. "I guess you can see now what happened. He didn't even have the decency to tell me. And he's obviously decided he has no obligation to take care of our children."

He sighed. "Now I understand the circumstances. I just need a promise this won't happen again. I can put you onto some groups who might be able to help."

I shook my head. "I have no idea what I'm going to do, but no, nothing like this will ever happen again."

"Where's Daddy?" Jack asked, standing in the doorway.

"I don't know, sweetheart. But, how about we have some dinner and watch some TV before going to bed?"

Jack nodded. He was used to his father not being around all the time, though he'd always picked him up. Maybe the excitement at riding in the police car overrode any concern.

I led Ben to the door, and he smiled at me as he paused before getting into his car. "I'm really sorry to see what's happened, Mrs Grant. Have you got anyone to help you out?"

"I'll sort something out. Thank you so much for bringing them home."

"You're welcome. They seem like good kids."

I grinned. "They are. Take after me."

At that, he laughed and I felt Thomas tugging on my skirt as I watched the car back down the driveway.

"Police," he said.

"Did you have fun in the police car?" I asked, scooping him into my arms. He wrapped his little arms around my neck hugging me tight.

"Love you, buddy," I whispered, closing the door. Right now it seemed that the love I had for my children was all I had left.

ONE JOB—EVAN had had one job to do that day. The same *one job* he'd had for the last couple of years. All he'd had to do was pick up the kids from school and day-care respectively. Not that hard, I would have thought. Thomas had only recently started day-care to get him used to socialising. *One job.*

It hadn't helped that I was running late. I'd just received my first pay from my new, higher-paying job and stopped to get groceries before coming home. I'd even splurged a little, buying steak we previously couldn't afford, and still stashed in the car was a bottle of Moscato wine. That was my little reward for myself.

Exhausted, I went out to the car, retrieving the wine. As I steamed the potatoes to mash them I drank straight from the bottle, not wanting to think about the whole screwed up situation. I could drink the whole bottle, but the thoughts wouldn't go away.

With Evan gone, my entire pay rise would be wiped out with increased childcare costs. There wasn't a hope in hell of support; he'd barely worked in the years we'd been together. Clearly he had found someone else to leech off.

Tipping the potatoes into a bowl, I took out the potato masher and began to thump them into submission. With a bit of milk and butter they complied, but the tension released in that simple act flowed out of me, giving me that tiny bit of satisfaction of winning at something.

I plated the food for the kids, taking it out to the dining table where they waited patiently.

"Where's Daddy?" Jack asked.

"I don't know, baby."

He frowned. "He's naughty."

"Eat your dinner, honey. It's getting cold."

I didn't know what to say to him, I didn't know how to feel myself. Evan and I had once hit rock bottom, to the point where I hadn't wanted to continue, but I'd kept going for Jack and Thomas. But, I thought we'd turned a corner the previous night when after all this time together, he'd shown me more appreciation than he had in years.

When the boys were tucked up in bed, I sat back, swigging the last of the wine out of the bottle on the couch, turning on the television for company and closing my eyes.

Tears rolled down my cheeks, but not because of Evan's treatment of me. He'd been taking me for granted for years and I knew it. I had been the one who took care of everything, the one who worked for everything, and none of it had ever been good enough. I just never thought he would hurt our children this badly. Clearly, he didn't even care.

Our relationship had been built on necessity rather than passion; I always knew that. Whatever he'd felt for me at the start had deteriorated pretty quickly. He'd taken responsibility when I'd become pregnant with Jack, but truth be told, he was a shitty husband, and an even shittier father.

And yet, I still felt his touch from last night, when I thought we'd started something new. When he'd climbed into bed with me and loved me the way he once had, all tender strokes and kisses that lit a fire in me that I'd thought long since extinguished.

"I love you, Olivia," he'd said.

And I'd been dumb enough to believe him.

2

THE NIGHT *before* I'd come home as usual, and cooked the kids' dinner. We had some chicken pieces in the freezer and I crumbed and baked them with creamy mashed potato and vegetables. It was basic and didn't cost a lot, but my boys loved it, and so did Evan.

Normally he'd have dinner with us and then go out. He'd come home any time of the evening, and there were times when I'd been sure I'd smelled perfume on him, but I didn't have the energy or inclination to fight. I was so busy with work and children and the house, on automatic pilot all the time.

After dinner, I'd dressed the boys for bed, and they'd brushed their teeth before I snuggled them in under their blankets, read them a story, and kissed them goodnight.

I'd not expected to find Evan still there and sitting at the dining room table, watching as I crossed the room.

I stood at the kitchen counter, running the water to wash the dishes.

Dropping the dinner plates into the sink, I picked up the dish brush to clean. He came up behind me, and I breathed in his scent as he wrapped his arms around my waist. This was different; Evan rarely showed any affection, and intimate contact was usually initiated by me.

"What have you done?" I asked.

"Can't a man hold his wife?" he whispered in my ear. He wore the musky aftershave the kids had bought him last Christmas. I recognised it because I liked it so much; I'd never expected him to wear it, though.

"It's not like you, that's all."

He grazed my neck with his lips, and for the first time in what felt like forever, tingles grew over my neck and arms, growing in intensity as his hands roamed my body.

"Evan. What's going on?"

He released me, and I turned around, brush still in hand. Evan took the brush from me and threw it in the sink.

His mouth claimed mine as he pressed me against the counter, raising a hand to one of my breasts, stroking it.

My breathing grew heavier. Maybe our relationship had been crappy lately, but my body still reacted to his. We'd been together for so long, there was nothing that we didn't know about one another. He knew just which buttons to press to get me going.

"Evan," I whispered.

"Forget the dishes. Let's go to bed."

I followed him, and he held my hand all the way to the bedroom. He was so tender, touching me as he had never done before, as we made love. Nothing like the frantic sex we'd had when we were younger, the crazy back seat rushed job that got us into trouble in the first place.

He fell asleep curled up around me, his nose against my cheek as I laid on my back and stared up at the ceiling.

Was this a turning point? It had seemed for so long that we were just cruising, waiting for an ending as it couldn't go on forever. The feelings I'd thought were dead had been revived in just one night.

He'd grazed my breasts with his teeth, and I smiled at the mark he'd left that would leave me with the memories of this night.

The candle, so close to being extinguished, ignited at his touch. For the first time in forever, I felt loved.

He woke me in the morning with kisses, just before the sun came up. Another half hour and I'd be out of bed and getting our children ready for school and day-care, dropping them off on my way to work.

"What's going on?" I whispered. He hadn't been like this our entire relationship, not even at the beginning when we were two awkward kids trying to work out what to do.

"I love you, Olivia," he said, his eyes so dark in the half-light.

My heart flipped as he kissed me again, his tongue dancing with mine as he stroked my body, and I was like putty in his hands as we made love again.

Later I stood at the stove, flipping pancakes for breakfast. The boys were out of bed and playing in the living room and I never heard a thing as he came up behind me again, his hand landing on my inner thigh as he reached between my legs.

"What is it with you?" I laughed, as he kissed my neck.

"Just loving my wife. I think she deserves it."

SLEEPING ALONE WAS WEIRD, even though I'd done it a million times before while Evan was out God knows where, doing God knows what. Waking alone was awful.

Thankfully, it was Saturday, so I had the weekend to prepare for Monday. Our drop-off routine could stay the same, but I'd have to speak to my boss about finishing early until I could shuffle the hours around at day-care.

I left the kids eating breakfast in front of cartoons while I took a closer look at what Evan had taken. His side of the wardrobe was completely empty, and my suitcase was gone too. I guess he needed the baggage.

Sighing, I caught a glimpse of my jewellery box out of the corner of my eye. It wasn't sitting the way it normally did, on the top right hand corner of my bedside cabinet. I shifted it back into place before lifting the lid. I didn't have much: a few things he'd given me over the years and my new pride and joy, a silver bracelet from my old work place. My leaving gift.

The box was empty. It wouldn't have been worth much, but my workmates had thought enough of me to give it to me the bracelet as a gift. It might be new, but their kindness gave it sentimental value.

Pain and anger growing in my chest, I picked up the box and slammed it against the wall. Jack appeared in the doorway, Thomas trailing behind.

"Mummy? You okay?"

I sat back on the bed. "Come on you two."

Jack jumped up on the bed with great gusto. Thomas tried to climb and I slid my arm around him, pulling him up beside me.

"Daddy's gone," Jack said.

"Yeah, looks like it buddy."

Thomas snuggled into me. At three, he probably had no idea what was going on, only that Mummy was sad. I closed my eyes as Jack snuggled in to my other side. At least my babies were safe.

Mid morning, I picked up the phone as I sat on the couch. It was best to try to sort out the work situation before Monday, and not just dump it on my boss. I prayed she'd be understanding.

I flicked through my phone. Missed calls from my best friend, Donna, but none from Evan when he hadn't picked up the boys.

Rebecca had called me herself to let me know I had the job. Her number was near the top, and I pressed dial, holding my breath.

"Rebecca Wallace."

"Hi Rebecca, it's Olivia,"

"Olivia? Is everything alright?"

I guess calling the boss on the weekend when you've just completed your first week of work is a bit unusual.

"Not really. It's not work-related. I've had somewhat of a crisis at home." The tears were coming again at having to explain what had happened when I couldn't even process it.

"You don't sound good."

"I didn't want to lay this all on you, but my husband left me last night." Here I was, crying down the phone to a woman who was still a stranger.

"Oh, God. Are you okay? Do you have someone with you?"

"I have my boys." I sniffed. "That's why I'm calling you. I need to sort out after-school care and changing day-care hours, but I'll need to finish work early for at least the next few days until I've organised it."

"Of course. Anything you need. I'm so sorry, Olivia. If you need anything else, just call me, okay?"

"Thank you," I whispered.

"No problem. I don't know you well, but he's an idiot."

I laughed through my tears. "Thanks."

I breathed a sigh of relief as I hung up the phone. At least that was sorted. I could call Donna. Her boyfriend, Craig, was one of Evan's friends, and over the years we'd bonded. But she'd always said I was too good for Evan, and I couldn't deal with the 'I told you so' she'd inevitably come out with.

I couldn't handle her today.

3

MONDAY DROP-OFF WENT FINE. Jack's before-school carers were more than happy to change his hours for the following week, leaving me with five days of early pick-ups. I could live with that.

Thomas was a bit teary, but that had been normal lately. I hated leaving him as much as he hated me leaving, but I had to work to support us, even more so now. There was a full-time position he could slot into, so at least that was sorted.

The sympathy I got everywhere I went was amazing. There was no hiding what Evan had done, and if anything, it helped get things sorted for the following week. The feeling of relief was immense.

And then I went to work.

I sat at my desk, staring at the papers, wondering where to start. I'd finished the week before feeling so organised, having a plan for this week, but the events of the weekend had been such a distraction, I felt as if I were starting all over again.

I'd been sitting there for around half an hour when Rebecca came by. I'd liked her the moment I met her in the interview, and we'd really seemed to click. I struggled to get myself together in the mornings, but she always looked immaculate: brown hair with perfect big curls, and lacquered nails that changed colour seemingly every couple of days. Today, they were blue.

"How are things going?" she asked.

"Good. I'm just working through these files I started on Friday. The system is similar to what I used in my last job, so learning it isn't proving to be too taxing."

She sat on the corner of my desk, frowning.

"I'm not talking about work. I'm talking about you."

"Me?"

"I haven't told anyone else what happened, but I was concerned that you didn't have anyone with you."

I shrugged. "To be honest, I do have a close friend I could have called. But she's been telling me forever how Evan wasn't good enough for me. I couldn't face her."

She smiled, nodding. "I get that. As long as you're going to be okay."

"I'll get there. I've got childcare sorted out for next week, so I'll just have to finish early this week. I'll be happy to work out a way to make up the time."

Rebecca shook her head. "It's fine. I think you have a pretty good excuse. I had a breakup recently too—spent days away from work. I can't even imagine what it's like with children."

"One of them is too small to really know what's going on." I held up the photo of my boys that I had on my desk to show her. "We'll get there. To be honest, I did most things myself anyway."

She laughed. "Good luck. I'll leave you to it."

I sighed when she was out of sight. It was so good to have a boss who cared and understood. My old workplace wouldn't have been as accommodating. Guess I lucked out.

Just before school was due to finish, I stood outside the gate waiting for Jack to come out. No one noticed me, even though I felt like the odd one out. Evan had been the one who always did the school run in the afternoon. Always the one at home while I worked, it was the one thing he did to help out.

The more I thought about that, the more it angered me.

"Olivia."

I looked up, and saw Craig coming towards me. Of course he would know by now; Evan had no doubt told his friends, even if he hadn't bothered to tell me.

"Hey, Craig."

His face was flushed, as if he'd been running. "I'm glad I caught you. I wanted to see how you were."

I shrugged. "I'm alive."

He sighed. "I know what you mean. This whole thing has been a bit of a shock. How are you and the boys holding up?"

In the distance, I could see Jack skipping happily along with his little friends, and I couldn't help but smile at how he was just getting on with things. The way we all needed to.

"Olivia?"

"Oh. The boys are a bit confused, but we just have to deal. I'm sorry I haven't called Donna. Dealing with changing day-care hours has been enough to keep me pre-occupied."

I looked back at him. His jaw had dropped and he was gaping at me as if I were the biggest idiot in the universe. "Craig?"

"Shit. I thought you knew."

"Thought I knew what?"

"Donna left me for Evan."

My anger burned all the way home. Thomas and Jack laughed and joked in the back seat as we weaved our way through the traffic, and all I could think about was Craig's bombshell.

All the times that Evan had been so cruel about Donna. All the times I'd defended her because she was my friend and I was often the only one in the group apart from Craig who gave a crap about her feelings.

Craig had adored her, spent years telling his so called friends to back off and leave her alone. And now she had left him for someone who had called her so many nasty names. The same asshole who thought it was okay to abandon his wife and children without a word.

I was fuming by the time we got home, and I bashed and thumped my way around the kitchen as I threw something together for dinner.

Bastard.

All I'd ever done was try to love him and our children. Ever since we were teenagers, wrapped up in each other, it had just been me with Evan.

And despite our relationship not working that well, we'd kept things together when I fell pregnant with Jack, and then again when Thomas came along. I should have seen it coming.

BY THE END of the week, I was saddened at the thought of not having the extra time with the boys anymore. Even the couple of hours more we'd had a day had been fun for all of us. Every night was camp-out night as they cuddled up in bed either side of me. There was no point making them move to their own beds.

On Friday, I went for the last of the school pickups, and spotted Donna somewhere behind Jack as he ran out the gate and into my arms. Turning towards the car, I set off at a brisk pace, with Jack running along behind me.

"Mum, slow down. You're going too fast," he said.

"Sorry, sweetie. I just want to get to day-care to get Thomas."

When we got to the car he mucked around, fidgeting as he climbed his car seat, his hands getting in the way of me buckling him in. "Come on, baby. We have to get going."

I turned as I closed the door, just in time for Donna to reach the car. She was panting at the effort to get to us in time, and grinned at me.

"Olivia, wait," she said, bending to catch her breath.

"I don't have time for this, Donna. I have to go and get Thomas from day-care."

She looked up at me. "I wanted to check and see if we were okay."

All around us people were walking to their cars, but I couldn't help it. After what Craig had told me, I wasn't about to be civil.

"Why the fuck would we be okay, Donna?"

She chewed her lower lip. "I just thought that if Evan explained everything to you, that you would be able to move on. I mean, I'm really sorry; neither of us wanted to hurt anyone."

"Explained everything? Donna, if that's what he's told you then he's lying to you too. Good luck with that."

I went to walk around the car, and she grabbed my arm.

"What do you mean? He said he talked to you and you were okay. It's not like you were really together."

My anger spilled over, and I pulled my arm away. "He told you that?" My voice rose in volume and I couldn't control it. "Did he also tell you that when he left, he didn't even have the decency to let me know that he wouldn't be picking up the kids, and I came home to the cops in my driveway? The school and day-care both called them as a last resort because Evan didn't give enough of a shit to take them home."

She frowned, her brow wrinkled in confusion. "That's not what he said."

"I don't give a crap what he said. My reality is that my husband left me without a word. He just took his stuff and left when I wasn't home, leaving me to pick up the pieces. Same as always."

"But Olivia ..."

"There are no *buts*, Donna. He is reckless and irresponsible, and you are welcome to him. Don't ever talk to me again."

I walked around the car, opening my door. "And for the record," I yelled, "he fucked me the night before he left, so don't tell me we weren't really together."

She paled at the words and I grinned, sitting down and slamming the door. To hell with her and everyone else. I would take care of my boys and me, no matter what.

"Mum? Are you okay?" Jack's voice from the backseat made me cringe. He would have heard every word.

"I think we should stop and get ice cream on the way home. What do you think?"

I looked at him in the rear-view mirror. His face had lit up at the thought of the treat that was usually forbidden.

"YAY! Can Thomas have some too?"

That was my boy, always thinking of his little brother. Both of them were so sweet.

"Of course. I think we should all have some. Maybe we can sit down by the beach and watch the sun go down with fish and chips and ice cream."

"Can we find a playground?"

I laughed. "Sounds good to me. Let's go get your brother."

4

THAT NIGHT I sat on the couch, watching a movie with the boys, eating popcorn as the day turned to dusk outside. The front door handle rattled, and then there was silence before it rattled again.

Thump, thump, thump.

"What the hell, Olivia? Let me in."

I went to the front door and opened it to find Evan, red-faced and fuming on my doorstep. He hadn't told me he'd left, I hadn't told him I changed the locks.

"What do you want?"

"I need to grab some things I forgot. I left my razor in the bathroom."

I took a deep breath. "The electric one? The one I gave you for your birthday."

"Yeah."

"Can I have my bracelet back first?"

He froze, his eyes roaming my face, but I wasn't going to give an inch.

"I don't know what you're talking about."

"The new bracelet I was given. It's gone from my jewellery box. In fact, everything is gone."

He shuffled from foot to foot, looking at the ground. "Maybe one of the kids took it out."

"Cut the crap, Evan. Let me guess: you've already given it to Donna."

I heard him swallow, hard, his Adam's apple bobbing in his throat. That was exactly where it was.

"Why did you change the locks?" He looked back up at me, narrowing his eyes.

"Are you for real? You. Left. Thankfully, the police were available to pick up our children from school and day-care because you fucked off."

His jaw dropped, and he gaped at me while my frustration grew. Prickly heat traversed my body, building up in my chest. He'd never seen me this angry, but then I'd never been in this position before. Being deserted—our children being deserted.

Do you even give a crap?

"I thought they'd just call you."

"I hadn't updated my contact details. Sure, I should have done that, but you should have been there. You're their father."

Tears rolled down my cheeks. Not for me; they'd never be for me, no matter how tender he'd been with me the night before he'd left. All for my boys.

"Why? Why her?" My voice croaked as I said the words, but I couldn't help it.

"Can I come in, Liv? I don't want to stand out here."

"No."

The taste of iron filled my mouth as I bit down too hard on my lower lip, steeling myself to fend him off.

"Jack? Are you there, Jack? Daddy wants to see you," he called over my shoulder.

"Fuck you," I murmured.

"Mummy?" Jack's voice came from behind and I closed my eyes at the sound.

Please don't let this get nasty.

"Jack," Evan said warmly.

Two small hands grabbed onto my waist, and I turned my head to see my eldest boy glaring at his father.

"You left me at school."

Evan frowned. "I know, buddy. I thought Mum would get you."

"The policeman did. It was *your* job." He was insanely stubborn, and I could already tell Evan wouldn't get anywhere with him.

"Buddy ..."

Jack let go, running back inside the house.

"You can't stop me from seeing him," Evan said.

"I'm not going to try. But, it'll have to be somewhere other than here."

He rolled his eyes, turning on his heel. "See you in court, then."

They were empty words and I knew it. He didn't have the money or the inclination to take me to court. That would be far too much effort. Even if he did, I had the advantage.

And it was true. I wasn't going to stand in the way if he wanted to see his children. But I'd had enough of running around after him.

AFTER THE BOYS were in bed I started sorting through our things. Whatever I could sell without causing us discomfort, I would. I'd been in a position where I could start building a nest egg for emergencies. Now, more than ever, I needed one.

First thing in the box was Evan's electric shaver. He'd barely used it. No doubt Donna wanted him clean-shaven. Well, tough shit. He'd have to buy disposable razors or go without.

There were boxes of his things, and I shoved those in the back of the garage. If he wanted them, he could come only as far as there to get them.

As I worked, I built a pile of things I could sell. Furniture I'd replaced but not thrown out; things we just didn't need. It was cathartic just to throw some of the accumulated crap out. Things that reminded me of my life with him.

As much as I had pangs for him, that last night still fresh in my mind, I needed to made a break from the past. There was no turning back now. Tears hung around my cheeks as I dug through boxes, all those memories.

My marriage was over. Time for the new.

Then I found it. Right at the bottom of a box was something long-forgotten, something that had once meant so much to me, but had been set aside with the birth of Jack.

I'd written a book while in high school, and as far as I'd been concerned at the grand old age of seventeen, it was the best thing ever written. I had been going to submit it to a publishing company, make a squillion dollars and be the most famous person who ever lived.

And then I'd discovered I was pregnant.

In an instant all my dreams went out the window as I struggled with my changing relationship with Evan, my mother throwing me out, juggling working and pregnancy and starting a new life.

I flicked through the pages, memories of the hours I'd spent on it flooding through my mind. It seemed so long ago.

Maybe I should submit it somewhere.

But where?

It was time to call it a night. The living room was a mess of emptied boxes, and I didn't care.

What I wanted to do was to curl up in bed with my book and read, see what my seventeen-year-old mind had come up with. While I'd stopped writing, I'd never stopped reading, and I was sure there were a thousand ideas stashed away in my brain.

Maybe it was time to coax them out.

IN THE MORNING, I called a pawnbroker and arranged an appointment for him to assess the things I'd set aside. Nothing like getting on with your life.

Three hours later, a battered old van pulled up in the driveway making a loud rattling noise, and the boys squealed, not knowing whom it was.

I laughed at their reaction as I got to the door. "Shhh." I put my finger to my lips as I pulled on the door handle.

The man on the other side was as weathered as the van he drove. A long wispy beard couldn't cover the smile he had on his face.

"Olivia Grant?"

I nodded. "You must be Mr Johnson."

He handed me a wrinkled business card. It looked older than I did.

"Call me William. I understand you have some things for me to look at."

I nodded, opening the door wide for him to make his way through. The boys hid behind me, one on each side.

Thomas's eyes opened wide. "Are you Santa?"

My jaw dropped. "Oh my God, I'm so sorry, Mr Johnson."

His eyes twinkled as he looked between my little boy and I. "Don't worry about it. Sometimes I help out at the local shopping mall at Christmas time." He winked at Thomas. "Santa has to have lots of helpers."

Santa better have some money for us then.

"I've moved all the things I'm getting rid of into this room, if you could have a look through and tell me what you think I can get for them?"

He grinned. "Of course, Mrs Grant."

I chewed on my lower lip while I watched him examining everything. I don't know why I was so nervous; I think it was just that the more money I got for these things, the better it was for us. I had plans for some of it, and the rest would be put in the bank. Now I was by myself, if anything went wrong I was the one who had to take care of everything. And I couldn't do that with no savings.

The whole time he scribbled on a notepad, making notes.

After about half an hour he presented his list to me, and my jaw dropped at how much he was offering.

"If I were you, I'd get a second opinion on that dressing table. Just to check what I think it's worth. Everything else is straightforward, but that is a much older piece of furniture and solid oak. Given a bit of a clean up, that'll be worth a lot to someone."

I was touched. He could have offered me anything for it and I'd have been none the wiser. I'd taken that with me when I'd moved out of Mum's, and if I'd known it was valuable, I would have sold it years before.

Tears rolled down my cheeks before I even noticed, and I nodded. "Thank you so much."

"If you like, I can pay you for the other things and take them off your hands today. Just let me know about the other piece."

I had no words, just nodded at him again. He patted me on the shoulder. "I'm glad you called me. A lot of others out there would have paid you barely anything and taken it off your hands without saying a word. I haven't stayed in business this long by being dishonest."

"You are Santa," I said, laughing.

BY THE END of the week, I had another company in to value the dresser. This guy was humourless, and dressed in a suit and tie. I much preferred Santa.

He spent half an hour just looking at the piece of furniture, not giving anything away, until he handed me a piece of paper with a figure on it. A figure that was half of what Mr Johnson had offered me.

"Seriously?" I asked.

"It needs a lot of work." That was all he said, and I sighed as he just stood, staring at me.

"No thanks."

The first sign of emotion: he frowned. "It's a very good price, Mrs Grant."

"What makes you think that?"

His lips twitched, and his eyes flashed with annoyance. "You won't get any better."

"How about double?"

He stifled a sigh, and I smirked as I knew I had him.

"I could add another couple of hundred maybe, but I really don't think I can ..."

"Oh well, thanks for your help. I think I'll take up the other offer I have."

"Other offer?"

I pulled out the piece of paper Mr Johnson had given me with the much higher figure written on it.

Now I had him. His eyes nearly burst when he saw what I had, and he took a deep breath. *Gotcha.*

"I didn't realise I was doing a comparison quote."

I cocked my head, trying to look as innocent as I could. "Does it really matter?"

His lips pursed as he continued to look a the number on the paper.

"I mean, how much do you really want it? If you don't, then I'll just call my other contact and let him have it."

And that was how I got an extra thousand dollars for a piece of furniture I'd thought was worthless. It was such a relief to have the money. Now, to spend a little and make a new life.

We drove halfway across town to a computer store. I'd learned what I could in my last job. In the absence of IT staff, I was literate enough to understand some specifications when we'd had to buy new equipment or hardware.

The salesman looked bored, fiddling with his tie and looking at his watch as if he didn't want to be there.

"I need a laptop," I said.

"What are you looking for? There are quite a lot to choose from."

No shit, Sherlock.

"I don't want anything too extravagant. I don't have a huge amount of money. Just something I can use the Internet on and write with."

He nodded, still looking at me as if I were an idiot.

"Look. Something that isn't going to be so slow I'll want to punch it, but not top of the line."

"Can we play games on it?" Jack asked.

"Maybe basic things. It's not really for that, honey."

The salesman steered me to one in the corner, and I started clicking on things, while he stood, tapping his foot impatiently.

"Are you supposed to be doing that?" Jack asked.

"They're for demonstration, so why not?" I asked.

I loaded up the web browser and waited. And waited. The programme was showing no signs to coming up, and that was before we even got to look at the internet.

"Yeah, no. I want something better than this."

Our of the corner of my eye, I caught the salesperson rolling his eyes. I let out a loud sigh. "Let's go somewhere else."

I turned to go, and as I was leaving spotted a woman on the other side of the room, talking a million miles a minute at the salesperson she'd ended up with. His eyes were darting around as she threw acronyms and technical words at him. It would appear that she was schooling him. All with a baby on her shoulder.

By her side was a dark-haired little girl, and Thomas's eyes widened at the sight of her. He tugged at my sleeve. "Mummy, that's Mia."

"Who's Mia?"

"She's at day-care sometimes."

I smiled at him. "Do you want to say hello to her?"

He nodded enthusiastically. "Is that your girlfriend?" Jack asked.

Thomas frowned, probably not really understanding what Jack was asking. "Yes." He pouted.

I chuckled. "Come on then. From the looks of it, her mother can help us find what we're looking for."

We walked away, leaving the salesperson standing there beside the slow computer he'd tried to sell me.

"Mia!" Thomas called out.

The little girl looked at him and grinned.

"Who's that, sweetie?" her mother asked.

"Thomas. From day-care."

I drew closer, and smiled at the woman. "Thomas recognised Mia from across the room. I'm Olivia," I said.

"Rowan. And this is Charlie." She turned so I could see the baby.

"Nice to meet you. Say, you seem to know what you're talking about. Could you help me find a laptop? If you've got the time, that is."

She eyed the salesperson smugly. "I'm sure I can do that. I'm after a new one, too. Maybe they'll give us a discount if we buy two."

The man fidgeted, looking up at the ceiling. I couldn't see a discount coming, but I could see how uncomfortable we were making him.

I think I loved her. It was clear her knowledge was superior to these young guys they'd employed, and she went on to ask a whole bunch of questions that I had no idea about.

When she'd made her selection, she smiled at me. "So, what are you after?"

"Nothing expensive. Something that will let me write documents and use the Internet. Something fast enough that I won't want to punch myself in the face using it."

Rowan laughed. "Oh, you need something like this." In an instant she pointed me in the right direction and I reached for the laptop in question, clicking on the web browser that sprung open as soon as I clicked it.

"That is so much better than the one he was trying to sell me."

"I come here for the pricing, not because they know what they're doing," she murmured.

I laughed out loud, managing to get sideways looks from the salesmen.

She looked down at Jack and Thomas. "How exciting, Mum getting a new computer."

Charlie made a squeaking noise and she patted him on the back. "We'll be on our way home very soon, sweetheart."

"I'm sorry to have held you up," I said.

Her hazel eyes widened. "No, don't worry about it. I'm happy to have helped."

She made her purchase and Thomas and Mia waved at one another as they left. I turned back to the salesperson.

"That one, please." I pointed at the one Rowan had recommended.

Job done.

5

TAKING the laptop out of the box, I had a child on either side of me, jumping up and down with excitement. It felt so good to have something new that was all ours.

As I started it up and worked through the setup, their enthusiasm waned and after a while I realised I was sitting there alone while they'd grabbed a book and were sitting on the couch.

"Done," I said as it finally loaded.

All of a sudden I had my audience back as two very excited little boys were back with me. I'd bought a couple of games I'd been told would work on it, and I would use it after they went to bed. They could have a turn first; they deserved something new too.

"One day we'll have enough to have a computer each. Right now, we have to share," I said.

They nodded in unison. I'd always loved that they were so close.

It set them in good stead. Now they quietly took turns at the Lego game we'd bought, one cheering on the other. I'd never been more proud.

"Maybe next we get a console. Then you can have a controller each," I said quietly.

When they went to bed, I sat staring at the screen. Something in me wanted to write, but what should I write?

And then it happened. A tsunami of words washed over me as I began to type. Overwhelmed by recent events, the story of Evan and my relationship hit the screen.

The more I wrote, the more outraged I became. I'd been his doormat for so many years. He'd always treated me as if he were some kind of trophy, that I wasn't quite worthy, but somehow I had kept him. But now I saw who he really was. A selfish, lazy man who hadn't been worth it. I'd given him and our family everything I'd had. He'd taken it all and still hadn't been happy.

I looked at the time. The boys had been in bed since 7.30 pm and it was now 10.25pm. Three hours had flown by and my recount of my story had only just reached the point where I'd discovered I was pregnant with Thomas.

My face was wet with tears, as I read over the words. Seeing the cruelty I'd endured for all this time in words on the screen was unlike anything I'd ever experienced. How had I not seen our relationship for what it was?

I loved my sons more than anything else in the world. Evan had used me, exploited me for everything he could get.

And then he'd left.

I tilted my head, looking at the screen as I pondered what I'd written. Could I turn it into a story for publication? Where, God knew, but I'd cried the whole time writing it. Surely someone else would feel that emotion, relate it to his or her own experience. Maybe I could help someone stuck in a similar situation recognise it for what it was.

At the thought of writing the next part, I paused. My pregnancy with Thomas was the hardest part of our relationship. At least, I'd thought so at the time.

I sat on the bed, waiting nervously for Evan to come home. When he did, he smelled like he'd emptied the fridges, and wanted sex. He was the father of my children, and I still loved him. The first boyfriend

I'd ever had, the first man I'd ever slept with, the one I'd thought would love me forever.

We were always working on it, trying to make things better. It just took me a very long time to realise: there was nothing to work on.

"Why, Olivia? Why did you do it again?" He sounded exasperated, as if he had lost patience with me over some tiny imagined misdemeanour. He was talking about our child growing inside me.

"You were involved too. I didn't just magic this child up."

"How do I even know it's mine?"

My blood ran cold as he said the words. Even if I had wanted to look elsewhere, where would I ever find the time or the energy? When I wasn't at work, I was at home.

Bursting into tears, I gritted my teeth and fisted my hands. "You know damn well you're the only man I've ever slept with. Just stop it, Evan. Please."

"You know this makes it harder for me to find a job. I'll have to stay home with the baby again so it doesn't cost us a fortune in childcare."

And so we went around in a circle. Once again I'd be the one to provide for my family. I didn't mind that; I didn't even mind if he wanted to stay home with the children. But for the right reasons, not because he couldn't be bothered doing anything to help.

But that was he. That was always him.

I sat back and stared at the words on the screen. After that night, Evan had never again voiced the opinion that Thomas might not be his. Of course he knew that was ludicrous. He knew I'd never stray, knew I was far too dedicated to him and our family to do anything to screw it up.

Saving what I'd written, I closed down the laptop. Time for bed and sleep. Maybe I could write some more tomorrow. Even if no one else ever read it, it felt good to get all those feelings out.

A peaceful feeling came over me, one I hadn't felt in forever. None of this mattered. I was still angry with Evan for leaving me this way, but the rest of my little family was intact and we were warm and dry and fed.

Not everyone was that lucky.

WHEN THE BOYS were in bed the following night, I read what I'd written the night before. I cried all over again, remembering all the bad times. All this time, and I never realised they outnumbered the good.

Two of the brightest moments were the births of my boys. Those two days were the best of my life, overriding anything Evan did or said to me. I smiled through my tears.

My heart swelled with love. This tiny little baby in my arms was mine. All mine. Evan was his father, but I would be the one to feed him, nurture him. At least for a little while. The thought of returning to work was like a punch in the gut. But for the moment I sat in the hospital bed, nursing my child in my arms, breathing in the scent of new baby. Nothing could make my life any more perfect right now.

One day. One day I'll share this story with my children. Maybe not the worst parts of my relationship with their father, but these bits. The lines to show them just how much their mother loved them from the second she laid eyes on them.

I loaded up a web browser and went looking for the information I needed about submitting books to publishers. Maybe there was hope for that old manuscript yet.

And then I stumbled on the biggest revelation ever.

I could do it myself.

Pages on pages of information. Editors, cover designers, everything I could ever want at my fingertips. I hadn't had any time for any hobbies or room for anything for myself for years. Now was my chance.

The more I read, the more excited I got. I trawled through forums, reading up about how to do it and who to buy from. It would take an investment to get started, but I could make it happen. I could really do it.

I needed something to give my life meaning. The boys were everything to me, but I needed something just for me, something that would give me the personal satisfaction I craved.

Downloading some free books, all different genres, I started reading. There were so many amazing novels out there, and I wanted to be a part of it. But I wanted to read what else there was, give myself an idea of what was popular, what people would read.

It didn't have to sell a million copies, but it would be nice to make my investment back.

The story I'd dug out of the box was a romance. They were popular, and some of the short stories I read made my cheeks burn with embarrassment. But I could do this. If anything, they were inspiring. I found myself laughing and crying, and all of a sudden it was midnight.

And I had to be up at 6am.

Reluctantly, I closed the laptop, promising myself more tomorrow night. Maybe I could buy a tablet or something to read on, catch up on my lunch break.

It had been a long, long time since anything had excited me so much.

6

I READ SO MANY BOOKS, short stories, and anything else I could get through that my head was spinning. This was what people were buying? I'd always loved losing myself in bookstores, wandering in and picking up anything that took my fancy, sometime flicking through the pages. None of those books were like this.

Loading up on free books, I spent hours curled up after the boys went to bed, reading, gaping, gasping, and crying.

Could I really do this?

Sex seemed to sell. I could write sex. I'd had sex. Quite a few times, in fact. Not always great sex, but in fiction, all sex was great sex.

I had life experience. I was sure I could make up some amazing, romantic, maybe even funny stories.

How about a broken heart? Yeah, I could write all about that. My mother broke my heart when she kicked me out, and then after the tenderest night of our marriage, even my husband, who had neglected me for so long, broke my heart. Just a little.

I'd bought a tablet to read on. My quest for knowledge led me from book to book and I consumed everything I could.

I made a list of ideas before settling on trying something new. All my reading had led to me realise that my seventeen year old writing wasn't really the best thing ever written. Now I wanted to write something different. It felt so weird at first; I'd been so self-contained for so long, but now I could pour my emotion onto the screen and let it all out.

A mess of sexual frustration compounded by my loneliness all fell out into the document. And there had to be a hero, a hero that was unlike any other man the heroine had met. One who would sweep her off her feet and love her forever, always be faithful, never be mean.

This felt better than anything had in a very long time. But would anyone other than me ever read it?

Sitting on the couch at work, sandwich in one hand, tablet in the other, I started to read over what I'd written. It wasn't that long, maybe 20,000 words, but it had a start, a middle and an end. What else did a story need?

Distracted, I didn't notice Rebecca until my tablet was snatched from my hand.

"Whatcha reading?"

She sat beside me, and read a few lines before her jaw dropped. "What the hell is this? Holy shit, that's hot."

I shrugged, reaching for it.

"Hell, no. I want to read some more. What is it?"

"Just something I'm reading."

"Yeah, but what's it called? I love romance books. I want to download it on my phone."

Shit.

"I don't know. A friend wrote it. I'm just reading it through for her."

She looked at me, raising an eyebrow and cocking her head. "What's your friend's name? Is there more? Can I buy it?"

"Rebecca, can I please have it back?"

Handing me back my tablet slowly, her eyes bore into me.

"What's the big deal? You go quite red when you're flustered." I looked down, and away from her gaze. "Look, Olivia, sorry if I crossed a line, I was just curious about what had you so engrossed."

I didn't know where to look. I raised my eyes to the ceiling. "I just … it's personal."

"Did you write that?"

I looked back at her, my cheeks burning with the embarrassment of being caught.

"Oh my God, Olivia, you did. Don't ever play poker; you'd get your arse handed to you."

Sighing, I rested my head on the back of the couch. "I just need something for me. After everything that happened, I needed a way to get out all my anxiety and frustration over the whole situation. I can't let the boys see what a mess everything is. I mean, I'm keeping it together, but inside I'm still screaming."

Her hand landed on my shoulder. "I get it. And you should have something for yourself. What are you going to do with this? Please tell me you're submitting it to somewhere to be published."

I shrugged. "I was thinking of doing it myself."

"Seriously?"

"Yeah, I've been reading all about it. I've found someone who sells book covers already made up, they just add the book title and your name."

She looked sideways at me, as if unsure whether to say something or not.

"What?"

"Do you want me to read through it? I have a degree in English Lit."

Uber businesswoman had a degree in English Literature? For some reason I picked her as having some business degree, or economics.

"Sure. If you want to. I mean, you've just read one of the hot parts."

She laughed, and stood, holding her hand out.

"Give it to me and I'll have a read through. I have a quiet afternoon, and I'm a quick reader. I'll give it back to you by the end of the day."

I sucked my lips in, suppressing a laugh. "I feel like I'm in school handing something to the teacher because I've been naughty and aren't supposed to have it."

She giggled, slapping her hand across her mouth. "I just want to read the rest. I'll mark anything that I think you need to fix. Proofread it, if you will."

"That would be great."

I handed her back the tablet, and she sashayed her way back out of the kitchen, presumably back to her office.

Sharing erotic fiction at work with your boss. Whoever thought that was a good idea?

AS I WAS LEAVING for the day, I wandered past reception and through to Rebecca's office. Her bag was still on the table, but there was no sign of her.

I glanced at my watch. I had to leave now to collect the boys on time and avoid paying penalty fees for being late. That was the last thing I needed.

Oh well, I guess I'll grab it in the morning.

When I got to my car, I looked back at the building. Her office light was still on. *Where did you get to?* I shrugged, climbing into the seat and started the car, chuckling to myself.

I was on cloud nine. Someone liked what I wrote. Unless she hated it and was avoiding me. Oh crap. What had I done?

Jack jumped in the car when I pulled into the car park. "Mum, have you got your tablet? I want to play that game before Thomas tries to take it."

I rolled my eyes. "Sorry, bud. Someone borrowed it today. I'll get it back tomorrow."

He pouted.

"Tell you what, I might let you play on the computer for a little while before bed tonight."

He nodded excitedly. That would be a real treat. I'd been glued to that laptop since I'd bought it.

As I drove to day-care, Rebecca was still on my mind. What she'd read hadn't even been the hottest bit, and I knew I'd pushed the envelope. What if she decided she hated it? What if I had been carried away with my fantasy and written something too sexually explicit and she decided to fire me? No, she couldn't do that. Could she?

Jack came in the day-care with me and when we did Thomas whooped, running towards us. "Mummy," he cried.

This had to be the best part of the day. The time of the day where I felt most loved.

"Tom, Mum said we can play on the computer when we get home."

A chorus of "YAY" followed me out the door and back to the car where I buckled them into their seats.

"Can we get pizza?" Jack asked.

"Not tonight, honey. Maybe on pay day."

He frowned.

"Tell you what? How about we cook cocktail sausages and eat them with heaps of tomato sauce?"

A resounding "YAY" came from the back seat and I laughed as I indicated to pull out. Sometimes it was the simple answer that turned into the most popular.

Thomas didn't even last through dinner. Stuffing himself full of the small red treats, he fell asleep at the dining table and I carried him gently to his bed, tucking him in and kissing him goodnight.

Been a long day for all of us. Hell, every day is a long day.

When I went back out, Jack was already at the computer, hammering the keys as he raced a car around a circuit. I watched for a minute before clearing the dishes and going to the kitchen to wash them.

As I scrubbed the plates, I watched him. I loved that kid so much, and his brother. When I looked at them, I felt as if my heart was going to burst with love and pride. Evan had made me feel useless, worthless. My children made me feel as if I was the most important person in the world.

It wasn't long before Jack was yawning and I moved behind him, watching him zoom around.

"Hey, you. Time for bed, I think."

Before Evan left, Jack would be straight home from school, on the couch watching television, snuggled up with a book when I got home. Now he went to after-school care. By the time I picked him up he was ready for dinner. *My poor tired boys.*

He didn't complain. Neither of them had since Evan had left. Both were so sensitive and yet they knew how hard this was for me, how much I had to deal with. Despite their young age, we just all put each other first.

It didn't take long for him to fall asleep and I sat down on the couch, flicking on the TV to see what was on. Switching channels, there just seemed to be nothing, so I left it on the news and lay down.

The combination of gentle sounds from the television, and the comfortable couch soon lulled me into a half-asleep haze.

I should give up and go to bed.

A sharp knock on the door woke me, and I sprang up, looking at the wall clock. Just after 9.30pm. I'd been lying there two hours. Who on earth could it be at this time of night?

Evan.

My stomach clenched at the thought of another confrontation, and when I peeked through the curtains, I couldn't see past onto the porch.

"Who is it?" I asked, approaching the door.

"Rebecca."

Rebecca? Rebecca was at my house?

I turned the handle, unlocking the door, and there she stood on my doorstep, my tablet in one hand, and a bottle of wine in the other.

I gulped, my heart pounding as a million thoughts ran through my head as to why she could be there. The bottle of wine indicated she wasn't expecting to be kicked out any time soon, though.

"What are you doing here?"

"I thought you might want this back?" She handed me the tablet. "I highlighted a few changes I think you need to make and some punctuation you need to fix. I mean, if you gave it to me as a word document, I can make the changes myself and go over it properly. I just had a quick read-through. I'm gonna need that for much, much longer."

Without even trying, one of my eyebrows crept up. "Thank you, I really wasn't expecting this."

"Can I come in?" She waved the wine bottle in my face. "I brought you a present."

I broke down, laughing and shaking my head. "Of course. Come on in. I'm pretty sure I have some glasses somewhere."

When I came back she was sat on the couch, looking around. "So this is your place? Where are your boys?"

"It's nine thirty. They're in bed, asleep."

"Holy shit, it's nine thirty," she said, gaping a the clock on the wall. "I lost track of time. I'm so sorry."

I shrugged. "It's fine. It's kinda nice to have grown-up company. I did come looking for you before I left work. Where did you get to?"

Taking the sparkling wine from her, I twisted the metal tie and popped the cork. When I looked back at her, she'd gone a deep shade of red and was looking at the floor.

"What?" I asked, grinning as I poured the wine.

"I had to make a pit stop."

"What are you talking about?"

"I spent all afternoon reading what you wrote. I had to take a toilet break."

Handing her the glass of wine, I nodded. It made sense, it was a lot to read in a short time.

"Reading all that sex, I had some ... uh ... tension I had to get rid of."

The mouthful of wine I was just about to swallow came flying out, spraying across the room.

Does that mean what I think it does?

"You've got a real way with words, Olivia."

Did I hear right? Did my boss just confess to slipping off to the bathroom to ...

I didn't have to ask. She nodded, shifting to spread her legs and flicking her hand in the air between to indicate what she meant.

"Holy crap," I said.

"I know. What if Grace had walked in?"

I let out a loud laugh at the thought. Grace was the receptionist at work and about 102 years old. At least, that was how it seemed. She was so prim and proper, and never found anything remotely funny. Everyone at work was pretty sure she'd been there forever. Maybe they'd even built the office around her. And right now, all I could picture was Grace walking in just as Rebecca ... well ... *that*.

"Sorry, I know this is *way* too much information, but you're so talented. I would love to help you if I can. I'm really glad I'm a nosey bitch."

I laughed again, shaking my head. This was nice, just having someone to talk to and laugh with. It felt like forever since I'd truly laughed, or found joy in anything other than my boys.

And that was how my boss became my editor.

7

MY WINE NIGHTS with Rebecca became a semi-regular thing. As I'd write, she'd go over it and tidy up anything she thought looked wonky, and our friendship grew.

Two or three nights a week we'd hang out at my place, sometimes watch a movie and all the while, we planned for my first book release.

Not only was she my boss, but she was my friend now too, and I cherished that just as much as all the help she'd given me.

When we got close to the end of creating my book, I started looking around for those final pieces to put it all together.

I found the perfect cover one night while sitting at my dining table.

It was just gorgeous. A man and a woman wrapped around one another. Sexy and romantic.

And for the life of me, I didn't know what to call it.

"Call it Tempting Fate. You know, that's what that girl does, taking a chance on the guy in the story. It's sexy and sweet, and open to interpretation. People who read that title will all take a different meaning from it," Rebecca said.

"I like that. But what do I call myself?"

"What do you mean?"

I sighed. "I'm not going to publish this as me. This is my secret thing, all for myself."

"Oh, right." She looked pensive. "I don't know. Let's just Google names and pick one."

I looked sideways at her. "That sounds scientific."

"Well, you don't know what to call yourself either, Miss Smarty Pants." She grinned.

"Hmm, you might be onto something there. I'll call myself M Smartypants."

She laughed, slapping me on the shoulder and leaning over to look at the computer screen.

"How about you just use your initial and a fake last name."

"Like what?"

"Something a bit rude, suggestive. How about O Rod." Rebecca raised her eyebrows, smirking as she tilted her head.

I got the giggles, and pretended to head-butt the computer.

"O Brother, more like," I said.

"Or just The Big O."

My face began to hurt from laughing so hard and the tears rolled down my eyes.

"O My." Rebecca moved from behind me, plonking herself on the next seat. I leaned back in my chair, shaking my head.

"Stop it," I said.

"I can't. This is too much fun." Rebecca grinned.

"Let's drink wine and think about it then."

She nodded. "I'm sure great ideas with flow after that."

"O Behave," I said.

She laughed as she made her way to the kitchen to get the wine from the fridge and the glasses from the cabinet. I enjoyed her company. It was so much better than having no one to talk to. And she cared, she genuinely cared about me and the boys. I loved her so much for that.

"What's your mother's maiden name? Don't writers sometimes use that as a surname?"

I had to rack my brain. It had been so long since I'd thought about anything to do with my mother, I couldn't remember.

"Knight."

Rebecca walked back in, cackling like an evil witch from a fairy tale.

"O What a Knight?"

I buried my face in my hands, laughing so hard I started to cry. "I don't know what to do."

"What's your middle name?"

"Elizabeth."

She patted me on the back. "How about Elizabeth Knight?"

I shrugged. "I guess. It's nothing too out there, but subtle enough to be different to my real name."

"You'll be hiding in plain sight."

I giggled.

"It just seemed like fun. Anyway, now you can set up your Facebook page."

I looked back at the laptop. "What Facebook page?"

"The one where you can make your announcements, somewhere for people to find you so they can see what you're doing."

I'd fiddled with Facebook, but hadn't used it for much other than playing a few games. I'd unfriended a lot of people when Evan left.

"Here, I'll show you. I'll even like your page. We'll hire that lady that made the cover to do a few more bits and pieces for decoration and away you go."

WITH ZERO IDEA of what I was doing, I leaned on Rebecca a lot. I might have only had one like on my Facebook page to start with—well two, if you count me liking my own page, but she was patient and I began to think I should be paying her to work for me. And at the same time, I'd found a friend who would support me through the good and the bad times. My life felt as if it were getting back on an even keel.

The night we pressed publish, I cried. And when the book went live, I clicked the refresh button a hundred times to see if I'd sold anything. It got so annoying, I handed it over to Rebecca to watch.

"We sold five overnight," she said as I came in the next morning.

"What? Holy crap."

"Yep. What does that make you? Ten dollars?"

I laughed, thrilled that *someone* had bought my book. The office worker in me silently calculated just how many copies I'd have to sell to get back my investment in my new little business. A couple of thousand would do it, a couple of million would be better.

Some days I sold none, some days I sold one. I found Facebook pages to share on and ways to advertise to readers for free. Slowly but surely, my Facebook likes trickled up.

And then Rebecca and I started something new to up the momentum.

The routine the boys were in helped keep my sanity. I hadn't heard from Evan again, his threats over custody had panned out to nothing as I had thought they would.

As little as we had, he probably had even less.

Within two months I had three novellas out and quietly growing sales.

Best of all, it made me feel better than I had in a very long time.

Now to sort out the rest of my life: get my head above water, raise my children, maybe meet a nice man ... actually have sex rather than just writing about it.

This was just the start.

For a few months I lasted in that house, paying the mortgage I could barely afford, no squeeze room in the budget. Our life there couldn't last forever. I was starting to make back the savings I'd spent producing my stories, but it wasn't enough.

This wasn't what I wanted for my children; it wasn't what I

wanted for myself. All the years I'd worked to make our lives better and we were back to square one. I'd worked so hard to buy this place and we'd managed to time it just right. I'd rather give it up than lose it though.

This place had been my dream. Our own home with room for our children to play and grow.

My reality now was much different.

I spent hours scouring the newspaper, trying to find somewhere we could live that I could afford. We'd have to rent; the mortgage was enough that anything I got out of it would cover expenses, but not a lot else.

At least I'd walk away with my dignity intact.

There was an apartment block nearby with vacancies that were an exact fit for what we needed. It would do.

With the place needing maintenance that Evan never did and I couldn't afford to pay someone to do, I got less for the house than I'd hoped for, but it was still enough that I didn't owe anyone anything. My boys and I would start with nothing, but it was better than less than nothing, which would have been the case if we'd stayed.

Even though I was being responsible, I felt like the worst mother in the world.

"What do you mean we have to move?" Jack's lower lip wobbled.

"We're going to move somewhere that's just for us."

Thomas's eyes lit up, as if it were the most exciting thing ever. "An adventure," he said.

Jack was seven, Thomas four. Old enough to know what was going on, but too young to really understand.

"That's right, baby. An adventure."

Jack snuggled up on one side of me on the couch, Thomas on the other. At least I'd have my boys we'd get through it together. I loved them more than anyone or anything else, and I'd do whatever I had to in order to protect them.

I called the moving company, and packed our things. And on the final day, I went from room to room, saying my own goodbyes to the home I'd made, the one I thought would be there forever.

For the last time, I locked the door behind me. Two stops to pick up the boys from school and day-care and we'd move into our new home. The moving truck would meet us there at three-thirty, so I had to get a move on.

"Goodbye," I whispered.

Concrete and metal, the block of apartments loomed over me as I approached through the courtyard. This was not what I wanted for my children, but it was the best I could do. For now.

"Is that our new house?" Jack asked, his eyes wide at all the apartments.

"It's so big," Thomas said, and I smiled at him.

"One of those is ours." I sighed. This must seem so awful to them after the place we had come from. It hadn't been huge, but there was a yard that was theirs. The closest thing to it here was the park down the road.

This is so unfair.

The moving company truck pulled into the car park and I took the boys up to the second floor and along the balcony to our room. The building was shaped in a semi-circle, overlooking the shared car park. We got an apartment and a park for the car included in our rent. It wasn't perfect, but it was a roof over our heads which would be warm and dry, and we could close the door and shut the whole damn horrible world out.

After unlocking the door, I watched as the kids ran in and took a look. There was a small living room, with a kitchen to the side, separated by a bench. It would be a squeeze, but we could fit in the lounge suite and the kitchen table I'd brought from the other place. The back half of the apartment consisted of a short hallway leading to two bedrooms and the bathroom at the back.

"Where's my bedroom?" Jack asked. Thomas grabbed my hand, asking me the same question and my stomach sunk into my knees.

"Well, there's one bedroom that you two have to share."

"That's not fair." Jack pouted, his younger brother following suit, united in their sadness.

"No, it's not fair. None of this is. But it's better than living in the car."

Jack wrapped his arms around my waist, hugging me. "Sorry, Mum." Thomas joined in, and I smiled, wondering if he had any idea of what was going on.

I bent down to hug both my boys. "Look, one day we'll find somewhere bigger. This will do in the meantime, won't it?"

Thomas nodded at me with all the wisdom of his four years. He was such a quiet little boy, and he'd say yes to anything either Jack or I said.

There were boxes everywhere soon enough, and I got the movers to put the furniture where I wanted it to go. For the moment, I set up the beds so we could sleep; the rest could wait until later.

This was home.

BY THE NEXT MORNING, the boxes were mostly unpacked. The apartment was a mess, with things everywhere, but now we could really settle in and make this as homely as we could.

I looked at the clothing lying scattered on the bed. So many of these things that I'd accumulated over the years had to go; there was simply no space for them. Besides, I hadn't worn so much of it in so long.

I picked up the small denim shorts on the top of the pile. Evan had loved it when I'd bought these, complimenting me on my butt and how good it looked in them. I hadn't worn them since before the boys and I idly wondered if I could still get into them.

Grinning, I slid them on and looked at myself in the mirror.
Not bad.

I was a little fuller figured than I had been before Jack, but they looked great, even if I wasn't sure whether I'd go out in public wearing them.

Curious about our surroundings, I thought about venturing down to the mailbox. I'd seen the rows of them at the base of the stairs and even if there was nothing in it yet, it'd be handy to work out there ours was. Besides, I could do with some fresh air.

I thought twice about whether I should wear the shorts and glanced at the clock. Six-thirty on a Saturday morning. There couldn't be that many people around, and I'd make it quick.

Grab the moment, Olivia. This is your new life.

I pulled on a shirt, looking at myself in the mirror one more time. A quick run down to the mailbox wouldn't hurt. Laughing to myself, I set off out the door. Jack and Thomas were both still fast asleep, and checking the mail just involved going down the stairs. I'd be back in a few minutes.

The complex looked deserted, and I trotted down the steps to my destination. It was only a short walk, but I took a deep breath, enjoying the morning air, and a few minutes of solitude.

I ran my finger over the steel boxes, trying to find mine. There were so many of them, and I finally found it, just below my knees. Bending, I unlocked the door, closing it again when there was nothing there.

"Good morning." A deep voice came from behind me and I stood up, turning towards the sound.

He was tall, and I raised my eyes, taking in his T-shirt which barely hid his chest muscles. His biceps were huge, and he had a tattoo on one arm peeping out from under a sleeve. At the top were these chocolate-brown eyes, the type you just want to melt into.

Stubble covered his chin and cheeks, meeting his thick dark hair by his ears. He was tough, but so beautiful. And he had one of those grins on his face that just screamed that he thought he was onto something. Hopefully me.

Cool yourself down, Olivia.

"Uh, hi."

"Logan Mitchell. I saw you come out of your apartment. I'm right next door …" He smiled. Oh God, his teeth were perfect too.

"Olivia Grant. We moved in yesterday. Seems like an okay place."

He raised an eyebrow. "We?"

"Mummy." I heard Jack call, and glanced up to see him at the top of the stairs looking down at us. Thomas trailed behind, sucking his thumb as he did sometimes when he was scared. I guess waking up and not finding me had done it. *Crap.* I hoped they hadn't locked our door.

"Sorry, guys. I just wanted to check the mail. I'll make us some breakfast now." I looked around, vowing never to do that again. Maybe not the best look to have them wandering around on their own.

Logan nodded stiffly. "I'll let you get back to your family." He stepped back, letting me pass, no longer smiling. It wasn't fair; I wanted to see that smile again.

Settle down.

"Thanks. Maybe I'll see you round." I smiled, climbing the stairs and ushering the boys back to our apartment.

"Who was that?" Thomas asked.

"One of our neighbours," I replied, reaching up into the cupboard for the flour. Making pancakes at the weekend was one of our traditions, and the change of scene wasn't about to stop that.

"Mum, your butt is hanging out of your pants." Jack giggled, and I rolled my eyes.

"They're short shorts. I'll go and get changed."

I went to the bedroom, peeling off the shorts when I got there, and flung them into a plastic bag with some other things I'd decided to pass on to charity. Most of the memories around them weren't that great, Evan had been a real dick about the way my body changed when I was pregnant. Mind you, he'd been a dick about a lot of things.

"You're what?" Evan looked at me in disbelief, and I wanted to shrink into the wall behind me, pretend that nothing existed.

"I'm pregnant," I whispered.

"Is it mine?"

My heart dropped. Was this the way he wanted to play it?

"Of course it is. You're the only guy I've ever had sex with. You know you were the first."

"How did it happen? Did you stop taking the pill?"

I shook my head. He'd never wanted to take any responsibility for birth control, and now he was about to back out of taking responsibility for our baby.

"Go home, Olivia. I don't even want to think about it. We'll make an appointment, go and get it taken care of."

I felt faint. My stomach ached, and it wasn't due to morning sickness.

"It's too late for that," I whispered.

"What the fuck? How long have you known?"

"I just found out." That was true too. My mother never talked to me about sex, never wanted to acknowledge me going through puberty, apart from throwing me a box of tampons and hoping for the best. Everything I'd learned, I'd discovered at school from other girls. That information had been sketchy at best.

"It's not my fault, Evan. You did it too. The pills just didn't work."

I started crying and he buried his head in his hands, not wanting to look at me.

"Evan, you know I wouldn't do this on purpose. My mother will kill me."

He sighed, and finally moved towards me, wrapping his arms around my shoulders.

"I guess you can move in with me. She's going to kick you out anyway."

I nodded, burying my face in his chest. He felt so warm, so safe.

If only I'd known how wrong I was.

8

IN THE EVENING, when the boys were in bed, I went out the front door to the only source of fresh air. The sound of laughter floated up to the balcony and I looked out, spotting Logan and a woman walking towards the building. She was tall, blonde, gorgeous—everything I wasn't. As she drew closer, I saw the tattoo she had from her hip, disappearing under her cropped top that stopped just below her breasts.

It was a snake, curling its way over her stomach, wrapping around her side and disappearing up towards her armpit.

So that was his type. About the opposite of me. She wore black denim jeans that sat low on her hips, and she teetered on six-inch heels, her stumbling disguised by supporting herself on Logan.

I leaned over the balcony, pretending to look elsewhere as they came up the stairs and past me. Drawing level, I heard him tell her to go ahead to his door.

He leaned over the balcony beside me, looking down at the cars I pretended to watch.

"You know, Olivia, your eyebrow will get stuck in that position if you keep watching me like that."

I glanced sideways, that damn grin of his making me laugh in response.

"Sorry. I was just out here getting some fresh air," I replied, poking my tongue out at him. I didn't know what it was about him that made me act like a child.

He rubbed his stubble with his fingers, raising an eyebrow at me.

"Watch out. I might think you're flirting with me."

"Looks to me like you've already got company. Goodnight." Before I could gauge his reaction, I turned and walked back inside, gently closing the door. I flopped on the couch and flicked on the TV, wondering what was going on the apartment next door, but then deciding it was best I didn't know.

He fascinated me—those beautiful sculpted muscles, how good he looked in tight pants ... it was enough to make a girl swoon. Well, this one, anyway. It had been so long since I'd been interested in someone, and even if he wasn't returning my affections, it still felt good.

When I climbed into bed, I realised just how much noise carried through the wall, and if they were too loud, I might just hear what was going on next door. I grimaced at the thought. The last thing I wanted to hear was two people having sex.

I picked up a book. Jack had borrowed *Charlie and the Chocolate Factory* from the school library, and we were reading it together. It was so different to everything else I'd been reading lately, and like diving into a big pool of nostalgia. This had been one of my favourite books when I was a kid.

After two chapters, my eyes were so heavy I couldn't fight them anymore. I snuggled down under the covers, and lost myself to sleep.

I woke to a loud thud against the wall as something hit on Logan's side. A woman started screeching, high pitched and loud. It was impossible not to hear the raised voices.

"What the fuck was that for?" Logan's dulcet tones resonated through the wall, and I sat up, leaning against it to hear more.

"What do you think it's for, you useless prick?" Something else hit with a thud and I sat back, staring at the wall as if it would give me some insight as to what was happening on the other side.

"Oh grow up." The disdain was clear in his voice.

"I don't need you. Stop telling me what to do."

"I'm not telling you what to do. You're an adult. Act like one."

My eyebrows were twitching as I drew closer again. I leaned in, pressing my ear to the cool plasterboard.

"I can't do this, I'm not strong enough." She was weeping now, her sobs loud enough for me to hear.

"You're so strong; you just don't know it. And you need to go back to your meetings. You'll never get better if you stop. I can't be your only support."

The sound of her crying came closer. I guessed she was going to him.

"I just want it so bad."

"I know you do. Let's get to your doctor and see what other rehab options you have."

She drew in two big breaths, as if she were hiccupping. "I'm sorry for being such a drama queen."

"You're hiding from your addiction. I'll help you, Kat, but I'm not going to jump back into a relationship with you. Even if it's just sex."

The raised voices dropped to a rumble, and I settled back into bed. So what was she? His ex? With some type of addiction problem? If he was as sweet as he sounded, that made him even more irresistible.

Stop it, Olivia. Just stop it.

He was the hottest thing I'd seen in forever, I'd sheltered myself from feeling anything for so long and the man next door was really doing it for me.

Although, maybe it was because he was the first man in a long time to offer me a kind word.

WE HAD A LAZY SUNDAY, the boys watching cartoons while I rearranged things and tidied up. I was down to finding a home for the last few unpacked items. It was a challenge, but I'd finally conquered the kitchen when someone banged on the door.

Logan stood outside my apartment, with plate in hand. It was covered with huge chocolate chip cookies.

"Thought I should welcome you to the neighbourhood properly," he said.

"You made these?" I looked at the plate again, they were beautifully cooked with loads of chocolate. Perfect. "I'm impressed," I said. "If you want to come in, I'll make coffee to go with them."

He grinned. "Of course I made them."

I smirked, shaking my head and turning from the door to go towards the kitchen to make the coffee. He trailed in behind me, following me as far as the counter that separated the kitchen from the living room.

The boys looked up from the television and Logan waved at them.

"Jack, Thomas, this is Logan from next door."

They waved back before turning back to their cartoon.

"There's a bakery just down the road. The cookies are amazing."

I laughed. "I appreciate the thought."

Jack came running through, and grabbed me around the waist. "Are there cookies, Mum?"

"You have excellent hearing," Logan said.

Jack nuzzled my side. "It's okay, Jack. Logan brought us some cookies." I picked up two from the plate. "One for you, one for Thomas. Okay?"

He grinned, grabbing a cookie in each hand and running back to the television.

"They seem like good kids. They don't seem to make much noise."

I smiled. "They're awesome. How do you take your coffee?"

"Milk and two. Hey, I wanted to say sorry for last night. You might have heard a disturbance in the wee small hours. I know how thin these walls are."

I poured the coffees and carried them to the table in the corner. He picked up the plate of cookies and followed, taking a seat as I placed the cups down.

"It's fine. I did wake up, but I went back to sleep pretty quickly."

Jack popped up and snaffled another cookie, looking between us with a huge cookie-stealing grin on his face.

Logan looked down at the coffee as I sat. "I'm still sorry." He took a bite of his cookie. "So, is it just you and the boys? Or …"

"Daddy doesn't live with us anymore," Jack said matter-of-factly.

"Oh. I'm sorry to hear that," Logan said.

The small hand started to creep across to the plate again, and I grabbed it, laughing. "No more for you. Take one for Thomas and that's it."

Jack grinned and nodded. "Yes, Mum."

"And as for what Jack said, don't be sorry. I'm not." I waved my hand as if to say no further conversation required.

"He must be an idiot not to be with you guys anymore. Unless you dumped him."

I nearly choked on the bite of cookie I'd just taken. Coughing, I took a sip of my coffee.

"Shit. Are you alright?" he asked, then looked around as if checking to see if the boys had heard him.

"I'm fine." I sounded as if I'd swallowed razor blades as I spoke, I was that hoarse. Damn cookie. I patted my chest to stop the cough, and Logan just looked at me with this big grin on his face, as if I were the biggest clown in the world.

"Sorry. I didn't mean to make you choke. And I don't mean to pry."

"He left me."

His expression blanked, and he nodded. "So he's an idiot?"

"I like to think so."

I took another sip of the coffee as I studied him. He really was very good looking, and something deep inside felt like it was waking after a long sleep. I'd never been one to pay much attention to other men when I was with Evan; half the time I was far too tired for them to register. Now my life was coming back into balance, it was time to appreciate the finer things in life.

"Kat's an ex. The woman that was with me last night? She's going through some stuff at the moment and I'm trying to help her. And failing."

He needs to talk. Holy crap.

"Sorry to hear that."

"I don't want to dump stuff on you, but I'm kind of torn between her and another ex and I'm wondering if you could be the deciding vote."

I frowned. Torn between them? What did that mean? And we barely knew one another. Why was he asking me for advice?

"Sure, if I can help. Seems a bit random that you'd ask me, though."

He grinned, shaking his head. "I have two headstrong women pushing me in different directions. Figured I'd add a third opinion to the mix. I'm a glutton for punishment."

His eyes twinkled with mischief, and I twisted my mouth while working out what on earth to say. "Try me."

Logan raised his eyebrows, and took a sip of his coffee.

"Kat has a drug problem. Can't keep clean. So, she asks for my help and I try my best, but she can't keep away. It's the whole damn reason why we broke up. I'm not into that shit."

The conversation I'd overheard was suddenly beginning to make sense, and I nodded to indicate he should go on.

"Anyway, another ex, Maddy, is telling me to stop picking up the pieces. That Kat has to sort herself out. And I know in a way that she's right. Every time I've tried, she's broken her word, and I can't let myself get dragged back into it. But I have to make sure she's okay. I couldn't walk away and then find out she's dead because I didn't help her."

That was a lot to take in, a heavy conversation for a virtual stranger to have with me. But it was clear he was hurting and lost as far as knowing what to do.

"Logan, I don't know what else you can do bar tying her up and not letting her go anywhere. I'm not saying don't be there, but you can't be responsible for her all the time."

He nodded. "That's what I think. I'd just feel so guilty if anything happened to her."

"You're feeling guilty now; it's written all over your face. You already said you're trying your best." Without even thinking, I reached across the table and placed my hand on his. "Sometimes nothing we do stops the inevitable."

I wasn't just talking about his situation, but my own. So many years I'd just kept going, trying too hard to keep a relationship together that was going nowhere.

Those beautiful brown eyes of his were so sad, as if he'd come to the realisation that maybe he had to let go.

"Are there any other rehab options?" I asked.

"Yeah, there's a place she can go. I was trying to convince her of that the other night. I can't force her hand."

I nodded. "No, you can't. Have you told her how you feel about all of this?"

"I've told her I think she needs help. I've told her that she needs more than what she's been doing. That she needs the support and I'm not enough."

I took a sip of my coffee and studied him. He had both hands wrapped around his cup, gazing into the liquid.

"There's only so much you can do. She's an adult."

He shrugged. "I know you're right. It's just hard to walk away." Logan looked up at me, that mischievous twinkle having returned. "So you mentioned tying her up. Are you into that?"

I gaped, the heat in my face rising as he took his turn studying me.

"I guess so. Lady has some kinks." He kept his voice low so the kids didn't hear him.

"Stop it." I laughed, shaking my head.

"Guess not then. What do you like, Olivia Grant?" Our gazes locked, and my heart pounded so hard I could hear it beating in my ears. "I mean in general. Not in bed. But I don't mind you telling me that too."

I rolled my eyes, laughing again, and he grinned.

"I don't know. I'm just trying to find myself right now," I said.

He ran his finger around the rim of the cup before picking up a cookie and dunking it. "Well, if you need a friend you know where to find one. I know I kinda landed it on you, but it's nice to get a perspective from someone not closely involved."

I got it. Sometimes it was the people outside the situation that saw it for what it was.

My situation? I saw it, but the end still caught me by surprise.

9

I SPENT all week looking forward to sleeping in on Saturday. The week dragged by, and on Friday night I treated myself to a bottle of wine on the way home. Something to take the edge off, though I would need no help to sleep.

We picked up fish and chips and gorged ourselves silly before both my boys began to yawn.

Friday night, 7.30pm, and I had peace, quiet, and a nice Sauvignon Blanc to keep me company. I sat on the couch and flicked through channel after channel, looking for something to watch on the television.

There's nothing on. Friday night isn't a night to be home alone.

I laughed at my thought. It had been years since I'd had a Friday night out, or any night out, for that matter. Looking down at the glass of wine, I swirled it around, watching as the liquid splashed. *Drinking alone. How sad.*

I took one sip, and then another; the alcohol had a fast effect. This was my second whole bottle of wine in months, and not being used to the drink, it made me warm and fuzzy. *So fuzzy.*

Thump, thump, thump.

My head pounded in time with the knocking on the door. Who was that at this hour? With bleary eyes, I checked the clock. 9.30am. Okay, maybe not so early then.

"Mum," Jack said through his teeth. He was so good; he and Thomas had done as I'd told them many times before and not opened the door by themselves.

I forced my eyes open. They stood beside the couch, staring at me like I had two heads. I'd never slept the whole night on the couch before. This must have seemed strange.

Stupid wine.

"Okay." I sighed.

I pushed myself to my feet, groaning at the effort. My knees ached from bending my legs all night, my neck ached from whatever weird position my head had been in.

I felt about a million years old and probably looked it.

Taking unsteady steps toward the door, I twisted the handle and pulled.

"I was beginning to think you weren't home." Logan stood on the other side, grinning with two takeaway coffees in a cardboard cup holder.

"I wasn't awake," I said. My voice was still thick with sleep, and he cocked his head, studying me closely.

"You okay?"

"I'm fine. I just had some wine to drink last night and it made me really tired."

"And you didn't invite me over? I could have drunk half the wine, left you with half the hangover."

I wrinkled my nose. "I don't have a hangover."

"Let me guess: you haven't had a drink in a long time and you're not used to it."

I might have laughed at that, but the throbbing in my temples was too powerful to ignore. "Something like that."

"Just as well I brought you a coffee, then."

What was this? I hadn't really flirted with a man in, well, forever. Was this what it was like, or was he just being nice?

"Thanks, I appreciate it."

He grinned, plucking one of the cups from the cup holder and passing it to me. "I seemed to remember you having milk and sugar the other day. Hope it's okay."

"I'd drink it black if I had to this morning," I muttered.

Logan laughed. "I came by to see if you wanted a tour of the neighbourhood. You know, seeing as you only just moved in."

He wanted to spend time with me? Us? What? No, maybe he was just saying thanks for me listening to him talk the previous weekend.

"What is there to see?"

"I thought I could take you three to the park. There's a playground there; the boys can let off some steam. You can sit in the sun, or under a tree while we kick a ball around, or you could kick a ball around with us too."

My stomach dropped to my knees, and not because I was feeling seedy.

"You want to play football with my boys?"

He shrugged. "Why not?

"I just didn't picture you as the playing-football-with-kids type."

At that he frowned, and I shook my head. "I'm sure the boys would love to go to the park. Let's finish our coffee and I'll get dressed." I turned my head towards the living room. "Hey, you two. Want to go and kick a ball around in the park?"

"YES," Jack screeched and I held my finger to my lips to quieten him. My head still wasn't too happy. He and Thomas jumped up and down on the spot. I glanced at Logan. It was as if he were spellbound watching them.

He had such a good heart.

"I can't believe anyone could leave kids like that," he said quietly. Our gaze locked. "Or you."

"It is what it is," I said, and took another sip of coffee. Thoughts of being out in the blazing sun weren't that attractive, but getting fresh air and giving the boys something to do other than sit around in the living room sounded good. The noise from the television would only add to the thump in my head.

I gave up sipping the coffee, and downed it while Logan watched, bemused.

"I needed that. Thank you," I said.

"That's what all the girls say." He winked and laughed.

I rolled my eyes. "Excuse me for a moment. I'll just jump in the shower and get changed."

As I walked away, I heard him call behind me. "Wear those shorts you were wearing when we first met."

When I shook my head, he laughed. *Flirty or friendly?*

I hadn't dated since high school, and I was never any good at working out whether boys liked me or not. Now it all seemed much harder.

I'll take it as friendly until such time it becomes obvious.

I flicked the shower on, twisting the water mixer until it came up to the right temperature. Peeling off my clothes, I stepped into the water, sighing as it caressed my skin, the heat relieving my aches and pains.

I grabbed a towel from the rail beside the shower and stepped out, running it over me and wrapping it around as I brushed my teeth. *Finally, feeling human again.*

It was then that I realised I had no clean clothes with me, and I frowned at the thought of the dash across the hallway to the bedroom. There was no guarantee that Logan would see me do it, but always a possibility.

I pulled open the door, peeking around to see what was happening. Logan had turned his chair to face the television and was laughing with the boys over something. I looked to the ceiling, saying a silent word of thanks before taking the three steps from one door to the other.

Grinning as I closed the door behind me, I finished towelling myself off.

Pulling out a pair of jeans from the chest of drawers, I made a mess trying to find the right top to go with them. Finally I settled on a loose-fitting shirt with a low, round neckline. Cute, but not too sexy.

What are you worrying for? He's just saying thank you. Get it together, Olivia.

I looked in the mirror. A face that seemed old for its age looked back at me. It had been so long since I'd taken care of myself. Screw it. It was time to start.

Taking a deep breath, I smoothed the fabric down, making sure it sat okay, hiding any bumps that lumps that might have appeared after my boys were born.

"Let's go," I said to the mirror.

Logan smiled when I walked back into the living room. "Ready?"

"We are," said Thomas.

I stared at him. My little mouse, so vocal all of a sudden. I smiled as I realised he'd put his pants on, but they were inside out.

"Baby, come here a second?" I motioned to him to come toward me, and he jumped all the way.

Kneeling down, I whispered in his ear. "We just have to fix your pants."

He frowned. "Okay, Mum."

I slid them down, turned them the right way in and ran them back up his legs. "There you go," I whispered.

"Thank you."

"Come on, then," I said.

Logan opened the door, and I grabbed my bag. Jack had his ball and we headed down the stairs and across the car park. Thomas and Jack walked either side of me, holding on to my hands as we ventured out to the street. We were led by Logan, who took us down the road and pointed out shops along the way that we might find useful.

"There's a takeaway place up that way that does the best fish and chips, and Chinese food. Their sweet and sour pork is to die for," he said.

"Sounds great."

"There's the bakery I told you about, the one with the amazing cookies."

The boys started skipping as we grew closer to the park, and when we hit the edge of the grass, I let go of their hands.

"This way," Logan said, leading us to the playground. There were swings, a climbing frame, and a huge slide that made Thomas's eyes as big as saucers to see. There were a couple of other kids playing, but it was fairly quiet. Perfect for a little boy about to tackle a slide so much bigger than him.

"It's a big slide, isn't it, bud?" Logan asked.

Thomas nodded, slipping his hand into Logan's to pull him towards it.

"You want to go on it?"

"Yes."

I watched as the pair of them went to the foot of the slide. Jack hung back with me.

"Don't you want to go?"

"Nah. Let Thomas go and then we can kick around the ball. That's what I want to do."

I ruffled his hair.

"Mum?"

"Yes, Jack?"

"Why didn't Daddy ever bring us to the park?"

I'd thought the worst was behind me, but standing there looking at him, I fought back the tears. I had no idea what the answer was either.

"Um, I don't know, sweetie. Maybe he just didn't like coming to the park."

His beautiful baby face screwed up. "I hate him."

Tears rolled down my cheeks as I pulled Jack close. I couldn't blame him. I knew exactly how he felt.

"Baby, I don't know why Daddy did what he did, but I do know one thing. When you were born, he was right there, holding you, and he fell in love with you just as I did. This whole thing—he might have behaved badly, but it's not about you or Thomas. It's about him and me."

There were so many other things I could have said, so many other stories I could have told that would have made Jack hate his father even more. But what I told him was true. The night he was born was one of those nights that Evan and I had been close. He'd looked at his newborn son in awe, unable just as I was to believe we'd made this child together.

That felt like so long ago now. We were just children ourselves.

"Okay, Mum." He looked at the ground, kicking the toe of his shoe into the dirt. I could barely believe that tiny child was my big boy now. The feeling I'd had that first night had only grown these seven years.

"Come here." I opened my arms and he fell into them, dropping the ball on the ground, and wrapping his arms around my waist. "Love you, baby boy," I whispered.

"I'm not a baby."

"Nope, but you'll always be my baby."

I closed my eyes, running my fingers through his hair.

"Mummy, look at me." Thomas's voice came from above.

Jack and I both looked up. He stood at the top of the slide, triumphant, and I shifted my focus to Logan. He was poised underneath as if ready to catch him if he fell.

"That's awesome, honey. We'll be right at the bottom," I called. I took Jack's hand, leading him toward the end of the slide.

Logan stood right under Thomas and slightly to the right so Thomas could see him.

"Come on. I'll follow you down," he said.

Thomas took a deep, loud breath as he sat at the top of the slide. I grinned at the sight of him. He struggled so much with self-confidence, and the sight of him being so brave and proud gave me shivers.

I didn't know if it was the location or the company we were in that was making him so happy, and I didn't care. He looked more full of life than he had in a long time.

I moved to the base of the slide and he pushed off, squealing as the slide took over and gravity pulled him toward me.

Logan ran as Thomas slid, joining me at the end as my boy reached the bottom, and jumped off to hug me.

"Mum, that was so cool. I was so high up and it was scary, and Logan said I didn't have to do it, but I wanted to do it." He babbled away excitedly, and I grinned to see him so far out of his shell. This was exactly what he needed.

I'll bring them here whenever we can come. He's having so much fun.

I bent, wrapping my arms around him, and kissing his little face. He brushed me away. "Mummy, stop it."

"I'm allowed to," I said, but pulled away. His eyes shone with excitement, and he grabbed my hand, squeezing it.

"Want to go kick the ball around now?" Logan asked.

"YEAH." The boys spoke in unison now, both so excited about playing. Oh, this did my heart good to see them like this.

Logan led us behind the swings and slide, to an area with goalposts and plenty of grass to run around on. I sat on a bench nearby to watch, and Logan joined me as the boys began to kick the ball around.

"They're having fun."

"They are." I looked up at Logan. All that flashy smiling stuff he did when he was being flirty was gone, and a genuine smile shone from his eyes as our gazes met.

"Thanks so much. We saw the park and had talked about coming here. They're really enjoying you playing with them."

He shrugged. "I grew up without a dad. I know how hard it can be."

"Yeah, me too. Never thought I'd have to deal with it with my own kids."

As stupid as it sounded, I hadn't thought of it that way before. This was history repeating itself. My dad had abandoned me years ago.

"My dad overdosed when I was seven. It's tough losing your dad, especially when you're a boy." He gaped. "Sorry, I mean, it can't have been easy for you either."

I shrugged. "My dad walked out on my mum. I was five, and devastated. I remember us being really close, and then there was nothing. My memories of him are really vague, but I still miss him sometimes."

Logan frowned. "See? I get that bad things happen in relationships, but walking out on a kid is really crap. How do you do that to your own flesh and blood?"

I shifted my focus back to the boys, who were laughing and joking while kicking the ball back and forward. "I don't know. I'd do anything for those two. Hell, I still can't believe I made two people."

He laughed and squeezed my arm. "They're great kids. I think they have you to thank for that."

"There are some days that are harder than others, but we're doing okay." I leaned back on the bench and took a deep breath of fresh air.

Why was it so easy to talk to him? Maybe because he'd opened up to me first; I didn't know. It was nice to find someone to talk to. It definitely didn't hurt that he was so cute, and seemed to actually give a crap.

"Logan, come and play," Jack called.

He stood, peeling off his jacket and handing it to me. "If you could look after this, I'll go kick a ball around with the boys. This'll be interesting. Haven't done this in years."

I laughed, shaking my head as he walked away then ran, clapping as the boys jumped up and down, excited to have someone to play with.

Every time we wanted to do something different, go somewhere as a family, it had always been me and the boys. I'd taken them to the zoo, to the movies, swimming. Everywhere we went, it was the three of us, barely ever the four. When Evan had come with us, he'd moan and complain about every little thing. I never saw just how much he'd put himself on the outside of our family until now. Now some stranger played football with my children in front of my eyes.

"Come and play with us," Jack called out.

I bit my lip. I didn't mind running around with them by myself, but I hadn't really come prepared.

"Just leave my jacket on the bench," Logan called.

The lure of playing and having fun with my boys outweighed the thoughts of making a dick of myself running around. I shrugged, dropping my bag and Logan's jacket, and ran out. At least I'd worn flat shoes.

Jack laughed, kicking the ball to me, and then launched himself in my direction. I kicked to the side toward Logan.

"So, are you any good at soccer?" he asked.

"Football."

He cocked an eyebrow, fending off Jack and kicking to Thomas. "Like that, is it?"

"My parents used to have that argument. Mum called it soccer, Dad called it football."

Logan grinned, the ball flying toward him again. Jack and Thomas piled on top of him, knocking him to the ground as he laughed. "You're not supposed to tackle me. We're not playing rugby."

"It's fun." Thomas laughed.

Nothing could be sweeter, hearing the laughter, seeing the smiles.

Watching the ball and not looking where I was going, I crashed into Logan, falling down in a heap at his feet. He fell too, landing almost on top of me, and we found ourselves nose to nose, looking into each other's eyes.

"Sorry," I said.

"I'm the one who's sorry. I clearly wasn't paying attention."

My breath hitched as I looked at him. His body was pressed

against mine, albeit at an awkward angle, but he smelled so good, like musky good, like oh-my-God-I-want-to jump-your-bones good.

"Olivia," he whispered.

"Yes?"

"Your shoe is sticking into my leg and it really freaking hurts."

I burst out laughing, kicking my shoe off from the half on position it was in. I couldn't feel it wedged into his leg, but I hoped that helped. He pushed against the ground and off me, my chest feeling as if it were releasing air for the first time in forever.

He stood, offering his hand for me to grab hold of. "Come on. I think that's going to be it for the day. Let's get you home."

I took his hand, pulling myself up and dusting myself off. We'd played for more than an hour, kicking the ball between the four of us. We felt more like a family than we had in a long time. All because of Logan.

"I think I need another shower after that. The ground is a bit dusty." I looked toward the boys, who stood a few metres away. "Come on guys. Let's get going."

"Awww, Mum," Jack moaned. As usual Thomas followed his brother's lead, but I shook my head.

"Come on. I'm sure Logan has other things to get on with. Let's go home and I'll make some lunch."

"Will you make me lunch too?" Logan asked.

I laughed, nodding. "Sure. I hope you like peanut butter sandwiches."

"They're the best," he said.

As we walked back to the apartment block, the boys wouldn't stop talking, chattering excitedly about the game. It warmed my heart to hear them, especially my quiet, little Thomas, who seemed to hang onto every word Logan said.

In one morning, Logan had paid more attention to my family than my husband had in years. And for that, I would be eternally grateful.

When we got to the road, I swear my heart stopped. Logan held out his hands for the boys to take and led them across the street. There was no hesitation on his part, and the three of them continued their chatter as we walked.

He just fitted in.

Two very tired boys slowly climbed the stairs back to our apartment. There weren't that many, but they were worn out from their play, and I teased them as I came up behind.

"Come on, you two. You've got young legs. You should be racing up these steps."

"Mum," Thomas whined.

"It's okay, buddy. Once we get inside you can have something to eat and have a rest."

Arriving at the door, I unlocked it, opening it up, and the boys raced in, both jumping at the couch. "So *now* you have energy."

Logan laughed. "So, are you really making me a sandwich too?"

"If you want one."

He leaned against the doorframe, smiling as I followed my children.

"I should probably go and do some work, but I'll take a raincheck."

I turned. "Maybe I'll pack you a lunchbox someday." His eyes bore into me, and I shrunk back, wanting to go back inside before I turned the colour of a fire truck.

He nodded. "Thanks for this morning, Olivia. Your boys are so much fun. I hope they enjoyed themselves."

"I think they'll be sleeping very well tonight, thank you."

He opened his mouth, looking as if he were about to say something before closing it again.

"I bet. See you 'round."

"Sure thing."

I closed the door behind me and turned toward the boys. One lay on the couch, the other on the floor.

"Tired, you guys?"

"Can we have lunch?" Jack asked.

"I'm just going to make some now."

As I grabbed the bag of bread and the jar of peanut butter, memories of the morning gave me a warm glow. Whether Logan was interested in me or not, my boys were happier than they had been in ages. Remembering what it felt like to be pressed against Logan made my heart race all over again. It had been so good to be so close to him; that smell would stay in my memory forever.

Whatever happened from here on in, this was one very special day.

10

BY MONDAY, I was still pondering our little outing, and wondering about Logan's motivation. Was he just saying thank you, or had there been more to it? Had I had my head stuck in my stories for too long? More than once, I found myself daydreaming about those muscular arms and how they'd feel, holding onto them while he ...

What the hell was wrong with me? I'd spent more time in the past few months writing about sex than getting anywhere near having it. And before that, my sex life with Evan had been nowhere near as exciting as my imagination.

"You ask me? You need to get laid," Rebecca said, wagging an index finger at me.

"By who? I'm not in much of a position to meet men. Besides, I don't want any complications. I don't want to confuse the boys by throwing someone new into the mix."

"And yet, you took them to the park with your next-door neighbour and rolled around with him on the ground."

I buried my face in my hands in embarrassment. "That's not quite what happened. I should never have told you that."

"What about What's-His-Name?" she asked, shrugging.

"Who?"

"That woman who your husband ran off with, her partner. He's alone."

I gaped at her. "You really think I should just sleep with someone? He's a nice guy, but I'm not interested in him in that way."

She sat down in a seat on the other side of my desk and put her feet up. "Your neighbour sounds interested."

Yeah, and I'm interested in him.

"I'm not his type."

"Really? Do you think that guys who think girls aren't their type take them and their children to the park *just* to hang out?"

I twisted my mouth, trying to think of what to say.

"Hey. Seeing as you're my boss, shouldn't you be leaving me alone to get on with my work?" I smiled sweetly, and she smirked.

"Nice avoiding the question, but yes, I have work to do too. Talk to you later."

Her feet slid off my desk, and she winked as she looked back at the door. "Maybe you'll have some gossip then."

If I'd had something soft, I probably would have thrown it at her.

LATER IN THE WEEK, I pulled into the car park, sighing as I opened the door to let the kids out. This routine was really getting to me; having to do things by myself was getting more and more exhausting. We'd had cocktail sausages and two minute noodles far too often lately.

I loved my job, my new friends, the life I'd made for myself. It was being alone that was tiring.

Lost in thought, I didn't see Logan at first. I looked up when the boys called his name and ran to where he knelt, doing something on what I assumed was his car. I wasn't much for noticing cars, but Evan always had his heart set on one of these and we could never afford it. It was a HSV Clubsport with full leather interior, painted silver, and pretty good-looking. If you liked that kind of thing. I bet it ran much better than my dirty old Mazda.

"Hey," I said.

"Hey Liv, how's things?"

I nodded. "As good as they're going to get."

His face lit up with a devilish grin, as if he were about to suggest something wicked, but he looked down at the boys, who were all but clinging to his legs.

"What are you two up to?" he asked.

"What you doing?" Thomas spoke up. He was growing in confidence all the time. I couldn't be more proud.

"I went to start this thing and she wasn't very happy. So, I went and got a part to fix her."

Thomas nodded, his big blue eyes gazing up adoringly at the man who had just answered his very important question.

"Mum's car sucks. It doesn't work very well," Jack spoke, looking at Logan with the same adoration his younger brother displayed.

"That's no good. Want me to look at it?" The question was directed at me, and I fell back under that intense gaze. I tried so hard not to look straight at him. With those black jeans and singlet, which showed all those impressive arm muscles, I'd be hot under the collar in seconds.

I shrugged. "It's just old. I'll probably drive it until it dies for good."

"If you ever need a hand looking for something new, I'd be happy to help."

"Thanks. I don't think that will happen any time soon, but I appreciate the offer." I smiled at him and he cocked his head, as if he were about to say something else, but he seemed to think better of it, looking down at the boys again. This seemed to be a habit of his. *Wonder what he wants to say.*

"How about we get inside and I'll get dinner started?" I said.

"Aww Mum," Jack said.

"You take care of your mother. She looks like she's had a long day," said Logan.

Oh great, I must look like crap.

They trailed along reluctantly behind me as we went up the stairs, and I paused to let them in the apartment first. I'd quite happily just heat up some frozen meals and collapse into bed tonight. At least it was nearly Friday.

"Olivia." I heard a voice behind me, and turned to see Evan walking in my direction. Nausea washed over me, I hadn't heard from him in months; what could he want now? He could leave my kids alone, that was for sure. I'd go into debt forever if I had to fight him for them.

"Evan?" I swallowed it down. Whatever he wanted, I was in the right. I had to remember that.

"What the hell are you doing here?" he asked.

I looked at him, confused. "What do you mean? We live here."

"I got your forwarding address from our old neighbour. There's some other people living in *our* house."

I took a deep breath, exhaling with a loud sigh. "It *was* our house. It stopped being our house a long time ago."

"So where's my money?"

"What money?"

"Well, if you sold the house, there'll be money from the sale. Where's my share?"

I shook my head. "There is no money. What I got for the house just covered what was owing. I am happy to show you all the paperwork, Evan, but there is no money for either of us."

His breathing quickened. I wondered for a moment if he'd been drinking—his eyes were that bloodshot. He raised his hand, and in an instant I thought of the fights we'd had over the years. So much yelling, him telling me how useless I was, calling me every name under the sun. The only thing he'd never done was hit me, and now that was about to happen right outside my apartment.

"Evan," I whispered.

A large hand appeared out of nowhere, grabbing hold of Evan's arm and pulling it back and away from me.

"What the hell?" Evan exclaimed as Logan came up level to him. Evan was tall, but Logan was taller, and he looked down at Evan with a scowl on his face.

"You really want to try that?" Logan asked.

"Get lost. It's none of your business. I'm talking to my wife."

Logan looked at me with an eyebrow raised before looking back at Evan. "You're almost on my doorstep. I think that makes it my business."

Evan shrunk back. "Olivia?"

"Go away, Evan. There's nothing here for you."

I felt someone behind me, and looked down at Jack, peeping out around the door. When he saw it was Evan, he disappeared back inside, and his reaction was enough for Logan.

"Olivia, if you want to talk to him, I'll stick around if you need me."

I shook my head. "That's not necessary. Evan is leaving."

I met Evan's eyes, and all I saw was irritation—not love, not regret, just annoyance that he wasn't getting anything from me.

He just looked at me for a moment. My skin crawled at the thought of him ever touching me, ever being that close. How on earth did I ever love him? "Whatever," he spat the word, turning on his heel. I watched as he went back down the stairs and across the car park, never looking back at the family he'd left behind. Typical.

As I turned, I realised Logan's gaze was on me. His eyes were full of far more compassion than my husband's had ever been.

"You okay?" he asked.

I shrugged. "Thanks for showing up when you did."

"Has he hit you before?"

I shook my head. "Never. Our relationship was broken for a long time, but he never laid a hand on me."

"Sorry for prying. I just don't get someone like that. To walk away from a family like you have. Man must be a total idiot."

I smiled, biting down on my lip to stop laughing. "You could say that."

"Any time you want to talk, Liv, I'm here."

I watched as he walked back downstairs to his car. He'd given me more in the way of friendship and companionship than my husband had in years.

We still barely knew one another.

SNUGGLED UP on the couch with the laptop, I stared, lost in thought, at the screen. The boys were fast asleep, and I was forming an idea for a new book.

As much as I fought the idea, Logan had stirred feelings in me that I hadn't felt in forever. If I ever did at all. Now to put the words together.

I looked up as the phone rang and sighed. Who could that be? It meant moving from my comfy spot. Then again, it could be important.

I shoved the laptop off my lap over to the other side of the couch and got up, making my way across the room to the phone.

I really should get another base unit to sit on the coffee table.

"Hello?"

"I thought it was about time we celebrated your moving with a bottle of wine." Rebecca's voice nearly deafened me, and I frantically pushed the volume button to quieten her.

"I don't know, I ..."

"Open your door."

There was a short knock on the door, and I rolled my eyes, grinning. There would be no waiting for her to arrive.

Sure enough on the other side of the door she stood with a wine bottle in one hand, her phone in the other. We hadn't had an evening together since I lived in the old house.

I looked at the phone in my hand and pressed the hang-up button.

Wagging my finger at her, I laughed. "You know, this is becoming a habit."

She shrugged. "At least I'm not drinking alone. Just one glass and I'll leave. I really wanted to come and check out the place."

"Welcome to Chateau de Grant."

Rebecca laughed. "Better tell the lord of the manor to fix this light along the balcony. It's not safe to have this big dark patch."

"Come inside where it's safe, then."

She looked around as she entered, her expression blank. I was pretty sure she was hiding that whole underwhelmed feeling. "Cosy."

"Yes, I know it's smaller than the last place." I closed the door, going to the kitchen to fetch a couple of glasses for us to use.

When I came back, the bottle was on the coffee table and she'd picked up the laptop. "Working on something new?"

"Yeah. I kind of got inspired today."

The cork flew out of my hands as I opened the wine, flying across the room and hitting the wall between my apartment and Logan's with a thud.

"Inspired by anything in particular?"

I laughed. "Maybe."

She cocked an eyebrow. "Oh, really? Pretty sure that shade is called fire-engine red."

My face felt as if it were melting. "Evan came by—"

Her jaw dropped. "No. You have not got back together with that cocksmack."

"No! Oh good grief, no. Never in a million years, no. But, anyway, he got all angry at me for selling the house. You know, the one I saved for and paid the mortgage on. I told him there was no money for either of us and he nearly hit me."

Rebecca placed the laptop on the table, frowning as I sat beside her, pouring the wine.

"I hope you called the police."

"Turns out I have a guard dog next door."

At that she squinted, obviously curious. "What?"

"My neighbour came to my rescue. Anyway, he stopped Evan in his tracks."

"Is this Mr Hot Neighbour who took you and the kids to the park?"

I grinned. "The very same."

"I have *got* to see this guy."

As if on cue, there was a knock at the door.

"You are popular tonight," Rebecca said, leaning back on the couch with her glass in her hand.

I went back to the entrance. "Who is it?"

"Logan."

I looked at Rebecca over my shoulder, raising an eyebrow. She shrugged as the grin took over her face.

Without thinking, I smoothed my shirt down, ignoring a faint laugh behind me before I turned to put my finger to my lips to indicate she should be quiet. She shook her head and I turned back to the door, pulling at the handle.

He stood on the other side of the door, his brows furrowed in concern. "Are you okay?"

"I'm fine. Why?"

"Just heard a noise, and something hit the wall. It was just a bit late, and I thought I'd better check it out."

I stifled a giggle. "That was me. We opened a bottle of wine."

His lips turned down, and I thought I saw disappointment in his eyes. "As long as you're all okay. I thought I'd better check. Especially with this damn light not working."

"We're fine. Thanks for checking."

He studied my face, looking for something. Maybe he thought I was hiding something after the earlier events. "I'll leave you to your wine."

"Are you sure?" Rebecca called. "I can only have one glass because I'm driving, and there's plenty left."

His eyebrow snaked up.

"I'm having a glass of wine with my boss, Rebecca. You're welcome to join us."

Now he lit up. "Sure. Sounds great."

The way Rebecca looked him up and down, I could tell I'd have some explaining to do. She was noticing him just the way I did.

"So, you're the famous Logan," she said as I retrieved another glass from the kitchen. I clapped one hand across my forehead. Sure, talk it up. I only had to live next door to him.

"I don't know about that. Liv?" Logan was looking at me with those beautiful brown puppy-dog eyes.

"I told Rebecca about our trip to the park. You have to excuse her, she's not quite all there." I smiled sweetly as Rebecca peed herself laughing in the corner.

I sat on the chair opposite the couch as Logan was now seated next to Rebecca. Leaning forward, I poured the wine into the glass and pushed it across the table at him.

"So you've been talking about me?" he asked.

"Now I have two of you ganging up on me? Great." I shook my head, looking at the ceiling. They both had their eyes on me.

"I have been telling Olivia that she needs to go out and get laid. You know, move on from her crappy ex-husband."

Logan's eyes were fixed on me as I looked back down, and he smiled that cheeky grin that made the butterflies in my stomach dance.

"Sounds like a great idea. Where do I sign up?"

It was only Rebecca's laughter that broke our gaze.

And I was struggling to find words.

11

I FIGURED it was my turn to say thank you to Logan, for defending me against Evan. That, and to apologise for Rebecca mouthing off. I knew she was just trying to push me, but it was a bit much at times.

After breakfast on Saturday morning, I set to baking cookies. When I'd been at home with Mum, I'd been quite a prolific baker. I loved working with dough, and who doesn't like making a mess?

The boys were wide-eyed at the sight. It wasn't something I did often, and both of them wanted to help. I resolved to bake more often.

Jack sifted the flour while Thomas added the chocolate chips. He painstakingly took each and every one out of the bag individually, placing them in the dough until I tipped his hand up and they scattered in the mixture, over the bench and all over the floor.

"Mummy." Thomas giggled.

"We can vacuum them up."

"Five second rule?" Jack asked.

I shrugged. The floor was freshly mopped. At least I knew it was clean.

Jack dived onto the floor, picking them up and popping them straight into his mouth, and I laughed as Thomas joined him.

"Just leave them, I'll sort them out. There's some left in the bag; you guys can have those when we finish." I cocked my head, trying to look serious. "Come back here and we'll roll out the dough and you two can use the cookie cutters to cut them into shapes."

By the time 10am rolled around, we had a tray of perfectly cooked chocolate chip cookies in all different shapes. I'd accumulated different cookie cutters over the years into a collection. Now the boys used every single one.

"These look yummy," Jack said.

"We're going to take some next door to Logan. To say thank you."

I turned my focus to the cookies, placing them one by one on the plate.

Jack tugged on my sleeve. "From when Daddy came?"

My little man—so wise beyond his years.

"Yes. Logan's been good to us, so we need to say thank you."

"I wish we could go to the park," Thomas said.

"Another day, baby."

I ran the vacuum over the kitchen floor, picking up the remaining chips before we gathered some cookies on a plate and left the apartment. Taking a deep breath, I knocked on Logan's door.

It took a while for it to open, but he was worth the wait. Clearly he'd just woken up from his still sleepy eyes, and he'd either slept in his jeans or he'd just dragged them on. He didn't wear a shirt.

There was that beautiful chest that made my stomach flip with excitement.

Down, girl.

"Oh, hey, Liv. What's up? Everything okay?"

My mouth went dry as I looked at him. I struggled to raise my eyes from his abs, my heart pounding hard.

"I ... um ... everything's fine." I thrust the plate towards him. "Cookies."

He smirked, raising an eyebrow. "Have you been to the bakery?"

"We made them," Thomas exclaimed.

"Really?" Logan grinned. "That makes them extra special. Come in. I can probably throw together a coffee, or juice for the kids."

We followed him into his apartment. I'd never seen it before, and I was struck by how empty it was. There was a couch along one wall, with a TV and cabinet opposite, a coffee table in the middle. A small table stood next to the kitchen area with a couple of chairs.

There were no decorations, no books, nothing. Not like our place, where I'd cut down on how much stuff we had, but it still seemed to be bursting at the seams.

I placed the cookies on the coffee table and followed him over to the kitchen.

"So did you really make the cookies?" he asked.

"It was a joint effort. There were a million chocolate chips all over my kitchen floor to prove it."

He laughed. "Sounds like fun."

"Mum, can we have a cookie?" Jack asked.

"Yep, one each."

Logan turned back toward me, a glass in each hand. "Here's some orange juice for the boys. Do you want one, or a coffee? I've just put some water on."

"Coffee would be nice, please."

Our fingers touched as I took the glasses, and I tingled at the connection. *Stop this, stop acting like a teenager. You're a grown-up.*

"There's a PlayStation there, if the boys want to play some games. I can turn it on so we can chat."

I nodded. "That'll be fun for them. We have a computer, but it's shared."

"Any time they want to play, just let me know. They're welcome to use it."

How much more perfect could he be?

"Thanks."

I went back to the boys, handing them their glasses. "Be careful you two. Don't spill anything."

They sipped at their juice, nibbling at the cookies.

"They're so good, Mum. We're awesome cooks," Jack said, grinning at his brother.

"You are fantastic cooks. Now to teach you to cook dinner." They giggled as I smiled at them.

Logan came in moments later, placing two cups of coffee on the table.

"Where are all your things?" Jack asked.

"Jack. Don't be so rude." My face was heating up.

Logan laughed. "It's fine. Most of my things are in storage. I'm just living here while I renovate my house. I bought an old place to do up. It's where I spend a lot of time on the weekends. It's happening slowly, because it's a part-time project, but I'm getting there."

"We used to have a house," Jack said, his lips downturned. "It was cool."

That stabbed me right in the chest. I knew he missed the place, I did too, but to hear him say that hurt more than I'd thought it would.

"Well, bud, I think your mum is doing a pretty good job keeping a roof over your heads. You gotta do what you gotta do." Logan winked at me. "Now, how about I turn that PlayStation on. There are a few games that are probably a bit too grown-up for you, but I think I've got a Lego one here."

Jack's eyes widened. "Awesome."

I watched as the three of them sorted out controllers and started the game. Pretty soon the boys were ripping into it, bashing Lego blocks as they went, squealing and laughing, and my heart grew still again. That was, until Logan joined me back on the couch.

"At least I can't fall on you, sitting here quietly." He grinned, and took a sip of his coffee.

I laughed, shaking my head as I met his eyes.

"I mean, unless you want me to. But your children are right there."

Rolling my eyes, I took a drink and turned my attention to the boys. They were bouncing around as their characters onscreen broke up the blocks, so full of energy and fun. This whole experience had brought us so close together.

"Your friend is pretty full on."

I glanced back at Logan. He cocked his head, looking at me curiously.

"I was really lucky to find her. All this happened after I started working for her, and she has been amazing. But yeah, she's a lot to get used to."

He nodded. "She's looking out for you."

"I don't know what I'd do without her." *For a variety of reasons.*

An unwanted thought hit me. *What if he's interested in her?* Time to test the water.

"She's single, if you're interested." There. I said it. Not that I wanted a positive answer.

His eyes darted from me to the boys and back again. "I'm sure she's great, but I am looking for someone a bit more quiet, someone who is just happy to snuggle on the couch. I get the feeling that any guy who took her on would end up naked and tied up somewhere."

I laughed so hard that I snorted, and I held my hand over my nose, blushing at the sound. He just grinned and shook his head.

"Mum, check this out," Jack said as he built some great Lego structure and then blew it up to beat the bad guys.

"Those two are awesome," Logan said quietly.

"Very much so." I ran my finger around the rim of the coffee cup, looking at the brown milky liquid.

"I meant what I said. Any time I'm at home they're welcome to come and play like this. I have the odd night when I relax and play PlayStation, but I'm usually working or at the house."

I looked up. He was so kind, it was unbelievable. "Thanks. What do you do for a job?"

He nodded. "I'm a mechanic. I own a garage over on Beach Road."

Business owner with his own house. "Nice. So ..." I took a sip of coffee and swallowed, smiling sweetly. "How old are you?"

Logan laughed. "All these questions. Are you interested, Ms Grant?"

Retreat, retreat, retreat.

"I was just curious. Your own business, and you own a house. You look like you're around the same age as me, and I know what a struggle it was to buy our place."

"I'm twenty-three. The business was my father's. A friend of the family ran it until I was old enough to take it over, but I've worked there since I left school. And for the record, the house was really cheap because of the work that needed doing to it. Most of the structural stuff is done, and now I'm working on the tidying up and then the interior. Does that answer your questions?"

I nodded. "Most satisfactorily."

There was that grin again. The one that made me want to abandon my self-respect and pounce. I'd never had that feeling with anyone before, or if I had it was so long ago, before I'd had to grow up.

"So how far apart in age are we? I mean, I'm guessing you're older, having had Jack, but are we talking cougar or what?" he asked.

I nearly spat my coffee out. "Ha ha. I'm nearly twenty-six."

"Oh, damn. I thought I was onto something there."

Slapping his arm with my palm, I shook my head at him. I'd never been that good at making friends; Donna and now Rebecca were the exception. But Logan made me feel so comfortable. It was weird and good.

"So, what do you do?" he asked.

"I work in administration. Mostly accounting, and, well, anything else my boss needs doing."

"And you used to have a house?"

I sighed. "Yeah. I had to let it go when it became just me. I tried to make it work ..." I didn't even know how to finish that sentence. Giving it up was too raw after all I'd done to buy it.

"I'm glad you guys moved in. You've definitely brought some fun to this place, and you've only been here five minutes." Logan punched my arm, gently.

"The boys have been telling me how much they loved the trip to the park."

His gaze was intense. "Just the boys?" he asked.

I looked back down at the coffee. "Maybe me too."

12

THAT NIGHT I dreamed of him for the first time.

Maybe it was the way he'd intervened when Evan had turned up. Maybe it was his kindness and gentleness that made me melt. Maybe it was the way my boys had grown so attached so fast, and he never had a harsh word to say to them, even when they must have been a pain in the butt.

But that wasn't what I dreamed of.

I dreamed of him, holding me in his arms, kissing me as if his life depended on it, touching me.

His hand stroked my bare skin, fingers dancing over the exposed flesh. He was only one of two men to ever see me this way, and yet I knew he saw so much more than I had on display.

He grazed his lips down my neck, kneading my breast as I gasped for air. His touch woke something in me that had been dormant, awoken briefly the night before Evan left me, but sleeping for so long before that.

My body tingled in the morning, an after-effect of the vivid dream I'd had. I slowly opened my eyes, half expecting him to be there, lying beside me. Rolling over, I'd been disappointed to find that I was alone in a cold bed.

I yawned, and closed my eyes for just a few more minutes, hoping to extend my dream. Instead, the alarm blared and I reluctantly climbed out of bed.

All day I thought about my dream, smiling to myself, my workload just that little bit easier to deal with as memories of how my body had reacted to Logan's imaginary touch drifted to the surface.

I stopped for fish and chips on the way home, eager to start my new story. This time I had the most amazing source material. I wanted to write what I'd dreamed, the way Logan's hands made me feel, the way his kisses burned on my skin.

I'd felt as if I'd been forcing it all this time, trying to create passion but never truly feeling it. Now? Now I ached to write down every emotion, ever reaction my body had. Even if it was just a dream.

Nearly everything I'd written had come from reading, studying the Internet for graphic descriptions of how people touched each other. I'd experienced some of it myself, but Evan was selfish, from what I could tell now, always putting himself first. From what I'd read, I'd missed out on *a lot*.

I sat at the keyboard, wondering if I dare ask Logan for details. What he did to make a woman feel special. Holy shit. Why did I think he was any different to Evan?

Because he just was.

He was sweet and caring, a gentleman. He'd be the type to give you fifty orgasms before worrying about his own needs. Okay, maybe that was a slight exaggeration. All I knew was that when he was close my heart beat faster, and my sweat glands went into overload.

Too much information, Olivia.

I laughed out loud at the thought of using that in one of my stories. Who wants a sweaty heroine?

And then I began to write.

"ARE WE KEEPING YOU AWAKE?" Rebecca asked on Monday morning

I was on my third coffee for the morning and it was only 9.30.

"I was inspired last night, stayed up late writing. In fact, I wrote most of the weekend."

She nodded. "That would do it. Just don't overdo the coffee or you'll never get any sleep tonight either."

"That's not a bad thing, I have more I want to get out. It's just pouring from me right now."

She started chewing on her lip.

"Rebecca, you don't have to worry about my work. I think you'll find it's still up to my usual standard. I'm just a little tired."

Rebecca sighed. "I'm not concerned about your work. I know you well enough already to know that. I just don't want to see you stretch yourself too far. You've got a lot on your plate with everything that's happened. And Olivia, you're my friend. I don't want to see you wear yourself out."

That meant so much, after what I'd been through. She'd helped me with so much and just kept on giving. I'd never be able to repay her.

"Thanks, Rebecca."

"I want what you've written so I can check it out. I need something to keep me company at night."

Shaking my head, I laughed as she left the room. She'd been such a godsend to me, just when I needed her. I'd take better care of myself.

I emailed it to her when I got home that night. I'd managed to get a lot written after our little visit to Logan, and as I reread it, I felt every emotion, remembered every lustful thought.

After dinner, I tucked in the boys and got back to the laptop to write.

A sudden shrill noise made me jump, and it took me a second to work out the phone was ringing. I rubbed my forehead, and wiped the drool off the laptop where I'd fallen asleep.

My bleary eyes tried to focus as I looked at the clock. *11.30pm. This had better be good.*

"Hello?" I mumbled.

"Oh. My. God, Olivia."

I exhaled. Nothing major then.

"What are you doing, Rebecca?"

"Reading your story and holy crap, you are onto something. This is so freaking hot. And sexy. And sweet. I would just want to hump this guy into next week if he was real."

He is.

"You really think it's good?"

"Yes. I stand by what I said earlier. You need to not work so hard. But this one is a real winner. At least, it gets me going."

I rolled my eyes, resting my forehead in my hand.

"Thanks. I'm going to bed now. I fell asleep at the computer."

"Good. Rest up. Oh, and Olivia?"

"Yes?"

"The only part that needs work is the oral sex scene. You should ask your muse for tips. Maybe he can demonstrate." She laughed.

When I hung up the phone, I slumped back in the chair, staring at the ceiling. She might have been joking, but she was probably right. I wasn't that experienced when it came to receiving pleasure, it was usually about giving. Could I even ask about that? I mean, I thought we were having this little flirtation, but would Logan stretch so far as to speak to me about his actual sex life?

I'd think about it in the morning.

13

ON FRIDAY we came home to Logan on the doorstep, his hands full of plastic takeaway containers.

"I figured I'd have Chinese, and it's cheaper if you get the special deals. I always end up with a whole lot of leftovers to get through."

"Uh-huh." I smiled to myself. I could almost pretend this was a date if I tried hard enough. Or if I got really brave I could ask him the question I had to help me with my book.

I unlocked the door, and the boys pushed past me and into the apartment. I shook my head.

"After you," Logan said. I smiled and led him inside, helping close the door afterwards.

"Right guys, we need some plates and knives and forks," I said, wearily. It had been a long week, not helped by the hours I'd been putting into my writing. I loved doing it so much, but it was taking a toll. It'd be worth it when the book was finished and released.

"Do you just want me to put these on the table?"

I looked up. Logan stood over the open laptop, and I held my breath before realising it would have gone to sleep while I was at work.

"Yeah. I'll clear the computer away."

I walked around the table and grabbed it, taking it to my room and dropping it on the bed.

Whew.

"Now. Where were we?" I asked as I returned with a smile. My secret was safe for the moment.

The sound of clattering cutlery came from the kitchen. Jack was going through the drawer, finding forks and knives and spoons to serve up the food. I didn't have the heart to tell him we didn't need everything he'd pulled out, but it didn't matter if we used it all. He was so proud he'd helped. I grabbed the plates and we placed the whole lot on the table and stood back.

We all just looked at each other.

"Now what?" Logan laughed.

"I'll get the boys' plates done and then we can have ours. If that's okay with you."

He nodded. "That's all good with me. I'm sure they're hungry."

I started to open the containers.

"That looks yuck," Thomas declared.

"It's so yummy, Thomas. I promise," Logan said.

"It's got green stuff in it."

"Yummy green stuff." Logan nodded as Thomas shook his head.

I laughed. "You've had broccoli before, just not like this. It's nice, sweetie."

He twisted his little mouth, looking between us as if he didn't believe it.

"Okay," he finally said.

As he rounded the table to take a seat, Logan met my eye with a smile. Here we were, back with family time again, him making up the four. I loved how good this felt. How right this felt.

Wonderful.

BOTH JACK and Thomas had eaten themselves silly, and Thomas even declared the broccoli 'yummy' before I made them brush their teeth and go to bed, despite their complaining.

"Thank you," I said to Logan as I came back out of their bedroom.

"You're welcome." He sat on the couch and I sat down beside him, picking up the remote control.

"Wonder if there's anything on television?" I clicked the remote and started to flick through the channels.

"If there's not, we could just talk."

I kept my eyes on the television, not wanting to look at him. I just knew he'd have that caring, earnest look in his eyes. The one that told me he was genuine.

Part of me wanted him to be flirting with me because that seemed to just be him. And part of me wanted it to be so much more. As much as Evan had hurt me, I didn't know if I was ready to plunge myself into something new.

I'm scared.

"Oh, *Die Hard*'s on. I love that film," I said with a big smile.

Hated that film. Why the hell did I say that?

I glanced at Logan. He smirked, leaning back on the couch. "I haven't seen it in a while. Great film."

"I think I've got a bottle of wine in the fridge if you want some." *Might as well find some way to enjoy this now I've painted myself into a corner.*

"Sounds good. I'm not much of a wine drinker, but I'll give it a go."

As I reached the kitchen, I could only find one wine glass when I knew I'd had at least three out before. Great. *Put them away somewhere and forget where they are.* The rest of the set were in a top cupboard. Logan watched curiously as I retrieved a dining chair.

"What are you doing?"

"Getting a wine glass for you."

He followed me back into the kitchen, leaning against the kitchen counter as I climbed on the chair. He nodded as I located a glass, and bent to place it on the surface before stepping down.

"What?" I asked.

"Just admiring the view."

Do you ever stop flirting?

I laughed, and popped the cork on the wine, pouring it into the glasses.

"Here you go."

He took the glass, studying me closely. "Thanks. You should learn to take a compliment, you know."

"What do you mean?" I asked.

"You barely acknowledge any time I say something nice. You blush, so I know you've heard. Didn't anyone ever say anything nice to you before?"

I shrugged. "Not very often."

Walking back to the couch with the wine bottle in one hand, glass in the other, I set the bottle down on the coffee table and went back to looking at the television.

"Well, I think that's crazy. There are a lot of nice things to say about you."

"You barely even know me."

"I've seen enough."

He sat back down beside me, and I turned my head toward him.

"You're a good person, Liv. I only have to see how much those boys adore you to know that. And you're strong. Look how well you've held it together for them."

I shook my head. "I lost our house." The wine smelled amazing as I took a deep breath in my glass, then took a big mouthful. I swallowed the sweet, fruity liquid to give me strength. *How do you perform oral sex on a woman? Stop. It.*

"But you didn't lose them. The three of you are together and that's awesome. You're awesome. I'm glad we're friends."

Friends. He said we're friends. Not that he wants me. We're friends.

"So am I," I said.

As the movie went on, I finished my glass of wine, and followed it with another. Logan cradled that first glass in his hands and I wondered if he really liked it, or if he were drinking it for me.

Soon enough, the whole bottle was gone and I had enough liquid courage to conquer the world.

"I should do the dishes," I said.

"I'll give you a hand with them. You wash, I'll dry?"

"Sounds good."

We worked in silence for a while, before I finally found the guts to ask him my very important question.

"Logan?"

"Yes?" he asked.

"What do you do when you go down on a woman?" I asked.

He gaped at me in disbelief. "Why are you asking that? Planning on doing it?"

I blushed and laughed, shaking my head. "Just a discussion that we were having at work with the girls. They were discussing technique and I was just curious about yours."

Logan stood, and moved behind me as I continued to wash the dishes. "We could always have a practical demonstration, Olivia."

When he used my full name, a shiver went up my spine. He was so close I was sure I could feel the electricity between us.

Just friends.

"Just tell me."

He placed his hands either side of me on the kitchen counter, giving me enough room to continue what I was doing, but standing close enough I could feel his breath on the back of my neck.

"Well, I kiss her inner thighs from her knee, all the way up slowly. Anticipation is the key to success."

I laughed. "Is that right?"

"Then, I start with my tongue, slowly. I am such a tease, Olivia, I really am."

My heart was pounding. His nose nestled in the nape of my neck and he inhaled as if he was taking in my scent. I hadn't been so aroused in such a long time.

"It sounds like it," I whispered.

"Then I flick my tongue over her, licking her like a cat licks cream from a bowl. By then she's gasping, wanting more, and I give it to her, pushing my tongue as far as I can into her and then licking her like a lollipop."

My entire body was on fire, and I wished I'd taken him up on his offer of a practical demonstration.

But that wasn't going to happen any time soon. He enjoyed teasing me too much, and I had seen the girls he went for. They were nothing like me.

Snap out of it, Olivia.

"Is that right?" The words came out as a half cough, and I tried to find the strength to behave like a normal human being, instead of an incredibly horny single woman who hadn't been laid in forever. Not that Evan was into oral—at least, not him on me.

"Are you feeling okay, Olivia? I haven't finished telling you what I do. Want me to leave so you can touch yourself?"

His teasing words snapped me out of the haze I'd fallen in to. "Don't be gross. I need to get some sleep."

He stepped back, the warmth of his body fading.

I turned, looking at him. He looked uncertain, as if he'd crossed a boundary and I was pushing him away. Instantly regretting my tone, I reached out and took his hand. "Sorry, I didn't mean to snap. I'm just really tired. That wine was a bit much."

He grinned, looking down at his hand in mine.

"You know, I'm always available for a demonstration. Free of charge."

Part of me wanted to say yes, give in to the yearning I had to be touched by this beautiful man. Everything I'd been through with Evan leaving was still fresh, I'd moved on, but I was terrified of being let down, hurt again.

I pulled my hands away, looking down. "Thanks for the offer. I think I'll pass."

"Oh." He sounded disappointed, hurt even. "I should get going anyway, let you get on with your night."

He turned away, and my heart yearned to reach out for him. My head told me I would only get hurt.

And then he was gone, and I went to the laptop to type the words he'd inspired. Now I knew just how to write my scene. I'd felt awful asking him something so personal and then pushing him away. Using him. What must he think of me? How much had I hurt him?

I'm so confused.

14

"MUMMY, MUMMY."

I woke to find Thomas standing in the doorway to my room at midnight, a dark patch on his pyjamas where he'd vomited, tears streaming down his face. It was Jack that was calling, seeking help for his little brother.

"Oh, baby," I whispered, carrying him to the bathroom for a clean up.

His bottom lip stuck out as he tried so hard not to cry. I smiled, stroking his head and brushing a stray hair off his face.

"We'll get you out of these pyjamas and find some new ones. You can come and hop into bed with me for the rest of the night, okay?"

He nodded, wiping his nose with the back of his hand as he sniffed.

I pulled the wet pyjamas off and ran some water in the basin to wash his face and hands. A bath could wait until tomorrow. Jack appeared with another pair of pyjamas.

"Thanks, sweetie. You get back to sleep. I'll come and clean Thomas's bed in a minute."

Jack patted Thomas on the head. "Get better soon." Proud that he'd helped, he raised his head as he skipped back to his bedroom.

"Come on," I whispered, towelling him off and pulling on his pyjamas. He looked so miserable I hugged him tight, giving him a kiss on his forehead. He was a little warm, and going nowhere in the morning.

"How about you climb in bed with me, and we'll snuggle up? I'll get you a container for if you're sick and we can stay home tomorrow."

He nodded, frowning all the way back to my bed. I lifted him in, and retrieved an empty plastic container before returning to my room.

Everything ached as I traipsed back to bed, my own tiredness turning my thoughts to Evan. When he was with us, life carried on as normal with a sick child. Sure, I'd have more to clean up when I got home, but I could still work and the rest of our routine remained the same. Five days sick leave a year wouldn't stretch very far between the three of us and I couldn't afford to miss too much work.

Damn you, Evan.

It wasn't that I resented having to stay home with a sick child; I loved being able to mother them. Now, it was one more burden I had to carry by myself. All because my husband cared more about himself than his family.

Stop it. Stop wallowing in self-pity. Your babies need you.

I climbed in bed beside Thomas. His little face was flushed, and his eyelids were trying to force themselves closed.

"Get some sleep, sweetheart. I'm right here if you need me."

He nodded, his eyes closing slowly as he gave in to sleep.

Me on the other hand? I'd rather be ill myself than have either of those two sick, at least they wouldn't be miserable and uncomfortable. I'd be lucky to grab a wink of sleep tonight.

BEEP, *beep, beep*

The alarm wouldn't stop, no matter how many times I thumped it. Sitting up and pressing the 'off' button, I looked next to me. Thomas was sleeping peacefully, and I had some distant memory of waking several times during the night to help him. Hopefully this was the end of it, but we were going nowhere today.

I still needed to get Jack ready for school and take him, and I climbed out of bed to call Rebecca and let her know I was staying home.

Jack was at the table when I got up, waiting for his breakfast, and I opened the pantry, finding the missing wine glasses I'd obviously left there in an absent-minded moment. Sighing, I poured Jack a bowl of cereal which he gulped down.

"Hungry, baby?"

He nodded. "Want some more?"

Jack shook his head, and climbed off his seat. "Good boy. Go brush your teeth and we'll get you into your uniform."

I picked up the phone and dialled Rebecca. The hum of her car was in the background. She was always in the office early.

"Rebecca, it's Olivia."

"Oh, hey, Olivia. Is everything okay?"

I sighed. "No. Thomas has some pukey bug and I'm keeping him home today. Thankfully Jack hasn't got it. I'm about to get him dressed and take him to school."

As I said the words, a loud cough-hiccup-burp noise came from the bathroom.

"Scratch that."

"I could hear him from here," Rebecca said. "Just take care of yourself and don't come back until you're all over whatever it is."

"Thanks, Rebecca." I could never express just how grateful I was to have her in my life.

"No problem. You work so damn hard. Don't be too worried about taking time that you're owed."

I breathed a sigh of relief.

"I'll have to keep them home tomorrow too, but I'll see you the day after hopefully."

"Let me know how you go. I'm here if you need me." I nodded, rolling my eyes at the realisation that she couldn't see me. "And Olivia? Press that publish button.'"

"Maybe, if I have time."

As soon as I hung up the phone, I raced to the bathroom. Jack stood over the toilet, no colour in his face, but a grin from ear to ear.

"Oh, honey."

"I got to the bathroom, Mum."

"Yeah, you did. Just as well you're still in your PJs. Want to lie down?"

He nodded. "I'll get you a container in case you're sick again and bring you a glass of water." I felt his forehead. He was a little warm.

Must have the same thing as Thomas. It's going to be a long day.

After making sure he was snuggled up in a blanket on the couch, I sat at the computer. No time like the present.

I posted on my Facebook page to tell people I was publishing, uploaded the file and pressed the publish button. Everything had been set up and ready to go, so at least I hadn't left myself with a bunch of things to take care of. All I wanted to do was get some more sleep.

I felt sick as I pressed publish. I had the story I wanted, but at what cost? I'd pushed Logan away when that was the last thing I wanted. I wanted him near me, getting to know me, maybe one day loving me.

And then I played the waiting game of seeing what happened.

I couldn't look. I closed the laptop and went back to bed to grab whatever sleep I could.

EVERYTHING GOT in the way of me checking on it that day, but the boys were my priority. Jack was sick a couple more times, but by the afternoon both he and Thomas had the colour back in their cheeks and I was relieved to see them smiling, even joking with one another.

At least it wasn't serious.

We all cuddled up on the couch in front of the television, a boy on each side of me, and did nothing for the rest of the day but relax. The boys would have to be home tomorrow too, as both day-care and school had rules around returning after being sick.

Thomas fell asleep first, and by the time I tucked him into bed and came back, Jack was asleep. My poor babies needed their sleep, and so did I. When Jack was in bed, I opened the laptop and then closed it again. My eyes already tired; I didn't want the screen to contribute to the strain.

I'll take a look in the morning.

I'D FORGOTTEN to turn the alarm off, and it was screaming at me while I tried to find the 'off' button with my eyes closed.

Cartoony sounds came from the living room, and I knew the boys were up and feeling better before I'd even seen them. Sure enough, they were lying on the floor with their pillows and blankets glued to *SpongeBob*.

"Morning, you two. Feeling better?"

"Yes," Jack said. Thomas nodded.

"That's good. You have to stay home today, and we'll have showers and make ourselves not feel so yuck and sick. Sound good?"

I spent the day changing the beds, washing the linen and the boys, and spending time with them while I could. It wasn't until late afternoon that things went a little crazy.

Coffee beckoned in the kitchen, and I stared at the wall while I boiled the water. *Holy crap, my book.* I'd almost forgotten about it.

I poured the coffee and sat at the table, expecting to maybe see a handful of sales if any. What I saw made me shriek.

It was selling, selling beyond my wildest dreams. The sales graph had steadily climbed overnight. I'd never seen anything like it.

I couldn't breathe for crying. This was it. It was our way out of the financial hole we were in. I could build up our nest egg.

"Mum, are you okay?" Jack and Thomas were by my sides, and I turned around so I could gather them both in my arms and into a big hug.

"I'm pretty damn wonderful, you guys."

"What happened?" Jack asked.

"Just good stuff. Only good stuff from now on. Now, I need to get dinner on and maybe we can go out to the park before it gets dark to get some fresh air."

Thomas's eyes widened. "Really?"

"Sure thing."

"Can Logan come?"

I looked at my youngest child, his eyes so full of hope that his new best friend would come with us. My stomach churned. I hadn't seen him since the night before last; what if he didn't want to talk to me? How would that effect Thomas?

I'd let him into our lives, and been mean to him, as my boys would say.

I had to find a way to make it up to him. For Thomas's sake, and for my own. My heart ached over the end of our last conversation.

We got our things together once we'd eaten, and I took a look over the balcony as we went outside. His car wasn't there.

"Can we knock on the door?" Thomas asked.

"Sure thing, buddy. Just don't be too disappointed if he's not there. His car's gone."

Thomas ran the rest of the way to Logan's door, pounding on it. When there was no answer, he pouted. "Maybe next time?" I ventured.

He nodded, enthusiastically. "I want to go on the biiiiig slide."

"You can go on it a couple of times. We'll have to be quick; it'll be dark soon."

They played until we'd wrung every last bit of light out of the day, and we headed back as evening fell, all of us nearly asleep on our feet. My mind kept returning to my book, and part of me wanted so badly to race home and take another look, but the fresh air was doing us all so much good.

Logan's car was parked in his spot when we came in the car park. The boys were still laughing and joking, and we made our way slowly up the stairs with me telling them to quieten down. We got to the door and I fumbled with the key.

"What are you doing out in the dark? It's not safe."

Logan's voice out of nowhere made me jump, that damn light not working on the balcony leaving me without warning that he was there.

"We were at the park, and stayed a little later than I meant to," I said. Slotting the key in the lock, I turned it and the boys tumbled inside. I flicked the switch in the living room on and light flooded the balcony.

"Well, don't. This isn't the worst area in town, but it's not the best area either. I don't want anything happening to you." There wasn't a hint of friendly, flirting Logan in his tone, just irritation.

Was he really growling at me? Apart from our growing friendship, it wasn't really any of his business, and he was really beginning to rub me up the wrong way.

"I'm fine. Jack and Thomas are fine. Don't worry about us."

He sighed, moving into the light, and ran his fingers through his hair. "I am going to worry while you're under my watch."

Oh.

"Under your watch?"

"You do live right next door, and it's not like we haven't been getting to know one another."

I took a deep breath. I was doing it again. He shows an interest, I act all bitchy. "I'm sorry. I don't mean to dismiss your concern. I've just had a really long day. The boys have had some stomach bug and we've been home a couple of days. I think we all just got cabin fever."

He looked pained, his face downturned in empathy. "I'm so sorry to hear that. I hope from that giggling that they're better."

I nodded. "They are, and I didn't pick it up, so there's that."

He gave me the smallest of smiles. "I'm happy to hear that. Wouldn't want you feeling ill. I'm glad you're safe, Olivia."

"Thank you for checking on us."

He turned to walk back to his place. "Logan?"

Half in the dark, I could see his eyes shining. "Yes?"

"Last time we saw each other, I wasn't very nice. I'm sorry. The last person I want to drive out of my life is you."

He chuckled. "As if that's going to happen."

My heart did that skip-a-beat thing where I think I'm going to pass out, and I gulped at those little words and the meaning they could hold. Maybe. If I was reading him that way.

When the boys were in bed, I opened up the computer and nearly passed out. The sales hadn't stopped, and I swear I could see the future. A future where we could be in a little house again, with a garden, and a room each for my boys. I mean, you do what you have to do when you don't have much, but everyone dreams of something better.

I didn't need to earn a huge amount to achieve my dreams. A couple of thousand dollars extra a month would go a very long way. It would move us from the having enough money to live to being able to enjoy ourselves a little.

Maybe this was a one-off; maybe I'd never do this well again, but for the moment I was on top of the world.

I wasn't really all that surprised at the knock on the door.

Rebecca stood on the other side. "I'm so sorry I don't have any wine this time, but I had to see you. I've been online all day watching your book."

I didn't care about the no-wine thing. I was just so glad I had Rebecca with me to celebrate. It felt so good to find a friend after the whole Donna experience.

"You know I'm going to be a zombie at work tomorrow," I said.

"You and me both. Do you really think I'm going home to sleep? I'll be watching your damn book rank."

That she cared so much warmed my heart. "Thank you. Thank you for everything," I said.

Rebecca slid her arm around my shoulders, squeezing me. "You're welcome. You've been through a shitty time; it's nice to see some good things happening for you. And this is a fantastic thing. I'm so proud."

When she was gone I sat in front of the computer and took a deep breath. Logan may not know he was responsible for the longing and desire I conveyed on the page, but the rest of the world would. Even if they didn't know who he really was.

I opened the blog page and started to type.

Today has been one of the best days of my life. You are all so amazing and supportive, and I love the reviews that are coming in.

This will just be a short blog post. It's late and I'm tired. Not that I'll sleep.

I want to say thank you so much to Rebecca. She reads my words and makes them make sense. I am so lucky to have found her.

And most of all ...

I stared at the screen. Should I name him? Oh hell, no one knew who I was. Now was the chance for me to say just how I felt without embarrassing myself.

Thank you to Logan. You are my inspiration. My knight in shining armour. Though I may only admire you at a distance, you are what made my story what it is. A story of love.

My palms were sweaty as I pressed post and I sat for a moment, closing my eyes and thinking about him.

How stupid, crushing on someone like this. I'm supposed to be a grown-up.

Closing the laptop, I stood and sighed. All this excitement and no one to share it with.

I didn't mean like Rebecca. That was great, but it wasn't the same as having a partner, a companion to share my life with.

I missed Evan. Although, it wasn't him I missed. There was no way I wanted him back, even if there was any future opportunity. He'd burned his bridges there. I missed having someone to snuggle up in bed with, even if they weren't always there. I missed there just being a warm body beside me. I just missed someone.

Then again, I also couldn't let just anyone into my life. They had to be approved by Jack and Thomas, and I wasn't about to introduce them to any random person. Logan was different. Logan had become a part of our lives due to his proximity.

I wished he were even closer.

15

I TOOK FRIDAY OFF. I had some leave owing and a long weekend sounded wonderful, especially if I could get a little time to myself.

Dropping the boys off at school and day-care, I stopped to grab some groceries and headed back home. I'd thrown on sweat pants and a T-shirt, not really caring about appearances. Soon I'd have a little money to buy new clothes. It had been so long since I'd done that.

I pulled into the car park, parking next to Logan's Holden. I looked at it curiously—normally he was gone in the morning before I left. *Guess he's having a day off too.*

Grabbing the bags out the back, I started up the stairs.

"Well, look who else is taking a day off." Logan stood in his doorway, watching as I came onto the landing.

"I fancied a long weekend."

He gave me a most affectionate look, one that made me warm from my head to my toes. Even with my raggy old clothing.

"Me too. I've got a friend coming over for a visit. You look comfortable, anyway; I would never have guessed you weren't going to work."

I laughed. "I'll have you know this is the height of fashion."

"Doesn't matter what you wear. You'd look gorgeous in a sack." My heart raced and my face grew hot. This whole *being friends* things sucked so bad, but I didn't know if he really wanted me or was just teasing. "Although, I still think you should wear those shorts more often."

He licked his lips. *Oh crap.* I bit down on my bottom lip and shook my head. "I'm way too old to wear those. Besides, the boys tease me that my butt hangs out of them."

"What's wrong with that?" He shrugged, and I pushed at his shoulder, laughing.

His focus shifted somewhere behind me and he straightened up, cocking an eyebrow at whoever was behind me. I turned. Oh great, another gorgeous blonde.

A blonde with a very new baby in her arms.

"I'm Maddy," the blonde said, smiling at me. She rocked the baby on her shoulder, and rolled her eyes at Logan. "You're so rude, Logan. Invite us in."

He grinned. "When did you ever need an invite? Did you turn into a vampire or something?"

I laughed, and the corners of her lips quirked as she tried to hide her amusement.

"I was being polite. Do you know how to be?"

Logan shook his head, shifting his focus to me. "Excuse me, Liv, apparently I have a couple of guests. Maddy, this is Olivia."

The baby let out a loud squawk and Maddy rolled her in her arms, stroking her little face. "Sorry, baby. Are you hungry?"

My heart swelled as I looked at the baby. My boys were once that small, and I'd held them in my arms, taking in the scent of them. I realised I was staring a little too much and drew my gaze away. *What's wrong with me?* If I didn't know better, I'd think I was clucky.

"This is Carly," she said, smiling at me.

Little Carly waved her arms and legs, gazing up at her mother with big blue eyes.

"May I?" I asked, reaching a hand out to stroke the blonde fluff on her head.

Maddy nodded, and I ran my finger up the tiny person's face, revelling in the softness of her hair under my skin. "She's beautiful."

Maddy beamed. "I'm rather partial to her." She looked over at Logan. "Got somewhere for me to sit?"

"Go on in, Maddy. You know you're always welcome."

"It was nice meeting you," she said as she sashayed her way past him and into his apartment. For a woman who had apparently given birth recently, she looked amazing in her short skirt.

"She seems nice," I said.

"She is."

Is that your child? No, you said you'd never leave your family, it can't be. What's the connection? Oh good grief, Olivia, this isn't any of your business.

"Maddy and her husband live in your old house," he said.

Now it was my turn to lift an eyebrow, and a chance to satisfy my curiosity. "What? How do you know that, and how do you know her?"

"She was my girlfriend once upon a time. We kept the friendship after we broke up, but we're not as close as we used to be. Not now she's married with a kid. Your ex turned up on their doorstep one morning looking for you, must have been just before he turned up here. She was worried he might do something stupid, tracked you to here, and realised you were right next door to me.'"

I nodded, not knowing what else to say. Was that why he was so protective? Was it to take care of me, or reassure his friend that I was safe?

"I should go. Madam will be expecting coffee."

He held my gaze, his lips snaking into a smile, one of those smiles that made my heart race. "We'll talk later. Hopefully you'll have taken my advice. You're far too beautiful to hide yourself away."

My stomach lurched as he turned and walked to his door.

He thinks I'm beautiful? A stark thought hit me. *No one's ever said I'm beautiful.*

The urge to write hit me like a tsunami, my head swirling with ideas. If only I could tell him just how much he inspired me.

Maybe one day.

I stared at his closed door door. Would I ever get brave enough to tell him? Would he ever do anything beyond the flirting? We were such good friends—would this ever become more than that? Or was I just destined to watch other women come and go while he joked with me?

I hammered out a couple of thousand words in a frantic writing sprint, and then with no kids around, I made the most of their absence, cleaning the apartment. The temperature in the living room was about a million degrees, so I opened the door to let some fresh air in.

The tiny breeze that flowed through made it slightly better, and I left the door open while I went back to vacuum cleaning.

I don't know how long he stood watching me, but out of the corner of my eye, I realised Logan was there. He stood in the doorway, resting one arm on the frame and peeking in. As he pointed at the vacuum, I flicked it off, curious about what he wanted.

"Hey. Um, this might sound a bit random, but I have a party to go to on Saturday. One of my work suppliers. Thought you might like to come with me."

I gulped. He was asking me out?

"I ... umm ..."

"Relax. It's not a date or anything, I just got a plus-one invite, and I thought you could do with a night out. I mean, the boys and work keep you pretty busy, and you seem quite the recluse at times."

My mouth was dry, and I licked my lips trying to think how to answer. *What was I doing?* There was only one reply.

"I can't. I don't have anyone to look after the boys."

"I'm sure Maddy could babysit."

I shook my head. "My boys don't know her."

"Yet."

I sighed, rolling my eyes. "Logan, it's really nice that you asked me, and I appreciate the gesture. But it's just a lot to ask. They're still all over the place after the upheaval, and ..."

"And their mother should stop making excuses. Come on, Liv. A night out—get dressed up, have a few drinks, live a little."

This was more tempting than I could say. I'd never really been on a date. Not that this was a date. It was just a thing that Logan needed a partner for. Of course he couldn't take Maddy with him. Not with her married and with a young child. I guess it made sense for him to ask the next best thing.

"Fine. But I want her to come around and meet the boys before we go. Get to know them a little before I head out the door."

He grinned, those perfect teeth all on display. *God, he's gorgeous.* "She's just left, but I'll call her now. Make sure she's available. They live a pretty quiet life now Carly's here, so hopefully she's not doing anything else."

I exhaled for what felt like the first time in forever as he walked away. A night out with Logan? Holy crapballs. It didn't matter that it wasn't a date—just spending time with him was enough to quench my thirst for him.

Whoa. Where did that come from?

I clasped my hands together tightly, closing my eyes.

I needed to write again.

THERE WAS nothing in my wardrobe suitable for a night out. I had clothing for work, skirts and shirts, but no dresses. And I wanted a dress.

"I've got some things that might look good on you," Rebecca had said during the weekend.

We took over the employee bathroom on Monday for me to try on dresses. Not only did it have cubicles for me to get changed, there was a big mirror along one wall to look at myself in.

Nothing seemed right. They were too tight or too baggy, and one sat so uncomfortably I would have been adjusting myself all night. No. I needed something that would fit well and be no hassle to wear. Rebecca and I were clearly not exactly the same size.

And then she pulled the last one out: a cute little dress of deep blue with enough of a plunging neckline that I could show off some cleavage. Hopefully it would fit.

It was meant to be. The soft fabric floated down me, clinging to the right places, a little flowy in the wrong places, and showcasing the most impressive boobage look I think I'd ever had.

"Cinderella," said Rebecca, standing behind me as I looked in the mirror. "You shall go to the ball."

I couldn't believe it and wanted to cry at just how perfectly it fitted.

"You can keep that dress if you want to. It doesn't sit right on me. Looks amazing on you. Versatile too, you can dress it up to be glamorous, or wear it with flats and a cardigan to be smart casual."

Excited, I flung my arms around her and hugged tight.

"He'll love it too. You look so pretty."

I looked back in the mirror. My long, dark hair was up in a ponytail, scraped off my face so it didn't annoy me. My mornings were mostly so rushed I didn't get time to brush my hair, so there was bound to be a knot or two in it.

My makeup-free face looked tired, small smudges of purple under my eyes that showed my lack of sleep.

"You should go and get your hair done. And your makeup. I know a place you can go to not far from where you live that does both."

I shrugged. It'd be a while before I received any money from my writing. I didn't really want to take any money out of my savings if I didn't have to.

"Olivia, make the most of it. Even if you're not out to impress Logan. Enjoy yourself."

I smiled, and Rebecca tugged on my ponytail. "And get someone to take photos, I want to see you on the arm of that hunky neighbour of yours."

On the way home, I stopped at a department store and grabbed some basic makeup. *When had I stopped taking care of myself?* Right near the door were some beautiful hair pieces, perfect for twisting my hair into a bun, or something more tidy than my usual appearance. I didn't need to waste money on someone to do my hair and makeup; I'd take care of it myself.

After dinner I set to practicing, and went into the bathroom to apply some make up. I'd worn this stuff all the time when I was a teenager, but at some point life had just gotten too crazy and it all seemed to hard.

I ran the brush across my eyelids with the eye shadow that I thought would go nicely with the dress. It smudged a little, and I used the rubber end of my brand new brushes to wipe the excess away. A few goes at it, and I'd have my technique sorted.

Carefully, I applied the mascara.

"Mum, you've got your tongue hanging out." Thomas giggled as he pointed at me. I'd been so deep in concentration, I didn't even notice.

"I'm glad you think it's funny. Want to try some?"

"That's *girl* stuff." He disappeared back to the living room and the board game he and his brother were playing. It was Monopoly, but they were making up the rules as they went along.

I applied a tiny bit of blush on my cheeks, and then came the part I always found hard. Lipstick. Slowly, I traced the shape of my lips with the waxy substance, making them a pale shade of pink.

Perfect.

Lost in thought, I didn't hear the knock on the door at first.

"Mum. There's someone at the door." Jack was rolling his eyes at me as I came back out to get it.

I made my way to the door, looking down at their game as I went, squinting to see what they'd done. The little houses were lined up along one side of the board in a pretty little green and red pattern.

"It looks nice and tidy," Jack said with a grin.

I laughed. "It sure does." Turning towards the door, I called out, "Who is it?"

"Logan."

Crap. Was he here to cancel our night out? *Stop thinking the worst. Just open the damn door.*

I pulled open the door, smiling at him.

His eyes widened as he took the sight of me in. "Wow, you look ... *wow*."

Oh. The makeup.

"Just playing around with some stuff."

He seemed distracted, running his eyes across my face. "Um yeah, I wanted to let you know that we're all good for Saturday. Maddy will come around five and we'll go around six, if that suits you. Gives her a bit of time to sit with the boys beforehand."

I was pretty sure my heart exploded. "That sounds great. I'm looking forward to it. What do I wear?" I might have the dress, but how I wore it would depend on the answer.

"Smart casual. Bit dressy, but not too much. I think that's what it means. I'm looking forward to it too." For once he didn't wink or grin or look at me in that sly way that made my heart pitter-patter. He looked so earnest, and I still wanted to jump his bones.

Mind wandering.

I sighed without thinking, and the corners of his mouth turned up slightly.

"I'll leave you to it. See you Saturday at five, if I don't see you before."

I just nodded, not really sure what to say next. The tension between us was thick, but I didn't know if he saw the magic there or not. There were times when I felt like a teenager again, having missed those years where you go out and have all of the fun, along with all of the confusion that went with it. This was one of those times.

Logan nodded toward me. "Olivia."

One word. It was my name, but it left me undone. When I closed the door, I just stood there, staring at it, even though he'd gone back home. What was he doing to me? Did he even know? Was I that deprived of true companionship I was getting this all wrong?

Now I'd have to wait for Saturday.

16

SATURDAY COULDN'T COME FAST ENOUGH. Maddy turned up at 5.30pm, later than arranged, but not enough for me to have flown into a full-blown panic. She smiled when she saw the boys parked in front of the television, eating cocktail sausages for dinner.

"Those look amazing. Are there any for me?"

"There are some more in the kitchen," Jack said.

I laughed. "I usually do a few more just in case they want extra. It's my 'holy crap, I need to sort something out fast' meal."

Maddy cradled Carly in her arms, and I reached down to stroke the baby's downy hair.

"It's fine," she said. "I do the same thing and this one doesn't eat yet. Do you want to hold her?"

As soon as the boy's dinner was cooked, I'd changed and applied makeup, twisting my hair into a tight bun. It was early but I was ready to go, and I looked at the baby, sizing her up. Knowing my luck, I'd get her into my arms and she'd puke all over me.

What the hell?

"I'd love to."

She handed Carly over to me and turned her attention back to the boys. What was I worried about? Just by asking if she could have the same dinner as them, they seemed to have become instant friends.

"I'll show you where the sausages are," Jack said, so seriously it was hard to hold in my laughter at his straight expression.

Holding Carly so close, I started rocking back and forward, tracing my finger down her face. She was just so precious, those big blue eyes gazing at me, her rosebud lips in a pout as she weighed me up. Those same lips wobbled and turned down as she decided whether or not to cry before I started bouncing her, and she broke out into a smile.

"Such a mum thing," Maddy said as she returned with a bowl of food.

"I have done it twice." I laughed as I shook my head at the baby. "You're not going to cry for me, are you little one?" We jiggled for a while and I barely noticed the knock on the door. I looked up to see Maddy at the door, shrugging at me. With my arms full of her baby, I nodded and she opened it. Logan stood on the other side, his eyes locking with mine as he noticed me there with the baby.

"Hey Maddy, Liv," he said, never taking his eyes off me as he entered the apartment. Jack and Thomas both rushed to him, one latching onto each leg, and he ruffled their hair.

"Hello Carly," he said, leaning over her. She shifted her focus from me to him and screwed up her face again as if to cry.

"Hey, we had a deal," I said, her little head twisting back toward me as she tried to work out who to look at.

Maddy laughed. "I'll take her off your hands so you guys can get out of here. I'm sure we'll be fine." She reached for her baby and I passed her over, but not without kissing her tiny little hand and breathing in her baby smell.

"Oh, Maddy, she is so beautiful," I said.

She grinned at me, snuggling Carly in her arms. "She is so freaking cool. My sweet little girl."

Logan nudged me, tripping me out of my daydream. "You ready?"

I took a moment to take a look at him all dressed up. He still wore his black jeans, but instead of a T-shirt, he had a dress shirt on, ironed to perfection and buttoned up, but with no tie. Good enough to eat. I mean ... "I sure am."

He grinned, and I caught Maddy out of the corner of my eye stepping back.

"I'll just grab my bag." My heart was in my throat as I turned toward Maddy. "My mobile number is on the fridge. The boys usually go to bed around seven thirty, but if they're a bit unsettled, don't worry too much about getting them off early. Particularly Thomas; he might be a bit funny about me not being here. And ..."

"Don't worry. We'll be fine." Maddy looked over my shoulder. "Won't we, boys?"

They both nodded in agreement, mouths still full of food.

"Be good."

I got hugs from both of them, and grabbed my bag on the way out. Taking a deep breath, I turned to Logan. "Ready."

He took my hand in his, leading me out my apartment and down the steps to the car, opening the door for me before getting in himself.

"You look amazing," he said when we were alone.

"Thanks. You don't scrub up so badly yourself."

He laughed. "I'll take that as a compliment."

Starting the car, he reversed out of the park, turning and driving out onto the road. Nerves were eating me alive, the butterflies in my stomach turning into bees, flying around wildly and stinging me everywhere. This was so silly.

"The boys will have a ball with Maddy. She's a big kid at times herself."

"I'm not really worried about them. She just walked in and managed to fit in straight away. Oh hell, I didn't check my mobile, it's usually buried in my bag. It could be flat for all I know. I mean, what if something happens and Maddy can't call ...?" I knew I was babbling, but I couldn't stop it.

Logan reached across and squeezed my hand. "They'll be fine. If

Maddy needs anything, she'll call me. I've got my phone in my pocket. They'll be fine; it's just a few hours."

"THAT'S WHERE WE'RE GOING." Logan slowed as we approached the place. It was a car park, littered with marquees and cars.

"A car show?"

Logan grinned. "They're a company that makes lube for cars. Where did you think I was going?"

I shrugged, my cheeks heating with embarrassment.

He turned, his dark eyes twinkling. "It's a party within the car show. It'll be a mix of people dressed up and dressed down. Besides, you'll be the prettiest girl there."

I rolled my eyes.

"Come on. You'll turn every head in the place. I'll be proud to have you on my arm."

As he got out of the car and walked around to open my door, I took a deep breath. I hadn't socialised in forever; this whole thing was nerve wracking. I could only hope I didn't screw it up.

The door opened, and he stood there, hand extended for me to take. With a smile and another deep breath, I placed my hand in his as I climbed out, terrified I'd make a misstep and fall on my face.

Wherever we were, it was exciting as I watched people mill around the exhibits and the cars. I don't know if I would have called it a party, at least from out here, but I soon realised what Logan was talking about.

One of the marquees was closed off, with a bouncer standing at the entrance. As we drew closer, the thumping music sounds drifted through the air toward us. Whoever was in there was having fun.

"That's where we're going," Logan said.

I nodded, following his lead. When we got to the bouncer, Logan produced two tickets from his back pocket. This hulk of a guy looked us both over, raising an eyebrow no doubt at what I felt was my obvious overdressing, but stepped aside to let us in.

Inside was a long buffet table, with a bar at one end. A dance floor took up the centre, where a handful of people were moving to the beat. Most were scattered around the sides of the tent, deep in conversation, the occasional person glancing at us as we made our way to the bar.

"I'm driving, so I'm going to drink Coke, but you treat yourself."

I cast my eye over the selection. "Vodka and lemonade, please."

Logan moved behind me, placing his hands on my hips and leaned forward. "Be careful. I don't want you drunk when I take advantage of you." He looked up at the barman, speaking much louder this time. "Coke for me, please."

While we were waiting, I gulped, taking a deep breath to suppress my nerves and leaned back against him, relishing the feel of his hard chest. He lifted one hand, sliding his arm around my waist. "Now what am I going to do with you?" he asked.

I shrugged, laughing. *Whatever you want to do.*

I did not think that.

Yes, I did.

I sighed, and he pulled me in tight against him.

"Logan." A man's voice came from beside me, and we both turned our heads to look.

"Richard."

"I'm so glad you could make it."

Logan let go of me to turn and shake the man's hand. Richard, whoever he was, looked me over, his eyes lingering around my cleavage. Oh. Awesome.

"This is Olivia," he said. "Olivia, this is Richard King. It's his party."

"Nice to meet you."

He licked his lips. "You too. Are you Logan's girlfriend?"

The hair stood up on my neck as he ran his gaze over me.

"Yes," Logan said. "My amazing, beautiful, pain-in-the-butt girlfriend." He grinned at me, winking as I gripped his arm.

Threat disarmed.

"Oh. Well have a good night, you two. There's plenty of food and drink, and I want to see you out on the dance floor." That last part was directed at me. Maybe he thought he could look up my dress if I was out there dancing or something—he seemed that creepy.

Logan grabbed our drinks from the bar, and we found a quiet little spot near the buffet table to sit.

"Sorry about that," he said.

"There's nothing for you to be sorry about." I smiled as he passed me my drink.

"I saw how he looked at you. Like you were some prey to devour. I mean, shit, maybe I looked at you like that too, I don't know. You're so freaking hot in that dress."

The ice in my drink couldn't cool me down fast enough.

"You didn't look at me like that." I placed my hand on his arm, and he met my gaze as I gave him a small smile. "I don't feel uncomfortable with you. I never feel uncomfortable with you. Him, however? He can just slither on out of here back to wherever he came from."

Gathering up my courage, I leaned my head on Logan's shoulder, and after a moment, he leaned his head on mine.

"You make me feel safe," I said.

The room might as well have been empty. I didn't care about anyone else in it—didn't see anyone else in it. As far as I was concerned, it was just Logan and I, and I didn't care if he knew how I felt about him. He was what I wanted.

He reached for my hand, interlinking his fingers with mine and I knew he was feeling the same way.

"You make me feel like part of your family," he whispered, lifting his head to kiss my hair.

I sat up straight, sharing a smile with him. "As far as the boys are concerned, you are family."

"And you?"

I nodded slowly, coaxing out that grin of his.

"Let's get out of here," he said.

"What? I thought we were going to make the most of the free food and drink."

He glanced around the room, and whispered in my ear. "Now I'm here, this is the last place I want to be with you. Fancy a burger?"

I grinned. "McDonald's or Burger King?"

Logan shook his head. "Macca's of course. I don't know if I can hang out with you if you don't prefer it."

I tapped my chin with my index finger. "Let me think ..."

"Oh, you did not just have to think about it."

"McDonalds is fine."

LOGAN HAD INSISTED ON PAYING, and laughed as I picked the pickle out of my cheeseburger.

"I could have ordered it without the pickle."

Shrugging, I took a bite, tasting the burgery goodness and sighing. "I don't want to make a fuss. It's no problem."

"Just as well I like it." He picked the discarded vegetable off the burger wrapper and gobbled it up, waggling his eyebrows at me. "Now when Maddy asks me how tonight went I can tell her I ate your pickle."

I nearly choked on the next mouthful of burger, grabbing my Coke to take a large drink.

"You're trouble, Logan Mitchell," I said between coughs.

"That's the aim. You'll never forget me."

I shook my head, laughing. This was better than any party, and more like a real date, despite the lack of romantic setting.

"I've got a magic trick," I said.

Logan rolled his eyes. "Show me."

Opening my mouth wide, I crammed the rest of the burger in, holding my hands in the air and humming a 'ta-da' noise.

I'm sure the people around us thought we were nuts, but he laughed with me, and it was wonderful.

The beach was a different story. The sand was soft beneath my feet. We tracked footprints down the beach as we walked off the huge burger meals we'd eaten. The sun went down, and we never went beyond holding hands. But that was fine with me. He was with me because he wanted to be. Not because he was obligated to.

I'd never felt more free.

"We should bring the boys down here," he said. "Bring some buckets, build some sandcastles."

That he would think of them now touched me more than I could say.

"They'd love it. There's so much I want to do with them when we have both the time and the energy."

We stopped back in front of the car, and he held my hands in his, squeezing them gently.

"You're not alone, Liv. Don't ever forget that."

We leaned against the bonnet as the sun disappeared and the sky grew dark.

"Can I ask you something?"

I turned my head to see his gaze on me again. "What do you want to know?"

"Do you have anyone else who helps with the kids? I mean, you never have anyone over that I've seen other than Rebecca, and you just do so much."

I shrugged. "Nope. Just me. Mum kicked me out when I got pregnant with Jack."

He frowned. "Seriously?"

"Yep. And I lost the family friends in the divorce. Not that I can get divorced. Yet."

He sighed. "Man, that sucks."

"Yeah it does. You have to be separated for two years. Can you believe it? I think I should get time off for good behaviour." I laughed, pushing myself off the car.

"No. I meant that you're by yourself. I have my mother at least."

I turned and looked at him. "You're not likely to have been a pregnant teenage girl though."

He chuckled. "No, but I don't think Mum would have thrown either my brother or I out if we'd come home with a pregnant teenage girl."

"I guess I was just special."

"You are special."

I grinned. "Not that special. Don't you have a thing for blondes?"

He smirked, cocking one eyebrow. "What are you talking about?"

"Kat, Maddy, need I go on?"

"Are you jealous, Olivia Grant?"

I shook my head.

"You shouldn't be. Recently I've had a hankering for a certain brunette."

What I really needed right then and there was a fan to cool my burning face. A bucket of cold water might have worked as an alternative.

Logan moved toward me, his face inches from mine. "Let's get you home."

"It's still early." I didn't want him to take me home, I wanted every second I could get like this.

"What do you suggest we do, Ms Grant?"

I shuffled closer, leaning against him. "I don't know."

"It's 9pm. Don't you turn into a pumpkin or something if you don't go home?" He teased me, waggling his eyebrows.

I laughed, remembering Rebecca calling me Cinderella.

"We can take the scenic route home, around the bays and back again. It's a nice drive." Logan suggested.

I nodded. At least we'd be together.

The car ride nearly put me to sleep—that and the small amount of alcohol I'd had plus carb overload. This was bliss, Logan by my side as we drove the twisty road along the beachfront. And that sea air was so soothing. I hadn't relaxed in so long, I'd forgotten what it was like.

"Happy?" he asked.

"Very."

"I'm glad."

I sat back in the seat, resting my head on the gorgeous leather. I'd never felt so spoilt and lucky. The worst twist in my life had led to the very best.

Miles away, I didn't even click that we'd arrived home until the car stopped. Logan got out and came around to open my door, helping me out with a touch of his hand. This time I didn't want to let go.

"Let's get you home to your babies," he said.

We walked up the stairs hand in hand, and as we got to the doorway, he raised one of my hands to his lips, with that shit-eating grin on his face I'd come to love. My heart ached as I watched him, and as he cast his eyes over me again, that self-conscious feeling began to grow.

"Thank you for tonight, Liv. It was great having you with me."

"Thank you for inviting me. I had fun."

His eyes were so warm and welcoming. *Kiss me.*

"I'm glad you enjoyed yourself." He gazed at me, a tiny smile on his face, his head gently nodding. "I suppose I'd better let you get in to check on the boys."

Don't let go of my hand, don't let go, don't let ...

He gently placed my hand by my side, slowly moving his away, his fingers lingering on my skin.

I love you.

Shit.

Did I say that out loud?

I breathed out really loudly as I realised I hadn't. Thank heavens for that. Crisis averted. Tonight had been fun, but I wasn't like those gorgeous creatures I'd seen with him. I couldn't make him fall in love with me.

Retract back into shell and step into the apartment.

"Goodnight, Olivia."

He leaned over, brushing his lips against mine before I could stop him. *Wait. What?* I didn't want to stop him. I wanted him to keep going.

Holy shit. Get it together.

"Go inside. I want to make sure you're safe." Oh. My. God. He was perfect.

My cheeks were burning, and for once I was glad the light between our apartments was broken so I could hide in the shadow.

"Goodnight, Logan," I whispered, sliding the key in the lock. Slipping inside the door, I closed it quietly behind me, exhaling really loudly.

I'd completely forgotten Maddy was there, and she looked up at me, grinning at the sight of my discomfort.

"So. Did you kiss him?"

"What?"

"Logan. Did you kiss him? Because you look like either he kissed the crap out of you, or you're running scared. You really like him, don't you?" The words came flowing out as if she'd practiced them. I knew I didn't have a poker face, but I didn't think I was quite *that* open.

"Maddy, I …"

She waved her hand. "Relax. I'm not going to tell him. It was written all over your face, though. He likes the crap out of you."

I actually thought my heart was about to explode. She'd just confirmed everything I was beginning to think.

"We're good friends," I said, nodding, moving towards the couch. As if I was going to confide in his ex-girlfriend.

"No, he *really* likes you. Seriously, Olivia, you should give him a shot. He'd be in like a rat up a drainpipe if you gave him a chance. And he is good in bed. I mean, exceptional. He'd make you forget all about Mr Jerkoff-Turn-Up-On-Other-People's-Doorstep ex." She bit down on her bottom lip, eyeing me nervously. "Oh, shit. I've said far too much. That's not like me, I swear. Okay, maybe it is, but don't tell Logan I told you any of it."

Well, this wasn't uncomfortable at all. Speaking with someone who had seen Logan naked, shared a bed with him. No this was really freaking uncomfortable and Maddy was completely oblivious. *What?*

Carly was asleep on the floor, and Maddy picked her up gently, grabbing her bag from the couch. "The boys were great. They sat and played with Carly—well, picked up her toys while she smiled at them. They watched some cartoons and then went to bed."

"Thank you so much," I whispered.

"It was no problem at all. I left you my number on the fridge too. Any time you need a break, or want to go anywhere, call me. I don't have much of a social life right now, so I'm always available to babysit. And if there's ever any time I can't, maybe my husband can."

She stood, and I couldn't think of anything else to do but hug her, leaving a space for little Carly of course.

"Sorry if I butted in like that. I've just been holding that in all night, and seeing you walk in the door helped me put the pieces together," she said.

"Thank you for everything," I said. *Thank you for all of it, however much of it is true.*

She walked to the door, turning and smiling before opening it. Logan stood on the other side, that grin back on his face again, and I think my heart beat about three million beats per minute wondering if he'd heard what she'd said.

"Give a girl a fright," Maddy said.

"I thought I'd better wait and walk you to your car. I don't want anything happening to you, and I'm pretty sure Andrew would kill me if it did."

His gaze locked with mine over her head, and I saw another emotion pass over his face. Longing?

You've been writing too much romantic stuff. Stop imagining things.

"Goodnight again, Liv." He smiled a tiny smile, and I held my breath remembering what Maddy had said. *Exceptional in bed.*

"Night."

Maddy closed the door behind her, nodding at me with a smile as she did so, and I flung myself down onto the couch. My breathing became ragged at the thought of him, his hands on me, his mouth on me. In all my life I'd never wanted anything so much.

I sat for a moment, squeezing my hands together before reaching for the laptop. My muse had given me so much without even knowing.

One day I'll tell you everything.

17

WE WERE LYING TOGETHER, *my back to his chest. His arms enveloped me protectively, wrapping me up, claiming my body. His lips grazed my neck as his hand slid between my legs, touching me until I was a shuddering, whimpering mess.*

I was his.

I woke to the phone ringing beside the bed and rolled over, flopping my arm onto the bedside cabinet to pick it up.

"Hello?"

"Olivia Grant?"

A voice far too chirpy for this hour of the morning was on the other end of the line. I opened one eye and looked at the clock. 8.35am. The boys were probably settled in front of the TV watching Sunday-morning cartoons.

"Yes?"

"My name is Rachel Peterson. I'm a reporter for the *Central Star*. I was wondering if we could have a chat."

"What on earth for?"

"I'd like to talk to you about your books."

My blood ran cold. No way did I want to talk publicly about

them. I wasn't embarrassed by what I'd written, but I'd kept it so quiet.

"I'm sorry. I don't really want to talk about them."

"But you've done so well with this one. And I read your blog post about your inspiration. I'd love to get to the bottom of it, maybe even meet this man you rave about."

The size of the knot in my stomach was only exceeded by the knot in my throat. What had I really expected? People had to know some time, but not in this way. This should be my choice.

"I'm not interested, sorry."

"I'll leave you my number if you change your mind."

"I won't."

I hung up the phone and sat up, my chest aching. I shivered all over. How had she tracked me down? There must be a trail leading back to me. I knew that when I was setting everything up, but I'd kept myself to myself.

Oh well, I'd told her I wasn't interested. Now she could leave me alone and let me get on with my life.

THE WEEK TICKED BY SLOWLY, and apart from small glimpses of each other coming and going, Logan and I hadn't had a chance to catch up and talk about the previous weekend. Either he was really busy at work, or he was avoiding me. Apparently my imagination chose the latter. And I was still thinking about that damn phone call.

"You look miserable," Rebecca said. I'd been staring into space for at least half an hour with no motivation, my mind going back to the call.

"I'm fine. Just have a few things going on."

She walked around my desk, perching on the corner. "This might seem a bit random, but I go to the gym most lunchtimes. I wondered if you wanted to hang out? I realised that you might have found a new hobby with your writing, but it just keeps you indoors more. To feed your mind, you have to feed your body."

She grinned as I rolled my eyes. "I don't know, I've never been into exercise. Besides, I don't have any clothes for it."

"I've got a spare shirt and shorts that I'm sure will fit you, and I know you have your sneakers on. Come on, we can hang out on the treadmills and perve on the bodybuilders."

"Rebecca, I don't know …"

"Come on, Olivia. Live a little. Do something different."

She wasn't going to leave me alone. I loved it as much as I hated it. "Fine, I'll come with you."

"Good girl." She patted my hand. "I'll see you out at reception at twelve on the dot."

Nothing like a spontaneous change of direction for the day.

Two hours later, Grace sat at the reception desk, frowning at us disapprovingly. Rebecca already had her gym gear on, but I was still dressed in my normal skirt and blouse. I didn't know what Grace's problem was; she didn't seem to like anything.

"I don't know if I want to do this," I said.

Rebecca shook her head. "You're not getting out of it *that* easily, Ms Grant. Come on, it'll be fun."

Reluctantly I followed her out to her car, and we drove just down the road, stopping outside a gym.

"Seriously? You drive here? We could have walked," I said, confused.

"When we've worked out and your legs are aching, you'll thank me."

Inside, Rebecca handed me a shirt and shorts and I changed, stuffing my clothing in a locker. She was right, this would help get rid of some cobwebs, a little exercise never hurt anyone. It wasn't like she had asked me to run a marathon.

We walked out to the rows of exercise machines. They all looked brand new, and I was almost afraid to touch them.

After a quick rundown by a staff member, I eyed up the treadmill. I hadn't exercised since compulsory physical education classes during the last year of school. The ones that doubled as sex education classes, such as they were. *Clearly I'd failed at that.*

I pressed the buttons on the treadmill, setting it for a fairly sedate walk. No point in jumping in at some advanced level I couldn't keep up with. If I enjoyed this, maybe I could make it a more regular thing.

After a few minutes, I sped it up a little. That was more like it. It still wasn't that fast, but I soon started to build up a sweat. This was good, as if all the tension in my body was breaking out and I could just relax.

"Psst." Rebecca made a sound next to me, and I turned my head toward her. She nodded behind her. "That guy is checking you out."

I rolled my eyes. "Whatever. You're between me and him. It's probably you he's looking at."

She leaned forward and I glanced past her, accidentally making eye contact with the man she was talking about. He was lifting free weights, and smiled as our eyes met. I couldn't see his eye colour, but he had muscles for Africa. *Holy cow.*

Going back to look at the treadmill, my concentration was broken, and I stole another glance, almost forgetting what I was doing.

It all happened really quickly. I tripped over my own two feet, landing face first on the treadmill controls with a loud bang. The electronic tag linking me with the treadmill pulled away and the treadmill came to a grinding halt, me on my knees, and Rebecca gasping in horror as I tried to stand from the kneeling position I now found myself in.

"Are you okay?" she asked, turning off the treadmill she was on and rushing to help me up.

"Pretty sure I've given myself a black eye, but I think I'm okay."

The staff were there in seconds, and I was led out the back to be examined and given first aid. So much of it was a daze, my head still fuzzy from the impact of the fall. *How embarrassing.*

And as Rebecca led me to the changing room to shower and dress, she laughed as we passed back through the gym.

"What's so funny?" I asked.

She nudged my arm and I looked up. The guy who had been looking at me winked as we passed.

Thanks for the concern.

The shower water felt soothing, warm, but I couldn't stay in for long.

"I'll take you home," Rebecca called.

"I still have to get the boys. Just take me back to work."

Towelling my hair, I gingerly dried my forehead. It was painful to touch, and I sighed when I saw my reflection. The bruise extended from just below my hairline to my cheekbone on one side. It was red and blotchy. That was going to come up a treat.

"We can try to cover it with make up," Rebecca said, stroking my hair.

"That will just be great. Like I have something to hide. My boys are going to think I've been fighting," I said.

"They'll love it. They'll think it's some type of war wound."

I hated to admit that she was right.

Sure enough, Jack screeched when he saw me. "Mum, who did you fight?"

I laughed. "I knew you would think that. No one. I had an accident. Wasn't looking what I was doing."

"Oh." His face fell in disappointment.

"How about we order pizza when we get home? I don't feel like cooking, and I don't really want to show too many people this."

He laughed. "That sounds great, Mum."

Thank God it was Friday.

I WIPED the pizza sauce from Thomas's face, and he frowned, looking at my bruise.

"Can't we wipe that off, Mum?"

Shaking my head, I smiled. "No, sweetie. It's got to go away by itself. I've got some things I can do to help it, but it'll be there for a little while."

"Does it hurt?"

It ached like nobody's business. "Just if you touch it. I'll be fine."

He flung his arms around my neck, and I stood, lifting him. "You're so big now, Thomas. Love you."

"Love you, too."

I sat beside the bed while he drifted off to sleep, and Jack followed him a few minutes later. As much as I loved them, it was nice to have some peace and quiet. My head still pounded and all I wanted was to curl up on the couch and watch television.

Going into the kitchen, I poured a glass of juice from the fridge and retrieved some ibuprofen from the cupboard. With any luck, this and a good sleep would cure my pounding headache. Then there would just be the bruise to get rid of.

I flicked through the channels until I found a decent movie, and lay down with my head on the arm of the couch.

I'd almost drifted off to sleep when a soft knock on the door brought me back. The clock on the wall said 10.22 pm.

Who on earth is it at this time of night? There was usually only one person who visited me this late. *Rebecca.*

I sighed, shaking my head with a smile. "Who is it?"

"Logan."

My hand flew to my face. What would he think of this? I ran my fingers down my cheek and across until they rested on my lips. The warm memory of his hands on my arms, his lips on mine, brought a smile to my face and longing to my heart.

"Olivia?"

Shit. I hadn't opened the door. I nearly laughed out loud at how distracted I'd been.

I took a deep breath and opened the door. He was grinning, but Logan's face fell as he took in my injuries. "Liv?"

Nodding, I returned to the couch and motioning for him to sit with me. I'd explain my little accident. Maybe he could kiss it better, if I wished for it enough.

Instead, he closed the door behind him, following and standing right in front of me.

As I looked up, his eyes flashed with anger, and he made a sound that resembled the whimper of a wounded animal.

He kneeled before me and I closed my eyes as he reached out, touching my face with his gentle fingers, running them softly across the bruise.

"Who did this?" he growled.

"What?" I opened my eyes. His face was inches from mine, his breathing picking up the pace as he examined my injury.

"Who did this to you, Olivia? Was it that useless ex of yours? I'll kill him."

"No. No, no one did this to me. It was an accident."

His nostrils flared and he finally met my gaze, his eyes full of pain. "Tell me what happened."

"Logan, I ..."

"Tell. Me. What. Happened," he roared. I flinched, pulling away from him, and he closed his eyes, his palms down as if calming himself. "Olivia, I'm sorry. I just can't handle seeing you like this."

"I was at the gym. I got distracted and fell and hit my face on the treadmill. No one hurt me."

"Distracted?"

"Some guy was checking me out and I looked back, and ..." *Oh shit.*

His shoulders slumped as if he was disappointed, and I reached for his chin, pulling his face back to meet mine. "It was an accident, Logan. I just got distracted by someone else's actions. Nothing more. I'm fine. It'll just take a while to settle down. It could have been worse."

"I'm sorry," he whispered.

"What for?"

"For scaring you. Seeing you like this frightened the crap out of me. The thought that anyone could ever lay a finger on you in that way just got to me. Although, I can't say I'm impressed you were checking some guy out."

A smile played on my lips before I gave in to it. "I wasn't checking him out. He was checking me out. But then, does it really matter?"

In a moment, I found myself pressed back against the couch, Logan's lips on mine. His hands pushed on my shoulders, pinning me. His kiss was desperate, filled with the longing I'd felt too. I didn't fight it; I couldn't. I wanted this as much as he did, and I surrendered, raising my arms and clasping my hands around his neck to hold him right where I wanted him.

A chuckle came from his chest and he eased up, kissing my face, skimming the bruised parts. *Don't stop. Don't ever stop.*

He ran his lips down my neck, his body radiating heat against mine. "I hate the idea of anyone else checking you out. That's my job," he whispered.

This man. This man was about to fulfil every single fantasy I'd had about him. He moved his hands to stroke my bare thighs, pulling me hard against him. Through his jeans, I could feel how aroused he was.

"Logan," I whispered.

"Damn it, Liv. I've been waiting a long time for this. I couldn't wait any longer."

"If I'd known this was how you'd react, I would have tripped on a treadmill ages ago."

He pushed away again, leaning over and planting kisses on my legs, higher and higher as his fingers hooked the elastic of my panties under my skirt.

"Oh, God. Yes, yes."

I took a deep breath.

"Mum!"

"Damn it. Not now," I muttered.

"Mummy." Thomas's voice carried through the air, and Logan looked up at me, pleading with his eyes.

"I'm sorry," I said, shaking my head as I got a fit of the giggles.

"Go to him. He needs you," Logan said gently.

"Mummy, I had a bad dream." Thomas stood in the doorway, rubbing his eyes. He lit up at the sight of Logan.

Logan stood, and now I could see just how turned on he'd been as well. Timing.

"Hey, buddy. I'm gonna get going and you can cuddle up with your mother," Logan said.

"You don't have to go. It won't take long to get him back to sleep." I bit my bottom lip as I moved in front of him, my hands behind my back. I heard him gasp as I touched him, and he gave my neck a quick peck.

"No, seriously. I have to go, or I'll just embarrass myself. We have all the time in the world."

I laughed. "See you tomorrow, then?"

"You had better believe it."

As he made his way to the door, Thomas jumped onto the couch, and I sat beside him.

"Night," I said.

"Goodnight, Olivia," he said in such a way that made a shiver run up my spine. The effect that man had on me … "Make sure you lock this door when I've gone."

I nodded, wishing he was staying, knowing why he couldn't as Thomas clung to my neck.

Burying my face in Thomas's hair, I hugged him tight. "Want to climb into bed with me?"

He nodded. "The bad dream was scary."

"I bet it was. But, we're safe, Thomas. You don't need to be scared of anything, ever."

"Logan keeps us safe."

"He sure does, buddy. He sure does."

18

IT WAS early and the phone was ringing.

"Noooo, go away," I muttered, reaching for the phone, slapping the bedside cabinet trying to get hold of it.

"He—"

"Olivia. Get on the computer and check out the *Central Star* website. There's a story about you."

Rebecca barely took a breath as she spoke, far too full of energy for a Saturday morning. Especially at 8.15am.

"What are you talking about?"

"There's a story about your books. Did you talk to them?"

My head started to clear. "No. I got a call, but I told the reporter that I wasn't interested."

"Well, she doesn't appear to have listened to you. I'd call your lawyer if I were you."

I sighed. "Thank you for letting me know."

"Olivia. You need to talk to Logan. He's mentioned too."

My stomach sunk to my knees as she spoke. *Just when things were going well between us ...* This could ruin everything. But it could bring us together as Logan realised just how I felt about him.

"Okay, I'll take a look."

"Take care."

"You too."

I hung up the phone and rolled over. Thomas was fast asleep beside me and I smiled as I stroked his cheek.

Time to go and look at this mess.

First stop was the kitchen for an extra-strong coffee. I had a feeling I was going to need it. Sitting at the dining table, I opened my laptop and loaded up the browser. It wasn't hard to find.

I stared at the screen, not believing what I was seeing. There it was in all its glory, an article written all about me. I might not have given an interview, but they had obviously searched the Internet as it even included the blog piece I wrote about where I got my stories.

I am such an idiot.

What if Logan saw it? Seeing people at work would be interesting enough, but I'd mentioned Logan specifically. My neighbour and muse who gave me inspiration and information. I felt sick at the thought of him seeing this when I should have just told him.

Thoughts of the night before flashed in my mind. I had been so close to being intimate with the man I adored. I knew he loved me now, or at least he wanted to be with me. He knew all about the emotional baggage I came with, and wasn't put off by me having children with another man. He was perfect and I should have been honest with him.

I had to get some fresh air. This couldn't be happening. I wanted to tell him on my terms, not have my hand forced by some random person. My gut ached with the thought of revealing my secret. Surely he would feel honoured by it? But then he might feel used. I pulled open the door, going to the other side of the balcony and gulping at the fresh air.

After all this time, I wanted my little house back. Not Evan—he could stay away. But this wasn't home; it had never felt like it. The only thing that made this place feel welcoming was Logan. Tears streamed down my face as I leaned over the balcony.

When the boys were awake and dressed, I'd take them next door, head it off before he saw it and explain. I'd tell him he was my inspiration, but that I was also in love with him. When I'd calmed down, I went back inside to read the article and wait for the kids to wake. I think I'd read it twenty times before he turned up.

He didn't even knock on the door, storming through and waving the paper in his hand. Looked like it had made the printed edition too.

"Is it true?"

I looked at the floor, not wanting to meet his gaze.

"Olivia, tell me. Is it true?"

"Yes," I whispered.

He ran his fingers through his hair. The pain in his eyes made me ache to just hug him and tell him everything would be okay, but he was in no mood for that.

"All this time, all these flirty conversations. Last night we nearly ... Shit, I was an open book for you and you just used me."

"Logan, I'm sorry. It wasn't like that, though."

"Like hell it wasn't. Did you get what you wanted? Have you got enough for your stories?"

I stood up, walking towards him. "Please, can we just talk about this? It's not what it looks like."

"Did you write them?"

"Yes," I mumbled.

"And you asked me personal questions to help you."

"You're the closest man to me. Besides, even if my husband was still around, he did nothing like you told me about."

He sighed. "Damn it. When you say shit like that I just want to do everything we talked about with you, because you were never treated right. Hell, I thought you were just being flirty but cautious because of the kids. That was why I held back. Why I was trying not to push too hard."

"Logan, you have been such a good friend to me and the boys ..."

Shaking his head, he looked up at the ceiling, avoiding my eyes.

"We were getting closer. And last night ... Hell, Liv. I thought we were falling in love."

His eyes fixed on me, the tears welling.

"Just stay and talk to me." I would beg him if I had to. "I didn't know how strongly you felt."

"How could you not? I've been at your beck and call, always here to help with Jack and Thomas, always here for you. We've shared so many moments, and now I don't know what's real and what wasn't."

"It was all real. I didn't even know I was your type until the other night."

He shook his head. "What the hell are you talking about?"

"I'm so boring. Why on earth would you be interested in me?"

The cry that came from his lips broke my heart as my words brought his sorrow to the surface. "Because you're you. You're beautiful and warm. Caring and loving. Some of the best times of my life have been with you and your boys, and you haven't been in my life that long."

He tugged at his hair, looking down at the floor. "I can't do this." Turning towards the door, he walked away from me. My heart broke.

"Logan," I said, reaching for his arm.

Pulling away, he went out the door, and I sank to the floor, sobbing as I realised exactly what I'd done. If I'd been honest with him from the start, this wouldn't have happened. But, no. I'd had to hide what I was doing from the one I cared about. Shit. *The one I was in love with.*

I struggled to my feet and got to the door. Hearing a motor start, I looked down at the car park, and watched as Logan drove away.

"Mum?" I heard Jack's voice from inside and went back in, closing the door behind me and sighing.

"Hey, baby. Good morning."

"Was Logan here?"

I sat down on the couch, patting the seat beside me. He sat and I wrapped my arms around him, kissing the top of his head. "He sure was."

He looked up at me with eyes filled with hope. "Are you going to marry him?"

"I'm still married to Daddy."

"Oh." He frowned. "Can't you get a divorce?"

"Yes. It doesn't work that way, though. Logan and I have to want to marry each other."

He nodded, as if that remotely answered the question. "I like him. He's better than Dad."

I clung to him, fighting renewed tears that filled my eyes. "I know, baby. I like him too."

LOGAN WAS GONE ALL DAY, and I kept looking over the balcony to check. Jack and Thomas were distracted by toys and the house was a mess. I didn't care.

After dinner, I tucked them in and kissed them goodnight. They were amazing, and I loved them so very much. Their father rejecting them stung all the more tonight. They'd been so full of life, comforted by having a male figure around. Now, it looked like Logan would no longer be a part of our lives. If that was the case, they had no one but me again.

A familiar sounding engine came into the complex, and I went racing out to the balcony. Logan pulled into the car park, his laughter echoing through the courtyard. A girl got out the passenger side, and he put his arm around her shoulders as they walked towards the stairs, laughing and joking with each other.

This wasn't the same blonde I'd seen before, but she was pretty similar-looking, and made me feel plain all over again.

Distracted by his companion, he didn't see me until we nearly drew level. My stomach dropped as our eyes met and I tried to fight the tears flowing again.

They came to a stop, and the blonde looked at me with a cocked eyebrow. "Olivia," Logan said, nodding.

"Logan." I swallowed hard, struggling to keep it together.

"Excuse us," the blonde said.

I moved aside. "Sorry."

They walked past me, and Logan looked back over his shoulder. I could feel my face contorting beyond my control as the tears threatened to fall again, and I ran inside and shut the door before they took hold.

Inside I felt as if I could breathe again, and I curled up on the couch, pulling a blanket over me to hide under. Evan leaving me hadn't hurt this badly. Our relationship had been so awful for so long that by the time he left it wasn't me I felt sorry for, but our children. This time, I hurt for all three of us.

I DECIDED to take the boys to the park before taking them out for Sunday brunch in the morning. More than anything I wanted to get out of this place, get some fresh air, and think.

As I opened the door, Logan came walking past and the boys pushed past me to get to him.

"Logan," they both cheered, one clinging on to each leg. He laughed, bending down to talk to them.

"Where are you going?"

"Mum's taking us to the park. Then we're going to get food. Do you want to come?" Jack asked.

He looked up at me, and I almost burst into tears all over again. "I can't, but you guys have fun."

There was a squeal behind him and the blonde from the night before was standing at the door. "Logan? Hurry up and get the milk. I want coffee and to go back to bed."

I fisted my hands, clamping my lips together in an effort not to cry.

"Sure thing. Uh ..."

She rolled her eyes. "Nadine."

"Yeah, right. Be back shortly."

Jack and Thomas trailed behind him all the way down the stairs to the car park. We parted ways as we exited the complex, going in opposite directions, and it took everything in me not to beg him to come with us instead.

"Can't we go?" Jack pleaded, pulling at my hand to follow him.

"Honey, Logan's got other things he needs to do."

Jack pouted, and I looked over my shoulder at Logan. He must have heard my child, and stood still on the path, watching us as we walked away.

"Sorry, love. Logan has his own life. He can't always hang out with us."

One last look back at Logan. His face said he was miserable. But he couldn't feel as bad as I did.

Surely.

19

BY MONDAY MORNING, I still wanted to dig a big hole and hide. I didn't know if any of my co-workers had seen the article. The thought shouldn't have bothered me, and probably wouldn't if it weren't for my heart being so broken over Logan. If anyone had asked me about him, I would have turned into a puddle of tears.

Calling in sick, I dropped the boys off and returned home. Some part of me hoped that he would come around and talk to me, but all I could see in my mind was that other woman. He'd clearly already moved on.

Maybe he wasn't such a knight in shining armour after all.

Rap, rap, rap.

I jumped as the knock on the door broke through the silence.

Grumbling, I got up before hope hit me in the face like a brick. Maybe Logan had had a change of heart; maybe he wanted to make up. Maybe I'd get the chance and be strong enough to tell him just how I felt.

It was Maddy.

"Olivia, I'm so glad you're here. I'm so sorry," she blurted out.

Little Carly was in a front pack, her fuzzy little head poking out the top against Maddy's chest.

"What are you sorry for?"

"I called Logan about the story in the paper. I assumed that he'd be happy, excited for you. Lord knows, I am. I think it's wonderful."

I nodded, standing back to let her in. She moved through the door, cradling Carly's feet as she made her way to the couch. "Sorry for turning up like this, too. I felt awful when I found out how he'd reacted. It's all my fault."

I shrugged. "You're not responsible. If you hadn't told him, someone else would have. Do you want a coffee, or a juice or something?"

"Juice would be great. I'm trying to stay away from the coffee with this one." She lifted Carly out of the front pack and I smiled at the sight of the little girl. Her big blue eyes widened as she saw she was somewhere different, a grin growing on her face as she looked at me.

"She's so sweet. I can't even remember my boys being that little," I said. I turned towards the kitchen counter, taking two glasses out of the cupboard.

"She's growing like a weed. That's what my mother used to say. She'll be crawling soon enough; she's already trying so hard to roll over."

When I turned, Maddy had spread a small blanket on the floor and laid Carly down on it. The little girl kicked and punched excitedly.

I poured the juice, returning to the living room where I placed the glasses on the coffee table before sitting opposite Maddy.

"Thanks. I was really hoping you were home so I could apologise. I felt so bad," she said.

"It's my own fault. I should have told him what I was doing."

She looked up, her brown eyes full of sorrow. "He really liked you. I've never seen him like this before. He wasn't even this upset when we broke up."

I sighed. "I love him, Maddy. I just got so confused, you know? Every time I've seen him with a woman, they were nothing like me. I thought he just wanted to be friends at first."

"Flirty friends. Yeah, I get that," she said, picking up the glass.

She smiled. Carly let out a squawk and we both looked down at the baby. She was so precious, I was sure I could feel my ovaries screaming at me.

"It's okay, sweetheart. I haven't forgotten you're there," Maddy said.

I sucked in my bottom lip, watching them. "Logan told me you live in my old house."

Maddy laughed. "Funny how that worked out. Actually, I spent a few days trying to track you down before I found out you were here."

I cocked my head. "So I heard."

"I started looking after Andrew slammed the door in your ex's face. No one yells at me, especially when my husband is around."

She grinned as I laughed out loud. Evan would have gotten one hell of a fright.

"He turned up here," I said. "I was glad Logan was around. Evan was angry that I'd sold the house, but he left us, so screw him."

Maddy laughed. "Good for you."

"I haven't seen him since, either, thank goodness."

This was so good. She was so easy to talk to. Maybe if this whole mess was sorted, Maddy and I could become friends. The last thing I wanted was to come between her and Logan.

"Logan's miserable," Maddy said quietly.

"That makes two of us. I couldn't face work today. He seemed to bounce back pretty quickly; he had some girl with him on Saturday night."

Maddy's left eyebrow couldn't get any higher. "He came to see us yesterday and never mentioned that. I'll ask him."

I shook my head. "Maddy, please. I don't want my problems causing issues between you and Logan. That's the last thing that needs to happen. You don't even know me."

Her mouth twisted, as if she was trying to think of what to say. "Fine. But, if you need anything, you tell me. Logan will come around; I'm sure of it. He has a heart of gold that guy. He put up with me for a lot longer than he probably should have, and is still a good friend. He loves you, Olivia. I know that much."

She said the words. She said the goddamn words I wanted to hear but was too scared to.

"I love him, too. I guess you're right. If it's meant to be, it'll sort itself out."

"RACHEL PETERSON, please. Yes, I'll hold."

I tapped my fingers on the table impatiently. At the very least, I wanted the reporter to know just how upset I was.

"Rachel Peterson speaking."

"Rachel, this is Olivia Grant."

Silence.

"You know, the woman you screwed over by writing your shitty little story for your shitty little paper."

Oh, that feels good.

"I'm sorry you feel that way. I thought it was an amazing achievement."

"An amazing *private* achievement."

More silence.

"I want an apology ..."

I'd never felt so angry, so alive. "Look, you picked the wrong time in my life to piss me off. So I suggest you get your boss to call me, or I will track him or her down and tell them how annoyed I am."

I slammed the phone down. It didn't make anything better, but it helped get a load of my chest. None of it really mattered. It didn't matter if they apologised to me or not, if I had to get lawyers involved or not. None of it would fix my broken heart and repair my relationship with Logan. None of it.

Half an hour later, the phone rang.

"Hello?"

"Mrs Grant? My name is Anthony Prendagast. I'm the editor of the *Central Star*. I understand you have a problem with an article we printed."

I took a deep breath. "Too right I do. I got a call from your reporter and I told her no, I wasn't interested. And for whatever reason you printed the damn thing anyway. This was nobody's business but my own."

"You're right."

What? He agreed with me?

"I'll be printing an apology in the next issue. For what it's worth, you should be very proud of what you've done, but I understand you wanting to keep it a secret, considering the nature of it."

Tears ran down my cheeks. How could someone who unknowingly ruined my life be so kind? I couldn't very well yell at him anymore and I don't think Rachel would be in any condition to deal with my venom. And I had plenty more to spew at him.

"Thank you. I appreciate your honesty."

What else was there to do?

IN THE MORNING I got up and went to work. There was no sign of Logan, and all I wanted was to see him, talk to him, explain to him the truth. My heart was sick, and I knew no amount of crap I might get at work would make me feel any worse than I already did.

Grace gave me the biggest smile as I walked in the door. It was actually pretty scary, and I wondered what I'd done to deserve it. She beckoned me by crooking a finger and I walked over to her desk reluctantly, just waiting for some smart-arse comment.

"I downloaded that book of yours. It was amazing. The things that man did. When's the next one coming out?"

I gaped at her, not quite believing what I was hearing. Of all the people I knew I thought she would be the one who didn't approve.

"Uh, I don't know."

"Let me know when it's for sale and I'll buy it."

"Sure."

I walked toward Rebecca's office, past the staff room. A group of women were in there, making their morning coffees, and one of them spotted me.

"Olivia," she called.

I sighed, and turned back toward the door.

They started clapping and cheering, and my cheeks were blazing as I thanked them and kept going. Rebecca stuck her head out of her office, and smiled at me.

"What's going on?" I asked.

"What do you mean?"

"Grace tells me she loved my book, that lot applauding me ... It's like I'm living in the Twilight Zone."

She laughed. "They're proud of you, Olivia. Get used to it. How did Logan take it? Can he live with being the inspiration behind a best-selling book?"

Tears welled up, and she frowned, grabbing my arm and pulling me into her office. With the door shut, she sat me down on her couch and sat alongside me.

"What is it? What's wrong?"

"Logan hates me." I sniffed and she pulled a tissue from the box on her desk, handing it to me. I wiped my eyes and blew my runny nose that had gone out in sympathy.

"Oh, sweetie. What happened?"

"He thinks I used him. I love him, Rebecca. I love the way he is with Jack and Thomas; I love the way he is with me. He's so tender and loving and I am the worst person in the world right now."

She wrapped her arms around me, pulling me in tight while I cried. "No, you're not. You fell in love; that's what you did. And if he can't see that, maybe you're better off without him."

"It just hurts so much. And he's right. At least once I asked him a question to help me get a scene right. I should have told him. What if I ruined my chance at finding happiness?"

We sat with me cradled in her arms, patting my back like a child, caring for me the way no one else would right now.

"Go home," she said softly.

"I don't want to."

"Maybe you'll see him to talk to and explain."

I looked up at her. "He's not interested. He's already moved on."

She clamped her lips together, giving me a steely glare that I'd only ever seen her use on people she was trying to intimidate. "What?"

"He had some girl at his house on Saturday. We nearly had sex on Friday night and he'd replaced me the following day. How important was I?"

A growl came from her lips, and I sat up properly. "I just have to accept that he doesn't want me and move on."

If only it were that simple.

20

I GRUMBLED GETTING out of bed a few mornings later. My head was thumping, and I could feel a head cold coming on, but with no one to help I just had to keep going.

All day I felt as if I had a cloud wrapped around my head, and my brain was completely fogged over by the time I got home. I threw a quick dinner together for the kids, thinking only of my bed. Thomas crashed halfway through his meal, falling asleep on the living room floor. I lifted him gently, tucking him in and kissing him goodnight, all the while hoping that Jack and he wouldn't catch this awful cold.

"Are you okay, Mum?" Jack asked. He looked so worried, and I forced a smile on my face to reassure him.

"I'm just tired, sweetie. I've got a bit of a cold. I'm going to go to bed, so if you want you can read a book, or I'll let you have some extra television time just this once."

He smiled. It wasn't often I let them watch television, so this was a real treat. I saw the indecision in his face on whether to stay with me or not.

"I'll just be in bed, and if you need me you just come and get me. Okay?"

Jack nodded, kissing my cheek. "Love you, Mum. Hope you feel better in the morning."

"A nice sleep and I'll be as good as new."

I sunk into the soft bed, sleep overcoming me as I closed my eyes.

I'm sure I'll feel better in the morning.

My dreams were full of Logan, his arms warm and welcoming. And then I would feel like weeping at the thought of him no longer wanting anything to do with me. As much joy and money as my little venture had given me, it wasn't worth losing his friendship. Now I needed him, wanted him here more than ever.

Then I would see Jack and Thomas. My babies. I could weep for them, with their father who no longer gave a crap about them. It was my fault they'd lost Logan too. I never asked for him to act in that role for them, but he just had, as my friend.

I'd dreamed of his hands on me, his mouth. The thought of his kisses made me ache with desire. But what would he want with me now? A single mother of two with nothing to offer him? I'd made a bunch of money from my one book that had been moderately successful, but there were no guarantees that my good luck would continue.

Since our falling out, I hadn't felt inspired to write anyway. Maybe there wouldn't be a next book.

My head swum, and I struggled to sit up before collapsing into the pillows again. I had no idea what the time was, just knew that there was light creeping through a gap in the curtains.

"Mum?" Jack was by the bed, with Thomas by his side. I smiled at him, reaching up to stroke his face.

"Hey," I whispered.

"Are you feeling better? We're hungry."

"Of course you are. I'll get you something to eat. Though, I think I'm going to have to come back to bed afterwards."

Jack beamed. "We can take care of ourselves," he said. "If you make us breakfast, we can find toys to play with."

"I'm sorry I'm so useless today," I croaked.

"You're sick, Mum," said Thomas. "It's okay."

"I'm glad you're okay with it."

I climbed out of bed, wobbling as I stood. Jack stood next to me, pulling my arm around him. "Here, Mum. Lean on me."

Every bit of strength I had, I used to make them breakfast. It was just a drink and some cereal, and yet I was exhausted by the time I fell back into my bed. I shivered despite the warm room, but had no energy left to go and find the thermometer to take my temperature.

Taking a long drink from the glass of water I'd brought back to bed with me, I fell asleep again, unable to keep my eyes open any longer.

I hope the kids will be okay.

And then I was gone into the oblivion of my illness, still fighting to stay awake because even though they were confident they could look after each other, I was all my children had.

"LIV." Logan's soft voice broke through the dream I was in the middle of fighting. Evan and I were arguing, and I was crying, apologising for some wrong I hadn't committed, or something one of the boys had done. He'd spat the words, *"I never wanted any of this, I never agreed to have them."* And I'd cried, falling to the floor, consumed by the grief caused by his words. Neither of them were planned, but I'd loved them from the moment I held those tiny bodies against me. At the time I'd thought he loved them too. Now, I relived losing him again, and the horror that it wasn't just me that he was leaving.

"Liv." I heard it again, and struggled to open my eyes, coming out of the hell that was my marriage falling to pieces. A cool cloth to my forehead made it easier to focus, and I looked up to see Logan sitting at the side of the bed, his brows furrowed in concern.

"What?" I croaked.

"You should have called me. I would have taken care of the boys while you slept."

My eyes stung as tears welled up. "You're not talking to me, remember? I guess now you can tell me what a shitty parent I am, too."

He frowned. "You're not a shitty parent; you're just dealing with all this by yourself. That would be hard for anyone. I'm here now. I'll cook some dinner and I'll hang around until you're well enough to be back on your feet."

"Dinner?"

A smile broke through, and he tapped my nose with his index finger. "You've slept all day, sleepyhead. Jack knocked on my door when he thought it was time for lunch. Told me to get my butt over here."

I sighed. "I'm sorry. I told them to wake me if they needed anything."

"Liv, you can't do this alone. Not all the time. We'll talk when you're better, but I've missed you. More than I should."

I cocked an eyebrow, but moving my face ached so much I dropped it back again.

"Get some more rest. I'll bring you something to eat soon and then you can sleep again."

"You're being so good to me."

"You mean a lot to me, Olivia Grant. You and your children. If I don't take care of you, who will?"

He stood, and I grabbed his arm as he began to move away.

"Thank you," I whispered, squeezing his bicep.

He looked down at me and smiled. "I'll be here as long as you need me."

I watched as he walked out, Thomas chatting excitedly as Logan re-entered the living room. My boys were happy, and that was what mattered. And now I knew I could recover and not worry about them.

My heart leapt at his words. He had missed me, and now he was here for me. I didn't care if he just wanted to be friends, I was just so glad he was back.

Logan soon returned with a bowl of chicken soup he had made himself.

"You're so clever," I murmured, taking a sip. My stomach grumbled at the smell of the food. I hadn't realised just how hungry I was.

"Not really. I just want to take care of you."

His brown eyes were full of emotion, and I could see just how much he'd missed us. Well, missed the kids.

I still wasn't that sure about me.

Logan laughed at how quickly I got the soup down, and went to fetch another bowl. I loved the way he moved, his swagger in those jeans that fitted him like a glove. While my eye enjoyed the sight of him, my heart hoped for a resolution to our differences.

Maybe we could make a fresh start. But then again, was I hoping for too much? He said we'd talk when I was better.

What if it was to let me go?

21

I SLEPT WELL THAT NIGHT, but still dreams haunted me, both good and bad, but at least I got a few hours without worrying about anything other than getting better.

When I woke, Logan was sitting beside the bed in a dining chair, watching me intently.

Hey," I said, not sounding quite so croaky.

"Hey. How are you feeling?"

"Better. That soup and the sleep have really helped."

He smiled, and my heart ached looking at him. I wanted to reach out and try to make amends, but was it too early? Would he accept my advances?

"It's mid afternoon. Do you feel up to a bath?"

I closed my eyes thinking just how nice that would be—soaking in a hot bath with bubbles and not having to worry about a thing. Besides, my nightgown and sheets were all sweaty. Not that Logan needed to know about that.

"That sounds amazing."

Opening my eyes, I watched as he left and looked up at the white tiled ceiling. He wanted to take care of me. That had to be a good sign.

"Mum?" Jack stood in the doorway and I smiled at him, motioning for him to move closer to the bed.

"We got Logan. Is that okay?"

"It's fine, baby." I reached out, stroking his face with my hand. "I'm sorry you had to go and do that."

"We didn't want to wake you up."

"You guys are okay? You're not feeling yuck?"

He shook his head. "We're fine. Thomas is annoying, but we're fine."

I laughed. My big, responsible boy.

Logan poked his head back in. "Bath is done. Whenever you're ready."

The water felt amazing. That hot, sticky, sweaty feeling was disappearing and I scrubbed myself over with my coconut shower gel that I loved so much. I would come out of this feeling better, and smelling amazing.

After washing my hair, I climbed out of the bath, towelling myself off and slipping a clean nightgown over my head. I wrapped my bathrobe around me and pulled a hairbrush out of the drawer. As I brushed my hair, I looked at myself in the mirror. Could he forgive me? Could we put all this behind us? If we couldn't, a little piece of me would die inside.

Damn it, Olivia. You need to be able to move on from this if he doesn't want you.

I crossed the hallway to my room. Logan had changed the bed, and I could have wept at finding clean sheets and pillowcases to snuggle up to. Nothing better when you're sick.

Dropping the bathrobe, I slid between the crisp sheets, still unsure of what I'd done to deserve his kindness. He'd had every right to be angry about what I'd done, even if I did it out of adoration.

I snuggled down and closed my eyes.

WHEN I OPENED them again and rolled over, the alarm clock told me it was 8.40pm. I'd slept most of the day. I woke feeling refreshed and not the hot sweaty tangle I'd been earlier. If I'd dreamed, the memories of them were gone.

I was still getting my bearings when there was a tap on the door, and Logan's breath caught as he saw me, his gaze settling on my chest. I looked down, realising I was showing off more cleavage than I'd intended, and I pulled at my sleeves to adjust the nightgown. He stood for a moment, taking me in, before making his way to the bed.

Shaking his head as if to remove what he'd seen, he sat beside me. "How are you feeling now? Did that bath make you feel better? I came in a few times, but you were fast asleep."

I nodded. "It really helped. I feel almost human again."

His breathing seemed to speed up as he reached out to touch my face. Running his palm from my cheek to my forehead, he nodded approval at the improved temperature. "You feel much cooler."

"Comes from being taken care of." I smiled at him, his hand lingering on my face as he traced his way back down to my cheek, and then on to my neck.

A look of longing in his eyes, he continued, brushing his hand down to my breast, which he cupped, running his thumb across the hard nipple. "Olivia," he whispered. My heart pounded as I moved closer to him.

"I like it when you call me that."

His head jerked up, as if he had snapped out of whatever daydream he was having. He pulled his hand from me as if he had been burnt.

"I'm sorry." He stood, turning towards the door.

"Logan?"

"I'm not going to be fodder for your writing, Liv. Doesn't matter how much I want you right now. Get some sleep; I'll crash on the couch tonight and go home tomorrow if you're better."

He closed the door behind him, and the tears built as I stared at it. Our relationship, reduced to this. All I'd ever wanted to do was earn some extra money to support the kids, and yet I'd destroyed any chance I had of being with the man I was in love with.

I did love him, and I was sure he loved me now. Pulling back the bed covers, I stood and took a deep breath. I looked at myself in the dressing table mirror, and patted my nightgown down, taking another big breath. If I was going to do this, now was the time. He could walk out that door in the morning and I might never see him again. My knight in shining armour could choose to turn his back and walk away, thinking I only wanted him around for one thing.

I opened the door slowly, just in case it creaked. The apartment was still and I went in the boys' bedroom on my way to the living room. They were both tucked up tight and fast asleep. I knew Logan loved them, too; he'd said as much.

Kissing them both good night, I walked down the hallway to the living room. Logan stood beside the couch, shirt off and muscles rippling as he set the couch up for sleeping on. This was my muse, but this was also my love.

"Logan," I whispered, barely able to get the word out.

He looked up. "Liv? Are you okay?"

I drew closer. "I can't just let you leave in the morning. You need to know how I feel."

Logan closed his eyes. "I know you value my friendship, and you and your boys mean the world to me. But we both know what this is."

"I love you, Logan. I have from the moment you smiled at my boys and showed an interest in us. I screwed up not telling you of all people what I was doing, and what I wrote reflected the desire I felt, the electricity between us. You were my inspiration, but only because you are the best thing that ever happened to me. To us. I don't have to write another word if it means I keep you in my life. I couldn't write right now, even if I tried; my heart just isn't in it."

He frowned. "Don't you have anxious readers waiting for your next book?"

I shrugged. "You're more important to me than that. Nothing is more important, except for Jack and Thomas. They love you too. You've been more of a father to them than their actual dad." I fought back the tears, failing as my eyes misted over. His brow creased as his eyes grew sad. "I know you have to do whatever you have to if you feel uncomfortable around me. I just wanted you to know that I will do whatever it takes to keep you in my life. Even if it's just as a friend to my children."

A coughing fit caught hold and he stepped forward as I struggled to catch a breath. I held my hand out to stop him.

"I'm going back to bed, but just think about it, Logan. Please?"

I couldn't look at him any more, and I went back to my room, still trying to fight the tears. Slipping between the sheets, I gripped the pillow. At least I'd told the truth. What happened now was up to him.

The bedroom door opened. "Liv?"

"Don't worry about me; I'll be fine. Pretty sure I'm over the worst of whatever this was."

"I know that." He sat on the bed, and I pushed myself up to sit. "Liv, I love you too. I just felt so used, like you were only keeping me around for your writing."

"That's not true." My heart beat faster at him being so close. He'd said the words I'd longed to hear, but it seemed a hollow victory if I still lost him.

"Are you sure, Liv? I mean, you say you love me, but how do I know that it's real? If you've got writer's block I need to know that you're not just trying to cure that."

I reached out for his hand, placing my own over it. "It's not writer's block, it never has been. I never felt inspired when Evan was in my life, and losing you is like a piece of myself is missing. I'll give up the writing if you want me to. I don't need to do it. It was fun, but I just wanted to see if I could earn some extra money, buy the kids a few new things. We managed without it before, and we'll do it again. You are more important to me than that."

He looked down at my hand. "Did you really mean everything you said in those books?"

I raised an eyebrow. "Like what?"

"The guy in the last book. He was the love of the heroine's life. Not just some guy she met and wanted sex with, not just a loving relationship. So much more."

"You read my books?"

A grin slowly grew on his face. "I did. I had to know what you were talking about. Was that us?"

Now was the time to be honest, and I nodded. "I thought about you a lot. I didn't write everything based on you, but you were never far from my mind when I was writing. You're just so perfect; far too perfect for someone like me."

"What do you mean?"

"I'm a wreck. Two children with a man who didn't really give a crap about any of us. You have nothing holding you back. Your business is going so well, and you could have any woman you want. I don't even know how we became friends, but I'm glad we did."

I took a deep breath. If I told him everything and he still wanted to be free of me, I'd let him go. It would ruin me, but I'd know I tried to fight for us.

"I wanted to tell you how I felt before you left and I have. I didn't mean to make you feel used; that's not how I ever saw it."

He cupped my face, leaning in closer to me. "Tell me how you feel about me again."

My pulse began to race again. This man was so good for my heart. I shrugged. "I love you, Logan. That's all there is to it."

His lips touched mine, and the room seemed to spin as everything I ever wished for lay in front of me. I was still so tired from being ill, and yet I felt as if I could do this forever.

I loved the feeling of being kissed by Logan. He was warm and soft, and his arms wrapped around my neck, pulling me in closer to him as he claimed me.

Finally, he broke away, and I opened my eyes to see all the love in the world for me in his. "I love you too, Olivia. That's all there is to it."

I smiled. "Does this mean we get to start again?"

"Kind of."

"What do you mean, kind of?"

"I mean, if you're up to it, I'd like to stay in this bed with you tonight instead of on your couch. It's not actually that comfortable."

I laughed. "Is that the only reason you want to sleep in here?"

"Well, I think you're still not well, and need a lot more sleep. If it's okay with you, I'll watch over you tonight."

The way he said that made my whole body shake, and it wasn't from fever.

"Olivia, if we don't screw this up, we have the rest of our lives to get it right. Let's get you well, and take it from there."

He pulled the blanket back, slipping in to bed beside me. Holding his arms open to indicate I should lie down, I gladly went to them, nestling into the bed beside him. Stroking my arm, he kissed me again, probing my mouth with his tongue.

Growling, he pulled away and grinned. "What an idiot. As if it's going to be that easy to be this close to you and not want to make love. Are you worried about the boys finding me here? I can get up early."

I shook my head. "They love you. They'll be over the moon to have you back in their lives again. I should be more careful too. The last thing I want is to make you sick with this."

"It's a bit late to worry about that now." He laughed, and I stroked his stubbled cheek with the palm of my hand. He really was mine, and I could hear the words forming in my head at the joy I felt in his embrace.

My muse had returned; not that I would tell him. Not yet, anyway.

22

THE MORNING LIGHT crept through the curtains, and I woke to Logan kissing my forehead just like my mother used to, to see if my temperature was raised.

I laughed. "Mum used to do that."

"Are you comparing me to your mother??"

I shook my head. "No. You two are completely different. She doesn't love me."

He kissed my lips, lingering before smiling at me. "Well, I do. More than you can imagine."

His hand moved to my breast, stroking it through the thin fabric of my nightgown. My nipples stood to attention at his touch, and as our kiss deepened, he squeezed gently, making me gasp.

"So, how about it, Ms Grant?" he whispered, planting kisses on my neck.

"Yes," I whispered back. Right there and then, I would have agreed to anything. All I wanted was him, and now he wanted to make all my dreams come true. Nothing could be sweeter.

He ran his hand down my nightgown, pulling it up my legs and tugging at my panties, urging me to remove them. Hooking a finger in the waist, I pushed them down, before sitting up and pulling my nightgown over my head.

As I flung the nightgown down the bed, Logan's eyes lit up at the sight of my breasts. After two children I was still proud of how firm they were, and he bent his head to lick and suck at my nipples, his fingers probing between my legs.

He stroked me and I moaned, my body giving into his demands.

"Olivia," he murmured, his mouth finding mine as my body jerked at the peak of orgasm. I moaned into his mouth, his tongue battling mine, his fingers slipping inside me, and I bucked my hips, riding them, loving him.

He kissed his way down my body, running his tongue between my breasts, down my stomach, plunging into me. I hadn't had sex for months and now this beautiful man was going to make a meal of me.

"I've wanted this for so long," he said, kissing my thighs. "I knew that first day I saw you, out at the mailbox in those tiny little shorts."

I laughed. "You have a good memory."

He gently teased me with his tongue, and I ran my fingers through his hair, sighing.

He looked up and grinned. "All I remember is seeing this gorgeous brunette with the most amazing butt I'd ever seen. But then I got to know you and the boys, and I knew you were so much more."

"You can talk, Mr Muscle."

He laughed before going back down on me, plunging his tongue into me, just as deep as he could get it, and I made some other contented noise that made him laugh. Every nerve in my body was alive as he kissed his way back up my body, until he was back at my lips. "I told you I was a tease, and I appear to have made you very happy."

I laughed. "Just being with you has always made me happy."

And then he frowned, his lips downturned in disappointment.

"What is it?"

"I don't have any protection on me. I thought I was nursing a sick woman, not ending up in bed with her." He rolled off me. "Sorry, baby. I'm such an idiot."

"I have an IUD," I said, reaching for his arm."

"What?"

"After Thomas was born, we didn't want another accident. So, I got an IUD so I didn't have to worry about pills or condoms or anything."

He propped himself up on his elbow. "Are you sure about this?"

"Not really." I swallowed hard. "I don't want to know, but I need to know if you're safe."

He nodded. "Completely. But why ... oh ... Nadine."

I shrunk into a ball, pulling away instinctively. Knowing about her was one thing, naming her another.

"Shit. She's a friend of Kat's. I went out for a drink to forget about us and found her stoned out of her brain with some guy about to take her home, and she had no clue where she was. I tried to get her to her place, but she wouldn't tell me where she lived. So I brought her home with me and slept on the couch while she took the bed."

He closed his eyes. "I should have explained at the time. I wanted to, but I was so hurt that when you saw her I bit my tongue instead. I'm sorry for letting you think I was with her."

I let myself go, pulling his head toward mine so I could kiss him. "I believe you."

His eyes flickered open, a look of sorrow in them. "I wouldn't lie to you. I couldn't lie."

Tension flowed out of me as my tears streamed. Our gazes were locked and he nuzzled my cheek, before littering my face with tiny kisses, taking away the last of my anxiety. I pulled him close to indicate I was ready, that I wanted him, that it was time for us.

"I'll ask you again: Are you sure about this?"

I nodded.

"Now I know you haven't slept with anyone else, and you know I haven't been. If we're going to be together, we need to trust one another. And we don't need to worry about pregnancy, I got that covered. I can always show you the little card in my purse reminding me to go back and get it changed."

He shook his head. "I believe you. Besides, I doubt you want another child. Not this soon, anyway."

I smiled. Evan had stood over me while I'd had the IUD implanted. He never would have trusted me enough to do it by myself. I'd never lied to him, and yet everything had piled up on top of me as if I'd been the one keeping secrets.

Logan moved back hovering over my body, and I could feel him hard against my leg as he kissed me. "I can barely believe we got our shit together."

I laughed. "Let's just keep it together, shall we?"

"As if I'm ever letting go of you now."

He guided himself to the right spot, dipping into my waiting body. Closing his eyes, he began to move in and out, slowly at first, his face showing how much he savoured each movement.

This was wonderful. It took a few moments to adjust to being with a man again, and I couldn't help but smile at him being so much bigger than Evan had been. I think I'd keep that one to myself. I tilted my hips, rubbing myself against him.

"What are you doing?" he whispered.

"I think you forgot to finish something." I giggled, then gasped as he hit just the right angle, and I tumbled over the edge, closing my eyes as I lost myself in him.

When I opened my eyes again, I watched, entranced by the emotions he displayed. There was no love scene I could write that was as tender as what we now shared, no words that could express what either of us felt. When he looked at me and smiled, I loved him more than ever.

Pushing back, I drove him in deeper, fighting the sensation to close my eyes again. I wanted to feel him, see him, share this moment with him more than anything else ever. For just a moment I wished I'd only ever been with him.

"Damn, woman," he murmured, kissing me tenderly. Nose to

nose, we just looked at each other, moving in unison. We were one, and everything was perfect.

"I love you," I whispered.

"I love you too." He picked up the pace now, pinning me to the bed as his tongue sought mine in another kiss. We tasted each other, our bodies pressed together, our skin flush. He stiffened as his climax approached, and with a loud groan he came. I was his, and nothing could be sweeter.

He rolled to my side, holding me, caressing me, looking at me with such a sense of wonder that I knew was written all over my face too.

Sharing kisses like we were two giddy teenagers, this was so much better than any other intimate moment of my life. I was loved, truly loved, and I adored this man who lay beside me.

"Did you get enough material?" he whispered.

Confused, I looked at him with eyebrow raised. "What?"

"I was kidding. Making a joke about your writing."

"Oh, that. Yeah, I've got a recorder going under the bed. What the hell do you think?" I snapped.

"Sorry, Liv. I was just trying to joke."

"I thought you hated what I was doing."

"Not hated, just wished I'd known." He smirked. "If you'd told me I was your muse, we could have had sex a long time ago."

I slapped him on the arm. "Now you tell me."

"Think we can make it, Liv?" He looked at me thoughtfully. "I'd really like to be here for you and the kids. They are so freaking amazing too."

I smiled, kissing his cheek. "I think we can do anything. Especially now we're together."

23

BY MONDAY MORNING I was much better, but still weak from being ill, and Logan insisted that I stay in bed while he dropped the kids off to school and day-care. I called in sick, collapsing back into bed once the call was made, and fell asleep.

Rousing when Logan joined me again, I laughed as he growled, pulling me into his arms.

"I figured I could play hooky with you," he said.

"I'm not playing hooky. I'm trying to get over this horrid flu."

He grinned, kissing me softly. "I'll help you forget all about that. At least until it's time to go and pick up the boys. I can drop them off; I don't have authority to pick them up."

Logan raised an eyebrow. "It does mean you need to get dressed at some point today. I'd rather you didn't."

I laughed. "Pretty sure the last thing I feel like today is getting dressed. I really just want more sleep."

"Then sleep. I'll sort out the rest."

I slept most of the day, waking when Logan shook me gently. "Baby, we need to go and get the boys."

"Hmmm," I mumbled. "Fine, I'll get up."

I laughed as I spotted what was on the end of the bed. From the bag of clothes I still hadn't given to charity, he'd fished out those damn shorts.

Logan shrugged, grinning as I rolled my eyes and dug in the drawer for some clothes I could actually wear in public.

He'd even cleaned and dried a load of washing, and I pulled my jeans out of the washing basket, kissing his cheek as I changed. "You're wonderful. You know that, don't you?"

"You and your family bring out the best in me," he whispered, patting me on the backside.

He guided me to his car. I snuggled into the seat before realising the boys' car seats were in the back.

"You thought of everything," I said.

"I wasn't about to put them in danger. They mean as much to me as you do."

I couldn't speak, I was so overwhelmed by him. Instead, I sat back and relaxed as we drove the short distance to school.

Donna stood outside the gates, and I bit down on my bottom lip when she spotted me as Logan helped me out of the car. He linked his arm in mine, pulling me tight to his side. "If you need to lean on me, I'm right here."

"I'll be fine. It's nice to get some fresh air. But don't you dare let go of me," I said, smiling up at him.

We walked past Donna and through the gates. I didn't catch her eye; I just kept going, looking straight ahead. I had no resentment or irritation for her, just the pride that I felt getting on with my life. Being with the man I loved.

Jack's eyes were wide as saucers as he left his classroom, sprinting towards me and throwing himself at Logan.

"Hey buddy." Logan laughed, letting me go and swinging him around.

I loved watching them together. Over the time we'd known Logan, they'd bonded. Something still stuck in my gut thinking about Evan's relationship with Jack, or lack thereof.

"Are you better, Mum?" he asked.

"Much better. I slept all day."

"Yes, so now we're going to go and get Thomas and I'll cook you all dinner," Logan said.

He grinned, leaning over to kiss me as I snuggled back up to him. Walking back out to the car, past Donna again, who stood there with her own children, was more satisfying than I could ever express. I felt her eyes on me the whole way as Logan opened the door for me and Jack, and made sure Jack was secure in his booster seat before walking around the car to climb in.

I smiled, taking his hand in mine as he sat, squeezing it gently. "You see that woman at the gate? The one looking at us?"

He turned his head. "Yes?"

"That's my former best friend, Donna. The one Evan left me for."

He looked back at me. "I'm sure she's nice, but he's still an idiot. I'm really glad he's an idiot, though."

Logan leaned over and brushed my lips with his.

"Mum, are we going to sit here while you guys kiss?" Jack whined.

We laughed, and I shook my head. "No, baby. Let's go get Thomas and get home."

I WAS GOING BACK to work in the morning, and it was late. Once the boys were tucked up we had gone to bed to lose ourselves in this new thing we had started.

His finger made circles around my nipple, and I studied him as he seemed lost in thought, staring into space.

"What are you thinking about?" I asked.

Without skipping a beat he looked up. "This. Us."

My lips twitched as I itched to ask him exactly what, but I didn't know if I wanted to hear it. Was he having second thoughts? "When I first saw Maddy with Andrew, I finally worked out what it was she and I had missing. She looked at him as if he were the only person in the room. It didn't matter that I was there, or that we were sitting in a hospital with people coming by all the time. All she saw was him."

His eyes searched mine and I met his gaze, wanting to know where this was going.

"Then, I met you. And I got it. The boys were there, wanting to play and making noise, but it was always you I looked at. I never had that before, Liv. That's why it hurt so much when I thought you'd used me. I don't do secrets."

I reached out to touch his hair, stroking it between my fingers as he closed his eyes.

"I won't ever keep anything from you now," I whispered. "I'm sorry I ever kept things in the first place."

He lay his head just below my breasts, and I kept stroking his hair.

"I saw a future for us." He planted a gentle kiss on my skin, his voice choking up. "You know, when you came here and I found out what had happened with your husband, something ignited in me. I still don't get how anyone could give up anything so perfect." He raised his head, moving up to kiss me softly. "This. Being in this bed together means I'm not letting go now. You and me; that's it. I want us to be together. I want us to be a family. Maybe one day, well, damn it, I want kids with you."

His face was inches from mine, his eyes pleading with me to feel the same way.

"That's what I want too," I whispered. "The boys love you so much. I love you so much."

A few seconds of silence, and he grinned. "I notice you didn't say anything about that last thing I said."

I laughed. "Before Evan left, I thought those days were behind me."

"I saw how you were with Maddy and Carly. That little baby waved her magic wand over you. If I ever came close to telling you how I really felt it was that day, seeing you with her. I saw the longing in your eyes, as if you weren't finished. As if there were more you wanted to give."

I smiled, nuzzling his cheek. "She does make me clucky. That is one beautiful baby."

"One day we'll have that. You and me. I never wanted to settle down so much as when I saw your reaction to Carly. That, and your boys are incredible. You've done an amazing job with them."

With that he kissed me again, and I lost myself in the warmth and love of this man who was no longer just my friend.

He was everything.

24

"MADDY ASKED me if we wanted to go and have dinner with them on Sunday," Logan said the following evening.

"Did you tell her?"

"She called to see if I'd ventured over here to make up with you. I frustrated the hell out of her by being so stubborn. She was so determined to get us together."

I laughed. "I like her, I really do."

"I think she felt guilty about pointing me in the direction of that story."

I hooked my fingers into the belt loops of his jeans and pulled him toward me. "She did. She came and saw me to apologise."

"Really?" His brow furrowed.

"She just wants what best for you. Maybe you're just friends now, but she still loves you enough to not want you to screw up your life."

He cocked his head, running his eyes down my face.

"Yeah, well, I could have done that easily by being so stubborn. Nearly lost the best thing that ever happened to me."

When he said things like that my stomach still plunged to my knees. I'd gone from being someone's regret to someone's dream. I didn't know if I'd ever get used to that.

"Shall we go and see her?" I asked.

"If you want to. Might be a bit strange being in your old house, but I'd really like it if you two got closer. She still means a lot to me in a purely platonic way."

He kissed my nose, leaning his forehead against mine, and I knew the last bit of that sentence was for my benefit.

"Besides, then you can meet her husband. Who knows? Maybe you'll completely understand why Maddy adores him so much. He's pretty good-looking, for a dude."

I cracked up laughing, lifting my arms and wrapping them around his waist, burying myself in his chest.

"I think I like you better."

"Are you sure? You haven't met Andrew." He held me close as I laughed, planting kisses in my hair.

"I love you."

"Ahh, knew I could get you to say it."

"WHERE ARE WE GOING?" Jack asked.

"Our old house," I replied, looking over to the back seat. His eyes grew wide.

"Are we going to live there?"

I shook my head. "Maddy lives there now. Maddy and her husband and Carly."

When we pulled up outside, Jack squealed. "Look, Thomas."

This was weird. It was our old house, but it wasn't, if that made sense at all. Maddy and Andrew had made it all their own, and all remnants of my life had been removed.

It felt clean, fresh, and it did my heart good to see the building being looked after. The way we should have taken care of it.

Maddy sat inside on the brown leather couch, Carly in her arms as she breastfed. Andrew had opened the door and ushered us in with a big grin on his face.

"You must be Olivia, I've heard all about you."

He was tall, with blond hair that matched Maddy's. They were such a handsome couple, it was little wonder Carly was so cute.

"It's good to meet you. This is Jack, and Thomas."

The boys ran toward the couch, scrambling to see Carly. The little blonde head turned at the sound, pulling away from her mother.

"Oi. Little Miss Distracted." Maddy laughed.

Carly's arms waved, and she grinned at the boys before returning to her feed. I moved to sit beside her. "Every time I see her, she's so much bigger," I said.

"She's rolling over now. Won't be long until she's crawling. Then I'm in trouble." Maddy grinned.

"Won't be long and she'll be able to run around with the boys."

"Can we get a baby?" Thomas asked.

I froze. Where had that come from? Unable to answer, I looked to Logan for help. He laughed, shrugging. "Maybe one day," he said, meeting my gaze.

"Dinner's nearly cooked."

The unmistakable smell of chicken made my stomach grumble and my mouth water. I loved that smell; it made me remember countless roast dinners in this place. I loved cooking big dinners for my family, and yet we hadn't had anything like it since we'd moved into the apartment. I guess my heart just hadn't been in it.

"Andrew's roast chicken is to die for. He does the potatoes in the chicken fat. I could live on those," Maddy said, gazing adoringly at her husband.

"I love doing them that way," I said.

"Mum hasn't cooked that for aaaaaages," Jack said.

"Well, when we're in the house there'll be a new kitchen, and plenty of room to cook roasts and different things," Logan said.

Wait. What? We hadn't talked about moving in together, although I guess Logan's natural progression had always been to move into the house. I hadn't thought about us doing that; there was so much to think about. Moving in with someone was a huge step, and I hadn't even seen the place. Not that it made a difference; one of us moving from one apartment to the other was huge.

Was I overthinking it?

Apparently I wasn't the only one.

"Isn't it a bit early to be talking about moving into the house together? Poor Olivia, you've been with her for five minutes and you're taking over her life," Maddy said matter-of-factly.

Logan's hand landed on my shoulder, and I looked up to see him smiling down at me.

"Liv knows the score. I'm not talking about tomorrow."

Well, I didn't, but now I knew that was his long-term plan.

"Besides," he continued, "the house still needs a lot of work before anyone moves into it."

Whew. For a moment, I thought I'd have to panic about just how fast he was moving.

"Good. You don't want to push her, Logan. She's a good one." I looked back toward Maddy, and she winked.

"Anyone want a drink? I've got beer and juice in the fridge," Andrew asked as he made his way back to the kitchen.

"Beer would be great," Logan said. "Liv?"

"Just a juice, thanks."

Logan bent and kissed me before leaving for the kitchen to retrieve our drinks. I watched as he joined Andrew.

"I'm glad you two are together. He looks happy. So do you," Maddy said. Carly finished and Maddy covered up, pulling her to sit up all in one swift movement. "Listen to this," she said to the boys. Patting Carly on the back soon produced a big burp, and the boys giggled.

"I bet you guys did that when you were little," she said.

"We still do," Jack said, nudging his brother.

I loved watching them, so comfortable around Maddy and Carly.

Maddy placed Carly on a blanket on the floor. She started on her back, but soon rolled over to face me, grinning at me so proudly, as if she'd just achieved the greatest thing ever. I guess when you're a few months old, that was how it seemed.

"Liv." I looked up. Logan stood over me with my drink, and I took it from him and blew him a kiss.

He knelt on the ground beside me, and leaned over to talk to Carly.

"Aren't you clever? Yeah?"

Pretty sure my ovaries twitched looking at them. He couldn't be more perfect if he tried.

I caught Maddy watching me out of the corner of my eye and turned my head to smile at her. She nodded towards Logan, continuing to nod at me, and I didn't have to ask her what she was trying to tell me. I think she could see our future too.

WE CLIMBED the stairs to the apartment, tired and sleepy from our amazing dinner, and it was later than I would normally let the boys stay up till.

"Pyjamas, brush teeth and bed," I said as we came in the door.

Thomas yawned, and I ruffled his hair. "Come on, little man. Let's get you to bed."

Logan went to the kitchen, and the kettle whistled while I helped the boys get ready for bed. If I knew him at all, he'd be making us a hot chocolate before bed. He'd done it the last few nights.

Thomas and Jack were both in bed, the blankets covering them, and I kissed one and then the other to say goodnight. "Sleep well, guys. I'll try to let you stay in bed as long as possible in the morning. Hope you had fun tonight."

Thomas nodded, his eyes trying desperately to close, and I gave him another kiss.

"Hey you two, sleep well." Logan's voice came from the door, echoing my words, but I think by the time he said them the boys were already asleep.

I sat on the end of Thomas's bed for a moment, just watching them. For all we'd been through, they'd come out the other side stronger if anything. Jack tried so hard to help around the house now he was a little older, and Thomas had become more confident, more sure of himself. I was so proud of them both.

Standing, I turned toward the door. Logan had gone again, back to the kitchen I assumed, and when I came back out Logan was sitting at the table, his cup in his hands, and there was a matching one sitting on the other side of the table for me.

"Made you a hot chocolate."

"You're so sweet." I sat down and yawned. I was more tired than I thought I'd been too.

"Tonight was good, huh?"

I took a sip and nodded. "It was great. I can see what you mean about Maddy adoring Andrew. Those two are so cute together."

He grinned. "You and Maddy get on great. It's nice that two of the women who mean the most to me are becoming friends."

I cupped my face in my hands as I leaned on the table. His eyes narrowed. "What's going on in that head of yours?"

"I don't want you to take this the wrong way, but …"

"Oh. Shit. You hate her. She is really pushy, and she talks *way* too much at times."

I raised my head and shook it, smirking at him. "Logan, she's fine. Really lovely, actually. I don't have any problem with her."

He nodded. "Okay …"

"It's just weird becoming friends with your ex. I know it shouldn't bother me, but my husband did run off with my best friend."

Logan came around the table, squatting beside me. "You know there's nothing like that between us, don't you? Hasn't been for ages. And she has Andrew. Those two are freaking soul mates, if there is such a thing."

I clamped my lips together, looking at the floor. "I know, and maybe I'm being silly. I like Maddy. It'll just take a while to adjust to having her around and knowing that you and her used to—"

I didn't get a chance to finish my sentence as Logan kissed me, his tongue finding mine as he soothed my fears with a touch. I might have felt a bit weird about Maddy, but I knew how Logan felt about me, and I had zero reason to think he would ever play around behind my back.

"I think it's bedtime," he whispered, kissing me softly under my ear.

Nodding, I let him take my hand as he stood, leading me to the bedroom.

I don't think I'd ever been happier in all my life.

25

I WOKE with him spooning against me, one arm slid under my neck and the other over my waist. The hand he had free was between my legs, inside my panties, and making me gasp.

I lifted the hem of my nightgown. "Come on then, just a quick one before I have to get the kids out of bed."

Logan pulled me roughly onto my back. "Don't you get it, Liv? I never want just a quick one with you."

I shrugged. "I don't have much time in the mornings to muck around."

He kissed me, long and deep, making my skin tingle with excitement. Every nerve in my body instantly awoke.

Hooking a finger in my panties, he slid them down my legs. "You should sleep without those, by the way."

I laughed, reaching up to stroke his face. "Would that make you happy?"

"You on tap makes me happy." His lips curled into a grin as he leaned over to kiss me again. He rolled on top of me, kissing my neck. "You could lose the nightgown too."

"Years of habit."

"I want you naked in bed with me," he whispered in my ear. A shiver ran the length of me, and I was almost panting with desire. I just wasn't used to feeling this wanted.

He pushed himself up and I pulled my nightgown over my breasts. Logan ran a loving tongue across them before letting me sit to slip it over my head. My eyes met his, and I turned to marshmallow at the way he stared adoringly at me.

"Logan," I whispered.

"You're so damn beautiful, Liv. I just want to look at you all the time, feel you against me. I can't get enough of this."

I fought back tears. Not once had Evan said anything remotely close to this, not even in his most tender moments. Logan loved me more than anyone else ever had.

"Don't cry, baby. I know you're not used to this attention, but you'd better get used to it, because this is me." His eyes were full of longing as he examined my face.

His kiss was so tender, and I closed my eyes, lost in the moment as he trailed kisses down my neck. "Get on top."

He rolled off me, beckoning me to straddle him, lowering myself on his hardness. Now it was my turn to gaze down at him, see the love in his eyes, the love that was mine and mine alone.

"Love you," he whispered.

I wiggled my hips and he grinned in response, thrusting upwards, harder into me. I loved that we were literally joined at the hip, and I never wanted it to end.

"Earth to Olivia," he said softly.

I laughed. He'd noticed I was away with the fairies, in my own little world thinking about us.

"Tell me what you're thinking."

"I'm thinking about just how perfect this is. And I'm thinking that we still need to make this quick so that I can get the boys dropped off on time. And then there's work." I waggled my eyebrows to show him I wasn't completely serious.

Logan smirked, one side of his mouth twisted into a sly grin. "Forget work, come home and play with me."

I laughed. "As much as I'd like to, I have rent to pay."

"I'll pay the rent. You can be a kept woman."

I rolled my eyes, gasping as we moved together. Never in my life had I felt so connected with someone, and not just in the physical sense.

He stroked my breasts, my shoulders, running his hands down my back as if he didn't want to lose contact in any way. I didn't want him to either, but I knew that I'd have to return to earth sooner rather than later.

His hands on my shoulders pulled me down towards him as he groaned his release. I couldn't have been any more poetic and loving in a book.

My heart swelled at the realisation that this was my life from now on. *He* was my life.

"Logan," I murmured as I rolled over and snuggled up beside him. I never wanted this feeling to end, the complete and utter giving of myself to another human being. One who was prepared to give me just as much back.

He kissed me, the whiskers on his chin tickling my face. It was a kiss filled with more than just the passion that we felt for one another—it was a kiss filled with love.

And as much as I loved it all, the clock was ticking.

"You are going to hate me for this, but I have to get out of bed."

Bang. Back down we both came, but he just grinned at me and nodded.

"I know. You have to get our boys off to school. Liv, I understand you need your independence after everything that happened, but you don't have to work as hard anymore. You've got me right behind you."

Our boys—he called them our boys. Something told me Evan didn't care enough to be concerned about that. It felt weird, but so good.

Logan pushed the hair back that had flopped so inelegantly over my face, his fingers running through the strands as he gazed at me.

"Get going before I change my mind and tie you to the bed," he murmured.

I laughed, pecking at his lips before pulling away. It wouldn't take much more to convince me to stay, but this would have to wait until the evening.

"You don't think I'm serious?" He cocked an eyebrow as he pulled himself into a seated position, leaning against the pillows.

"I know you are. Why do you think I'm escaping now?"

I picked up my panties from the floor. "I'd better put these on too. They can always come off later."

"You know they will." Logan winked, those eyes full of love making my heart pound.

I sighed, overwhelmed by the feeling inside me. Nothing had ever felt so good. I'd thought I had it all before, but this time, I really did.

"Move it, missy, before I change my mind about letting you go."

I dropped my nightgown over my head so I could make my way to the shower. Logan sighed as it draped over my breasts, and I shook my head, rolling my eyes at his lost expression.

Leaning over the bed, I kissed him tenderly before making a move toward the door. "Want anything for breakfast?"

"I believe I've already had breakfast." He had such a cheesy grin on his face, I had to get out to stop myself from laughing.

If this was what real love was like, I wanted my life to be this all the time.

It was overwhelming and amazing, and at the same time scary. The thought of getting what I always wanted terrified me.

26

IT DIDN'T TAKE LONG for Logan to all but move in. As the days went by, he brought over clothing and the most important thing of all, according to the boys: the PlayStation. I even gave him a key so he could start preparing dinner. It all just felt right.

We couldn't get enough of one another, and it was almost as if he'd always been there, the way he naturally stepped into our world full-time.

Now I came home to dinner cooking instead of rushing to do it myself, and our apartment felt like a real home. I hadn't realised just how hollow my old life was. Logan had completed it.

We settled in to our new routine as if it were the way we'd always done things, and the month flew by as I looked forward to sharing a bed each night with him.

Tuesday night was Chinese takeaway night, and I grabbed some on the way home. The boys were chattering the entire car trip about their days and what they hoped would be their latest Lego conquest after dinner.

I rolled my eyes at them, but I loved how enthused and happy they were. They'd had so much to deal with during the past few months, but they were settled, and knew just how much they were loved.

Logan wasn't home when we got there. That was odd. His workshop was nearby, a five-minute drive away, if the traffic wasn't bad. I pulled my phone out of my bag, but there were no missed calls or voicemails.

Maybe he'd lost track of the time. I placed the food on the table and went to the kitchen to fetch some plates.

"Where's Logan?" Jack asked.

"He must be at work, baby."

He pouted. "Not fair."

"Jack, he has customers he has to take care of. I'm sure he'll be home soon."

I returned to the table, putting the plates down and taking the lids off the plastic containers. There was that lovely freshly cooked smell.

Making the boys plates up first, I put one together for Logan for later and plated my own dinner.

I sat on the couch as the boys sat on the floor, wolfing down their food, desperate to play that next level on their game. "Slow down you two, the game isn't going anywhere."

"But, Mum ..." Jack said, talking through a mouthful of food.

"Take your time. I said you could play the level."

When we were finished, I put the plates in the sink and lay on the couch to watch them. I loved how they were using team work to build things and demolish them.

It helped keep my mind of Logan not being home, and as the minutes ticked by I tried not to think about it, pretend that everything was fine.

An hour later I looked at the clock, frowning as it ticked over to 6.30pm. All those old insecurities began to grow as I called the workshop and got no answer. His mobile went straight to voicemail.

Torn between being worried about his safety and worried that he might be up to no good, my stomach ached. My heart told me he would never do anything to hurt me, but years of dealing with bullshit turned my head in such a way that the feeling ate me alive.

"Where's Logan?" Thomas asked.

"I don't know sweetie. Running late." I smiled as he grinned up at me.

"He's not Dad, Mummy," Jack said.

My heart caught in my throat as I gazed at him.

"I know, baby. Something must have happened. I'm sure he'll be home soon."

The nagging doubt stuck around until after they'd gone to bed. Where was he and why wasn't he answering my calls? The thought of him with anyone else stabbed me in the heart. I'd given myself to him heart and soul, more so than I had any other person.

I sat on the couch, flicking on the television while I waited. Eyes growing heavy, I laid down, resting my head as I looked at the images on the screen. Tears welled in my eyes. I'd been used to this with Evan; I never thought I'd have to deal with this with Logan.

A stream of tears rolled down my cheeks. I tried to fight them. There could be many explanations as to why he wasn't home, but the years of Evan going out in the evenings with no idea of when he was coming home pushed me to cry.

I closed my eyes, only to be woken by Logan's gentle kisses.

"Hey, beautiful," he whispered.

My eyes felt as if they were glued together as I pried them open.

"Oh, baby. I hope those tears weren't for me. I got home as soon as I could."

He pulled me up to sit, wrapping those big, strong arms around me, making me feel comforted even without explanation. He was home, and all was right with the world.

"I went to get parts this afternoon out east, and there was a huge accident. Must have been all over the news. Some poor woman got stuck in her car, and I stayed with her until the fire service managed to cut her out."

Holy crap. My breathing sped up as I released a sob, and he pulled me closer, stroking my back to calm me.

"I tried to call when I realised I was going to be a while, then found my phone was flat. I should have got someone to call you, babe, I just didn't think. I'm sorry."

"I didn't watch the news; we were having dinner and then the boys played their game. I just thought …"

"You thought I'd done what Evan used to do to you. Damn it, Liv, don't you know I'll never, ever do that?" He kissed the top of my head, resting his chin in my hair. "All I kept thinking about was that if it were you, I'd want someone to stay and hold your hand. No matter how long it took."

I wrapped my arms around him, hugging him as tight as I could until the sobs subsided, and I felt I could breathe again.

"I know I was being silly," I whispered.

"Never. You have every reason to feel this way after all the times it's happened before. If there is ever a time I'm not by your side when I'm supposed to be, there'll be a good reason. God knows, it's hard enough to say goodbye to you in the mornings."

I buried my face in his chest, laughing.

"Jack knew," I said, my voice muffled by Logan's warm body. "Jack told me you weren't like his dad."

"Jack's very wise. You should listen to him."

"He is, and I know you're not. I just panicked. I'm sorry."

He leaned back, letting go of me, and raised my face with his fingers under my chin to look into my eyes.

"There's nothing to be sorry about. I really want to have a shower and go to bed. Want to come with me?"

I nodded, and he bent his head to kiss my tears away, making me better.

"Then, I want to hold you close and dream with you. That woman today? Her husband was away on business. They couldn't even get hold of him to let him know. It made me so grateful that we're all together and nothing is ever going to separate us."

"I love you," I whispered.

"I love you too. Very much. Don't ever forget that."

He stood and reached out for my hand to pull me off the couch. With his hand in mine, I felt safe, loved, sorry that I ever thought the worst.

Soon after I examined his face as he slept peacefully beside me. What I felt for him still blew me away. I'd never thought anything was possible, but here he was, right next to me, loving me as if it were something he'd done his whole life, protecting me from harm, feeling the need to be with me as I felt for him.

And still, I was terrified.

Terrified of having something so perfect and losing it. Terrified of being left alone again.

I'd had to be stronger than I'd ever thought I'd have to be since Evan left. Now I had this big, strong man backing me up, wanting to fulfil my dreams.

I only hoped I could give him what he needed in return.

"I THINK it's time you met my mum." They were the first words out of his mouth in the morning.

The words freaked me out. Not that I wasn't committed to Logan, but I'd not had much luck with parents. My father had left, and my mother threw me out. Evan's parents had split up at some point, and his dad had died in a building accident. His mother was around for a while, but then she'd had a massive stroke.

Maybe I was just bad luck.

"Are you sure? I mean, I seem to either drive them away or kill them. Not that I literally kill them, but that's what it seems like."

His eyes smiled as much as his lips did. "Olivia, relax. She'll love you. You're the most chilled out, down-to-earth girlfriend I've had. You're not overwhelming, like Maddy, and you don't do drugs. And those boys? Man, she'll think she's died and gone to heaven."

I cocked an eyebrow. "Do you not think that's what I'm afraid of?"

He laughed. "I get my easy-going charm from her. you two are very similar."

"Easy-going charm, huh?"

"Well, it worked on you." He leaned forward and kissed me as I laughed. "That and I just know you were impressed by my wealth."

"What wealth?"

"Whoops." He waggled his eyebrows and kissed me again.

"I think I fell in love with your arm muscles first. They are pretty damn hot."

Logan frowned, looking hurt. "What? You only want me for my body?"

I nuzzled his nose with mine. "That's just one thing I love about you. You're loving, and kind, and exceptional in bed, as Maddy would say."

He pulled away from me. "You and Maddy have been talking about our sex life?"

I laughed, raising my finger to my lips. "That's for me to know."

"But that's not fair. You said you weren't comfortable being close friends with my ex, and you're talking about our sex life?"

At that, I just laughed harder, shoving his shoulder with mine. "No, we didn't talk about our sex life. That was one of the things Maddy used to talk you up."

Logan rolled over and out of bed. "Clearly it worked. Do I meet your expectations?"

He swivelled his hips, and I snorted with laughter. "Every one and more."

Retrieving some underwear out of the bedside cabinet, he pulled them on and with his hands behind his head, did it again. "Is that better?"

"Are you asking me if I like you jiggling while clothed or not?" I crawled across the bed toward him.

"Well?"

"I don't mind either. I'll take you whichever way you do it."

He leaned over, cupping my face in his hands. "As long as you know I'll only ever do it for you."

A quick kiss and he was gone, jeans and a clean T-shirt for the day in hand.

Mr Perfect.

IN THE EVENING we laid in bed, curled up together, sleep calling.

"Why don't I introduce you to the house on Friday night?" Logan asked.

"Sounds great. Why not Saturday?"

"Because we're going to dinner at Mum's place on Saturday. That is, if you want to go."

I got that puppy dog, hopeful look he sometimes gave me when he wanted to fool around and I was busy doing other things. My heart become this big melted puddle when I got that look—not that I had told him that.

"Sounds great." I yawned. Today had been so long. We were in the middle of an audit and between trying to do my job, find random things the auditor wanted, and Rebecca freaking out about everything, I was mentally exhausted.

Logan stroked my forehead, which just made it worse. My eyes tried so hard to close all by themselves and I had to force them open to continue the conversation.

"One day I'm going to make every single one of your dreams come true. We'll be in our home, surrounded by our children, and you won't have to run around after anyone else but me."

Laughter burst from me, shaking me out of the half-asleep stupor I'd been in. "I'd love to see the house."

"Good, because you're going to let me know how you want it decorated. If we're going to live there as a family, it's important to me that you're happy."

I ran my fingers through his hair, pulling his face closer to mine. "I love that you feel that way. It's your house, though."

Logan frowned and covered the gap between us to kiss me, his tongue tangling with mine as the fire ignited between us.

"Logan," I whispered.

"The house is ours, Liv. I've never been more serious about anything my whole life. We're living together anyway, it doesn't matter where we are."

"Okay, okay." I stroked his hair to soothe him, and he slid his hand up my body, resting it on my breast. My nipple stood to attention and he laughed, dropping his head to my chest to nuzzle it.

"So," he said, his voice muffled as his nose rubbed against the fabric of my nightgown. "Fish and chips at the house on Friday night, followed by dinner with Mum on Saturday."

I could barely concentrate on what he was saying as he reached down to pull my nightgown up and slide his hand into my panties.

"Yes, oh God, yes," I groaned.

He lifted his head, chuckling at something. I couldn't think what, given that my mind had gone blank at the touch of his fingers.

"Good."

Bewildered, I raised my head to query what he meant, but my words were lost as I cried out something, anything to express what I was feeling.

He had me.

WE PULLED up outside the house, and I swallowed down the thrill I felt at seeing it. It had to be half as big again as the little house we'd lived in before. This big, old white wooden mansion needed someone to make it their home. It needed us.

"It's so much bigger than I thought it would be," I whispered.

Logan laughed. "It's got four bedrooms and a tiny room that's no good for anything else, so I was going to throw a desk in there and make it an office. You can use it for your writing."

There was no garden to speak of, but the lawns were neat and tidy. All that was missing was the white picket fence around it. It was the most beautiful thing I'd ever seen in my life, other than my children.

"Liv?"

I looked at Logan. He was beaming with pride, and I wondered just how much work he'd done to get it to this stage.

"Sorry. I love it."

"Knew you would."

"Is that our new house?" Jack asked.

"Sure is, buddy," Logan replied, "so let's get out of the car, into the house, and eat this food before it gets cold."

I got out of the Holden, and went to the back to help Thomas out. He held my hand tight as we approached, Logan and Jack behind us with Logan carrying the paper-wrapped parcel of food.

He flicked the key up and unlocked the door, pushing it open for us to go inside.

"Take off your shoes everyone," I said, not knowing what was inside.

If the outside was beautiful, the inside was even better. The floors were wooden and rough. *Will these be polished, or carpeted?* The entranceway had a couple of rooms to the right, the living room to the left, I could spot the kitchen down the back, and there was a big staircase right up the middle. I fell instantly in love with it.

The inside walls were all new plasterboard, bare, still waiting to be painted. Devoid of all furniture, the rooms looked huge.

"Let's go into the living room and sit on the floor. After we've eaten, I'll show you around," Logan said.

I was on the verge of tears, but held them back. For Logan to want to share this with us was overwhelming.

By the time I turned around, he'd already opened the food bundle, and was spreading out on the living room floor. He squirted the tiny tomato sauce sachets in spots around the outside, Jack and Thomas already picking at the hot chips.

"Logan, it's amazing." I sat beside him, grabbing a chip.

"Before I met you, I thought about selling this place. It was a bargain because it was neglected and run down, and I thought it was a great project for my spare time. But meeting you and the boys changed that. I could see this house full of children and noise and love. I'm going to finish it for you."

I leaned over and kissed him gently on the lips. He knew my heart better than anyone, knew how much I'd love it.

"Can we pick our rooms?" Jack asked. He looked sideways at his brother. "Can we have a room each?"

"You sure can," Logan said, with a laugh.

Thomas lit up, his eyes shining with excitement. "My room?"

"There are four bedrooms upstairs. One for me and Mum, one for you, and one for Jack."

Jack held up his hand, counting on his fingers. I rolled my eyes. It was all for show; he knew how to add.

"There's one room left. Who's going to go in there?"

"It'll be the spare room. Maybe one day there'll be someone else to sleep in there," I said. Logan nudged my arm, he knew what I was referring to. There was definitely no rush for *that*. It was enough to have found him and be starting a new life without adding to it yet.

But we could in time.

27

IN THE MORNING we set off in the car to Logan's mother's place. She'd moved out of town a while ago he said, and had found a little place that was semi-rural. It was close enough to the city, but she'd found her peace and quiet.

We reached the end of the motorway and turned into what ended up a country road. Jack and Thomas loudly pointed out every cow, every sheep, and Logan and I laughed at just how excited they were.

"I guess they've never really been out of the city," I said. "We never had the time, and when I had holidays I used them to catch up around the house."

"They'll love this place. There aren't any cows or sheep, but there's a dog who's just a big gentle sap and loves kids. Mum's had him for ages. He's pretty old now, but he'll be over the moon to see these two."

I leaned back in the seat. It was nice to have someone to drive me around now; I'd always driven before. Now we could take turns—that was if Logan ever let me drive his precious car.

He reached across, taking my hand in his and giving it a quick squeeze. "Love you."

I squeezed his hand back, letting it go so he could change gear, and took a deep breath. After my initial hesitance I was looking forward to this; it showed just how serious he was about us, and I loved that as much as I loved him.

"Love you too," I said.

One more turn, and we slowed until we came to a long gravel driveway, tall trees either side. It looked so peaceful and beautiful. I adored it.

"It's gorgeous."

"Wait until you see the house," Logan said.

I looked back over my shoulder at the boys to see what they were doing. They were chatting excitedly the trees and how easy or hard they would be to climb There was a squeal of brakes and we all shot forward. I breathed a sigh of relief for my seatbelt before turning to see what had stopped us.

"Kat?" Logan said.

Logan's ex had come across the driveway and walked into our path. Only having good brakes had stopped us from hitting her.

"Sorry. I thought I had enough time. That damn dog of your mothers was in the way; I was trying to get him to move."

She looked across at me gaping at her, and smiled. "Hi. You must be Olivia."

"Uh, yeah."

"Do you want to get out of the way now? So I can get to the house?" Logan asked, his face tight with tension.

Kat smirked, and moved back. We drove past and in the side mirror, I saw her wandering up the driveway with the black and white dog padding along in tow.

"Before you ask, I had no idea she was here," Logan said.

As we pulled in front of the house he turned his head toward me, the stress clear in his eyes.

"I believe you. You sounded surprised to see her."

"I am. She got on okay with Mum, but they weren't that close. Especially after she developed her problem."

I nodded. With Logan's father dying of a drug overdose, I couldn't imagine that Kat's problems had gone down well with his mother.

Logan was with me now, I didn't need to worry about her. I squeezed his arm at what I saw.

He was right about the house. It was a cottage nestled among the trees, with plants and flowers growing up against it. he exterior was painted brown, and it almost blended into the background. The only things making it modern were the aluminium windows and the screen door at the front. Just beautiful. I fell in love with it as soon as I saw it; it was just so cute.

Logan grabbed my hand and squeezed it again. "Come on."

Taking a deep breath, I got out of the car. Logan had opened Jack's door, and I went to help Thomas out. He frowned as I helped with the car seat. "Where are we?"

"I told you, baby, we're at Logan's mum's house."

While he'd come out of his shell so much, there were still times he got shy. But then he saw the dog draw level with us and his eyes grew big.

"Patch. Come here," Logan called. Thomas climbed out of the car, and we ventured around the back in time to see the dog run to Logan. Logan rubbed Patch's head and stroked his ears, the Border Collie panting as Jack reached out to touch him.

"Can I go?" Thomas asked.

"Of course you can." I said, ruffling his hair.

He walked slowly towards them, and Logan looked up, holding out his hand for Thomas to take. "Come and meet Patch, Thomas."

His little hand shook as he reached out to stroke the dog, but Patch stayed still, maybe sensing his fear, and let him take his time.

"He's a good boy, but he's a bit old, so we can't go running around too much with him. I think he likes you two," Logan said.

"Patch loves children."

I didn't have to ask. The voice behind me belonged to Logan's mother. The butterflies in my stomach went into panic mode.

I turned. Logan's mother walked toward me—at least, I assumed that was her, unless Logan also had an ex in, I guessed, her fifties staying with his mum. She had a warm smile and those same brown eyes that he had. She took my hands in hers. "I'm Beth, Logan's mother. You must be Olivia."

I nearly burst into tears, she looked so kind. Instead, I nodded.

She looked over my shoulder. "This must be Jack, and Thomas. Whenever I speak to Logan, he never shuts up about any of you." Letting go of my hands, she walked to Logan, giving him a big hug.

"Hey, Mum."

"It's so good to see you. Did you have a good drive?"

Logan nodded. "Until I nearly ran Kat over in the driveway. You didn't tell me she was here."

We all turned as Kat came walking toward us, her sneakers shuffling in the gravel. She looked nothing like she had the night I'd seen her. The skin that had been exposed was now covered, and she looked a lot more comfortable in track pants and flat shoes than the stilettos she'd teetered on.

She wore an oversized shirt, hiding the tattoo I'd been so fascinated with, her hair up in a ponytail, off her cosmetic-free face. I don't think I would have even recognised her if it hadn't been for Logan identifying her.

"Your mother let me stay here for a little while. Just to get away from everything." She shot a glance at me under her eyelashes, no doubt wondering how much I knew.

He nodded. "Good. I hope it's helping." Instead of being laid-back, as he had been with her when I'd first seen them together, he was stiff, awkward, more than likely because of me. I had no idea if I should say anything, or say nothing, or just nod and agree without letting her know he'd told me everything.

"Liv knows, so you don't have to worry about not talking in front of her," he said. *Whew, that was that confusion avoided.*

"It's nice to actually meet you. I think we saw each other in passing that night that Logan tried to help me."

I nodded, smiling at her. After the conversation Logan had with me about her, I'd built up this picture of this woman, struggling with her drug addiction and losing. Whatever had happened since then, she seemed to have gotten her act together, and she looked healthy and relaxed.

"That was me. This is Jack and Thomas, my boys." I said.

"Let's get inside and I'll make coffee," Beth said, "and something for the boys. I'm pretty sure I have some cookies in the cupboard somewhere."

"Can we, Mum?" Jack asked.

"Of course you can," I said. Thomas slid up beside me, slipping his hand in mine. I squeezed it tight as we followed Beth inside.

The interior of the house was as charming as the outside. It had all the modern comforts, but with a rustic feel to it. Polished wooden floors graced the entranceway, and photos were hung all over the walls. So many pictures of Logan, and another younger boy. That must be his brother, Matthew. His mother was so proud of the pair of them.

The aroma of roasting meat filled the house, and some vague memory of our home smelling the same way rose to the surface. Back before Dad had left, before we'd struggled and everything fell to pieces.

Patch scrabbled on the floor behind us, trying to get a grip before getting to the carpet of the living room. I reached down and scratched his ear as he drew close, and he shook his head.

"I'm cooking for a small army," Beth said. "I hope everyone likes roast lamb and potatoes."

"It smells amazing," I said.

"You sit down, and I'll bring some coffee through." She smiled, and I wanted to just hug her and thank her for all of this, even though I knew it wasn't all for me.

"Come on." Logan took my arm and led me through to the couch.

I leaned against him, resting my head on his shoulder. "Not too scary, I hope," he whispered.

"Not scary at all." I turned my head to face him, and he kissed me gently. I watched as the boys sat either side of Patch, patting him on the head. He moved his head from left to right, revelling in the attention and making each boy squeal as he showed them favour.

"The boys are happy," Logan said.

"They are. Patch is so good with them."

"I hope you packed to stay the night. Just in case. It's a long drive home after dinner." Beth returned with a tray of mugs filled with black coffee, and glasses of lemonade. She placed it on the table, and Kat brought through a jug of milk and a sugar bowl.

"Help yourselves," Beth said.

Logan reached over first, spooning sugar into a mug and topping it up with milk. He handed it to me with a wink. Beth watched intently as he made one for himself while I called the boys over to get their glasses.

"What sweet boys." Beth smiled as they made their way to sit on the floor beside the table.

"Told you they were awesome, Mum," Logan said.

The hair on the back of my neck pricked, and I scanned the room, feeling as if someone was watching me. Beth and Logan were focused on the boys. Kat, however, had her gaze fixed on me, and smiled as I made eye contact. I had been prepared to meet Logan's mother, not so prepared to deal with his ex being there.

It's me he wants. Only me.

A hand squeezed my thigh and I looked up to see Logan smiling at me. He nuzzled my cheek. "Still okay?" he whispered.

"I'm fine. Stop worrying," I whispered back.

"So, I read about your story-writing, Olivia. Are you still doing it? I have to confess, I downloaded one of your books and read it. Absolutely loved it." Beth smiled widely at me, and I was momentarily lost for words wondering what she'd read, how much sex might have been in it, and had an oh-my-God-she'll-know-her-son-was-the-inspiration moment.

"I haven't lately. My life has changed since Logan moved in with us." I looked at Logan, and he gazed back at me with that loving look in his eyes.

"I'm sure these three keep you busy. Logan never stops talking about any of you when I call him. He's so proud."

He interlaced his fingers in mine. "I am. Ready-made family, just waiting for me."

Kat cleared her throat, and I shifted my gaze back to her as she smiled sweetly. *So uncomfortable.*

"Kat, dear, could you please go and check the chickens for eggs when you've finished your coffee? They must need feeding by now." Beth smiled.

"Sure thing, Mum," Kat said.

Logan squeezed my hand as if to tell me to ignore her, but it was really freaking hard to do.

"How about you boys? What year are you in at school? Do you enjoy it?"

Beth shifted her focus to Thomas and Jack. I think I loved her already.

Logan leaned over, kissing me under the ear. I smiled, twisting my head toward him. He raised his hand to stroke my cheek. It was reassuring and loving. Just what I needed.

Jack spoke first—he always did—telling Beth all about school and Logan and Thomas. Thomas couldn't get a word in if he tried.

"Thomas? How about you, sweetie?"

"Thomas isn't at school yet," Jack proclaimed.

"Thomas is a bit shy," I said. Thomas stood, making his way over to us, and Logan pulled him up and onto his lap.

"Well, that's okay. Logan used to be shy too. Nothing wrong with that."

She smiled as Thomas buried his face in Logan's chest, and my heart pounded as I watched them together. For Thomas to seek comfort with Logan was a sure sign that he was part of our family now.

"You ask Logan to show you the animals. There's a lamb out there, and the chickens. And you've met Patch."

"Patch is cool," Jack said.

She nodded. "He's very cool. He's been around a long time now."

Kat finished her coffee, gulping down the last part. Her focus went to Logan, who sat there rubbing Thomas's back, whispering to him that it was okay and he could take his time. She didn't register I was watching, and pulled a face as if she were sucking on a lemon.

As she turned, she caught me looking at her and gave me a half-hearted smile, but I'd seen it—the contempt she had for him being with my child, and by extension me.

I tried to blank my face, but I didn't have it in me to hide my irritation. She frowned, shrugging and leaving the room while I leaned over to give Thomas a reassuring pat on the back too.

"C'mere Patch," Logan called, clicking his fingers at dog level.

The dog came wandering over, and Logan patted his head again. "How about you give Patch some love, Thomas? I bet he really wants you guys to be friends."

Thomas reached out and touched Patch's head again. This was what would bring him out of his shell.

"How about we go outside and you can see the garden and the animals? Want to see a lamb?" Logan asked him.

He nodded excitedly and Logan stood, carrying him on his hip. "Want to walk, or do you want me to carry you?"

Thomas hugged him tight, and for a moment I thought he was going to completely retract and ask Logan to carry him outside. Instead, he straightened his legs to drop down, and took Logan's hand instead.

"Jack?" Logan asked.

Jack drained the last of his lemonade and jumped up. I watched as the aging dog seemed to get a new lease on life, standing too, and wagging his tail as if whatever they were doing was the most exciting thing in the world. Maybe it was.

"Coming?"

The word was addressed to me, and I nodded. "You bet. I have to check this out."

If the front of the house was enchanting, the back was magical. Beth had a huge lawn with pockets of garden planted all over the place. Different flowers were in each patch, and what looked like a large vegetable garden at the back.

There was a large pen with the lamb in it to the left, and a chicken run on the right. In the event of a disaster, this place would probably have been the perfect safe zone.

It was simply beautiful.

Kat was coming out the chicken run as we walked across the lawn, carrying a bowl.

She twisted her mouth, as if unsure whether to speak or not. Looking at Jack, she held the bowl out. "Want to see what I've got?"

His eyes widened when he saw the eggs. "Thomas *loves* eggs."

"Come and have a look, Thomas," she said.

Thomas took tentative steps toward her until his curiosity got the better of him, and he ran the rest of the way, gasping as he saw the bowl.

"Fresh out of the chicken," Kat said.

"That is so cool," Thomas said, turning back to address me.

"Better than the ones we buy at the supermarket, right?" I laughed.

"Take one." Kat smiled, actually smiled at Thomas, and for just a few seconds I was grateful to her. Then I remembered the way she'd looked at him and Logan together inside.

Thomas dipped his hand in the bowl and pulled out an egg, cradling it in his palms as if it were the most precious thing in the world. I slipped my phone out of my pocket, and lined up a photo. He looked up and grinned, laughing as I clicked.

"What have *you* got?" I asked him.

"Mum, look." He walked so slowly toward me, covering the gap between us. He looked up at me, excitement gleaming in his eyes.

Of everything I'd seen today, this was the best.

28

DINNER WAS AMAZING. The lamb was cooked to perfection, seasoned with rosemary and thyme. The potatoes were crispy and salted just right, and the vegetables were fresh from the garden. If I'd cooked it just for us, I would have eaten myself into a food coma. But other people were there.

"This is great, Mum," Logan said. "The lamb is amazing."

Thomas frowned, and I cocked my head, waving to get his attention. *What's wrong?* I mouthed.

"Is this the lamb from the back yard?" he whispered loudly.

Beth grinned. "No, sweetie. The lamb is still there; you can go and visit him again after you've finished your dinner. This is from the butcher."

His little mouth formed an O and he picked up a large slice with his fork and bit into it. "Good boy," I murmured.

He and Jack even asked for seconds. Running around outside in the fresh air combined with a good meal would make them both sleep like logs tonight.

As if she read my mind, Logan's mother looked over at them.

"You should stay the night. Those two look like they're falling asleep on their feet."

"Mum, I told you it would just be a quick visit," Logan said.

She sighed and stood, picking up her plate to take to the kitchen. I followed her lead, picking up my own and stacking the boys' plates on top.

"I'll take care of those," Beth said.

I smiled. "It's no problem. I'll give you a hand."

"Why don't you take the boys into the living room, Logan? They're about to nod off, and it can't be comfortable sitting at the dining table."

Logan grumbled, but did as his mother told him. Jack and Thomas followed along behind him, Thomas yawning wide as they left the room.

That left Beth, Kat and me. Not uncomfortable at all. I reached for Logan's plate to stack on the pile, but someone else had that idea. Kat and I looked at each other, both with one hand on the plate, before she shrugged and let go, sitting at the table instead.

Oh, this is fun.

Beth was already running water in the sink when I carried the plates in, and I placed them with the other dirty dishes, taking up the spot to her right with a tea towel I'd grabbed from the handle of the oven door.

"He's just being grumpy because he knows the right thing to do is to just put them to bed, and he thought he had it all planned," Beth said.

Laughing, I grabbed the first dish and began to dry. "He's just adjusting to being with us and having to work around them. I have to say, he's done an amazing job so far."

Beth pointed at a cupboard in the corner. The kitchen was as amazing as the rest of the house with so much cupboard space.

As she washed and I dried, she asked me all kinds of questions about my family and the boys. I had nothing to hide. When I got to the part where Evan left me, she put down the dish brush and hugged me.

Kat walked in as we were in this awkward embrace, my arms loosely around Beth, as I had a damp towel in one hand, a plate in the other. Kat brought in the remainder of the dishes from the table, placing them on the dirty side of the bench and stalked back out, giving me the evil eye.

Logan passed her in the doorway, turning as she went past and shaking his head as she walked away. He met my gaze, smiling that special smile that made me so freaking hot. Right when I was pressed up against his mother. I shook my head with a smirk, rolling my eyes and making him snicker.

Beth let go, tilting her head to look at her son.

"One on the floor, one on the couch, both fast asleep."

"Told you," she said smugly.

"Whatever, Mum. I have a bone to pick with you while we're alone."

Alone with me right there.

"We need to talk about Kat. You didn't tell me she was here," Logan said, his tone irritable and with good reason.

"I knew if I did you wouldn't come. I don't know about you, but I think you can get on with your life without worrying about her. She needed somewhere to stay out of the way of temptation, and this has been perfect. Look at how well she looks."

My skin burned as I sat in the middle of this confrontation. I didn't want Beth to think I was causing trouble over it, but at the same time I needed Logan to know I supported him. Having Kat here was a distraction; it was hard to just be myself when with a few looks I felt as if I'd have to grow eyes in the back of my head to avoid the knives.

"I understand, but I'm not happy about bringing Olivia and the boys here under these conditions. Me? Fine. But Olivia shouldn't have to deal with this."

"Katrina needed help and I helped her. I know that you did what you could for her until you didn't think you could help anymore, but I stepped in. She's doing so well, and I'm sorry for being selfish and wanting to meet Olivia and the boys. If it makes you feel better, I can see why you love them all so much."

My head shot up before I even thought about it, and we made eye contact. She looked at me so kindly, and whether it was sentimentality or not, it made me think of my mother and how we used to be a long time ago.

"Logan, I'm more proud than you can imagine that you've found someone so ... well ... normal."

I couldn't help the smirk that spread across my face, and her eyes twinkled as she kept her gaze on me.

"So. Are you staying the night, or are you going to make those poor boys take that long car trip in the dark? It'll be so uncomfortable for them sleeping in their car seats."

Oh goodie. Guilt trip.

He sighed. "Fine. Whatever. We can stay, if Liv is okay with it."

I shrugged. "I don't mind. Your mother is right. It's a long drive this time of night."

"There's plenty of room, and you two can sleep right next door to them," Beth said.

Logan turned toward me, his shoulders slumped. "I guess you're right. It just feels so awkward with Kat here."

"One night will be fine."

He reached for me, and with a light grip on my hair pulled me toward him for a kiss. Beth clapped. "So, it's settled then."

Logan rolled his eyes. "Guess so."

And then he grinned that damn devilish grin, the one that always got me into trouble.

We were fine.

He picked up another towel, and with his help we got through the rest of the dishes quickly and quietly.

"We should go and move the boys if we're staying the night." He sighed.

"I'll grab the little one. You grab the one that's too heavy for me to carry."

Beth laughed. "I'll go and turn down the beds so you can bring them right in."

"Thanks, Mum. I do appreciate it."

Thomas stirred as I picked him up off the floor, kissing him gently on his forehead. Following Logan up the hallway, we went to a room near the end where two single beds waited.

Tucked in, I kissed them both goodnight, as did Logan, and we came back out to the hallway.

"Little angels, those two," Beth said.

"They're brilliant. I don't know what I'd do without them."

She took my hand and led me back to the kitchen. "Coffee?" she asked.

COFFEE DIDN'T DO much to wake me up. I was as tired as I was sure the boys had been. It had been a long day, and although I would miss my own bed, the thought of sinking into any mattress was welcome.

"Come for a walk in the garden," Logan said, pulling me into his arms.

"I would, but I really want to check on the boys and make sure they're okay. I'm tired, too; must be this country air."

Beth laughed. "It does have that effect."

Logan kissed me, lingering on my lips and waggling his eyebrows before exiting out the back door. I sighed without thinking, prompting his mother to giggle.

"You've got it bad. So does he," she said.

"He's so sweet, and the boys love him, too. He's just been a perfect fit."

She nodded, flopping her arm over my shoulders. "I think you're just what he needed. From the sounds of it, he's just what you needed, too." She drew back, looking me right in the eye. "I love seeing him so happy; it's been a long time."

I smiled, and moved toward the door on my way to check on my children.

"I'll do that. You go out for a walk with Logan. It's a beautiful night out there."

"I can't ask you to do that."

She crossed the room, taking my hands in hers. "If I'm going to be a granny to those two, I'd better get used to it."

I couldn't help but grin at her welcoming us all with open arms. How could she be anything but wonderful with a son like Logan? This had been even better than I could ever have imagined.

"Okay," I said.

Beth grinned. "Get going."

I laughed as she let go of my hands. "Yes, ma'am."

Skipping to the door, I pushed it open and was overwhelmed by the sight. The garden was dark, lit only by the odd solar light, but the sky was full of stars, so many more than we ever saw in the city. I felt a pang of regret that the boys were asleep. Thomas in particular would love it.

I breathed in that heady night air and looked around for Logan. Hearing a noise in the far corner of the garden, I moved toward it, and spotted him leaning against a half wall that contained a small garden behind it. Kat stood between us, her back to me, and the closer I got, the more I heard of their conversation.

"You promised," she hissed, stabbing at him with a finger.

"It's not like that, Kat."

"Of course it is. You said we could be together if I kicked this, and I have."

He sighed. "I said that a very long time ago."

"You still said it. So now you have to ditch her and keep your promise."

I felt sick, not because I didn't believe in Logan, but because she seemed to think that I was something he could just throw away. But then again, he was a man of his word. What if he kept his promise and did the unthinkable?

My head was swimming with possibilities. She felt strongly enough about this to make a big deal about it. He'd admitted he'd said it. With every bone in my body I'd fought thinking the worst of him, and now it all came flooding to the surface again as he hugged her and said something too quiet for me to pick up.

I knew I should stay and push my way in but instead I went quietly back inside, sneaking in behind Beth so she didn't see me, and went to our room, undressing and slipping between the sheets as if nothing were wrong.

But it was. All I could see was them together. All I could hear were the words between them. The bedside lamp glowed in the corner, covering the room in a soft light. I laid on my back and stared at the ceiling, looking at the shadow cast by the warm yellow light. This sucked so bad.

My heart thumped as anger passed over me. I'd sworn to never be anyone's doormat. Screw it. I'd go out there and claim what was mine. *No doormat here.*

I rolled over and sat up, but before I could get out of bed and put my clothes back on, the door opened.

"Hey," he said softly.

"Hey." I knew I was abrupt, more than I ever had been, but seeing her with him like that had pushed my buttons.

He pulled off his T-shirt and slipped his jeans down, kicking them off and sliding into bed beside me.

"You okay?" He reached out and rubbed my back, his warm hand working its magic, even though he hadn't touched me in one of those naughty places only he was allowed to touch. I raised my hand to my cheek, swiping away the tear that had escaped my eye and quickly ran my finger across the other eye to stop the same thing happening.

"I'm glad we came. Mum just loves you and the kids. At least she won't be hassling us to have more anytime soon. We can take our time." His voice was soft and soothing, and I closed my eyes at the sound.

He didn't miss the deep breath I took. I didn't know what to do, whether to confront him. I'd been so determined to storm out and say something, but now he was here, with his hands so gentle and his gentle words, I wasn't so sure.

"Come here," he murmured, pulling me back and down into the bed, enveloping me with his arms. His skin smelled of coconut, from him using my shower gel that morning. Familiar and soothing.

"I've never loved you more or been more proud of you," he said.

I raised my head, locking gazes with him. His eyes scanned my face, and he frowned. I guessed he knew something was wrong, but wasn't sure what, and I was too scared to open my mouth for fear of freaking out at him.

"Hey. I'm sorry about Kat being here, too. I really didn't know. Sounds like it's been good for her, but not so good for you to have to deal with her being around."

His chest heaved as he took a deep breath, and I held mine as he continued. "A very long time ago, way before I met you, I struggled with Kat taking drugs. I broke up with her, she'd stop for a while, we'd get back together, and then it would start all over again. I got to the point where I told her we couldn't be anything more than friends until she gave up for good."

He lowered his head closer to mine, kissing my nose. "I made her a promise that we could be together if it stopped. But then I met you. And you turned my whole world upside-down. I walked away from my promise, and I don't do that lightly."

I exhaled for the first time in what felt like forever at his words, relief flooding through my system. "It's you, Liv. It's you, and Jack, and Thomas. You're the ones I give all my promises too now, and I'll keep every single one. I know there's still so much to learn about one another, but you're the one I want to spend my life with. That much is so clear."

My body shook as I released the tension that had been building, the tears falling onto him like raindrops, and his mouth claimed mine as he wiped my face with his thumb.

"I heard you out in the garden. I thought ..."

"You will never lose me. Even when we weren't together, you were still the one that owned me."

"Maybe I should have *Property of Olivia* tattooed across your chest." I laughed through the tears that remained.

"Maybe I'd let you," he whispered.

I snuggled in tight, as he ran his fingers through my hair before resting them on my back.

"Don't you ever forget just how much you are loved."

29

ONE YEAR LATER ...

OUR FIRST TWELVE MONTHS TOGETHER.

We'd been inseparable. Logan had made the final step to move in with us months ago, even though he'd stayed every night since the first night we slept together. After our rocky start, he did everything in his power just to be there for me.

We were more in love than ever.

As our first year together drew to a close, I was due to go and have my IUD replaced.

"Don't bother," Logan said. "Let's have a baby. We're so close to moving into the house that we'll have the space."

I shouldn't have been taken aback; he'd expressed the wish for us to have a child together someday, and the few times I saw Carly just made me more and more clucky. So I said yes.

I was pregnant in the first month.

We were in love, we were solid, and we were going to spend forever together.

I was thankful that the house was nearly finished. The apartment was small enough with the three of us, but four of us there for a year had just about driven me up the wall. The last of the renovations had dragged on, and I was champing at the bit to get some more space. The early stages of pregnancy were leaving me grumpy, tired, and I was over nearly everything.

On the upside, Logan's workshop was busier than ever and we were more than financially ready for me to take maternity leave. Logan didn't care if I worked or not up to the baby's birth, but I was going to work for as long as possible. After all that Rebecca had done for me, I wanted to give as much as I could back.

And as for Logan? He was my best friend, my lover, and a father-to be. He was still pretty much perfect. We were blissfully happy, and for the first time I dared to think that I might just get my happy-ever-after.

"You never write any more," he said as he dried the dishes. The boys were in bed and we were getting ready for another night of peaceful snuggling on the couch, making up for when our lives would inevitably become chaotic with the baby and the move.

I shrugged. "I put one book out a few months ago, and I still have plenty of ideas. I'm just tired all the time at the moment."

"I hope it's not because of me."

As I turned towards him, I found myself face-to-face with his chest, and took a deep breath. "I'm tired all the time because I'm pregnant, so it kind of is, in a way." I grinned. "Why would it be because of you?"

"Because of the way I acted when I found out. I know we resolved all that, but it bothers me that you stopped because of me." His fingers played under my chin, slowly raising my face to look into his eyes.

"It's not because of that. I used to pour out all my pent-up emotion on the page. Now I get to do that to you."

Logan laughed, and I raised my hands to indicate that I would hug him but for the dishwater coating them.

He rolled his eyes, and wiped my hands with the towel before throwing it towards the washing pile and wrapping his arms around me.

"Any time you want to write, I'll take care of the boys. Get them out of your hair if you need the quiet. You have to be yourself with me, Liv. I won't take anything less."

"Have I told you lately just how perfect you are?" I said.

He grinned. "I want you to have the freedom to do your own thing, and I have asked a lot of you lately, with the house and everything."

The house was his project, but he had consulted me on everything. I guess because we were going to live there as a family. Every time I thought of that, a warm glow began in my stomach and travelled upward.

"Maybe when we've moved and I have the study to work in."

He glowed. Damn that man's smile was intoxicating. And it was just for me, all for me. That warm glow began to move down.

"I so want to go to bed right now," I said.

He hugged me tighter. "I'll come to bed too if you need a cuddle. I know how crappy you've been feeling. A sleep would do you some good."

I grinned, poking his chest with my finger. "Who said anything about sleep?"

HE FOUND me in the bathroom in the morning. *Damn morning sickness.*

"Were you like this with the boys?"

I shook my head. "Not this bad."

"Must be a girl."

I laughed, cocking my head. "You think?"

"Isn't it logical?"

I pushed myself up off the floor and filled a glass with water, taking a long drink.

"Are you sure it's not because you want a girl?"

"Maybe."

He took my hand as we went back out to the kitchen. "I made you some dry toast." His brown eyes were full of tenderness. *Oh, how I love this man.*

"Mum, are you sick *again*?" Jack asked.

"It's just the baby making itself known. Just reminding me that he or she is there."

He laughed, slapping his knees. "How could you forget?" he asked.

I sat, taking tiny bites of the toast. Logan cleared away the breakfast dishes when the boys were finished. It was still so wonderful to have that support and not have to deal with everything myself.

"I can take the boys to school if you want," he said.

"It's okay. I've got to get to work."

"Babe if you feel that bad, stay home."

I shook my head. "I just have to get through this early stuff. It'll pass. I'll be fine."

He frowned, and I watched as he slipped lunch boxes into the boys' schoolbags. He'd thought of everything.

The drop-off went okay, and the morning was tough, but then the morning sickness drifted into the afternoon and I'd had enough.

Exhausted and feeling ill, I made my way down the hall to see Rebecca. I didn't even have to tell her what was wrong.

"You're grey, Olivia. Go home and come back when you're feeling better and not before."

"Thanks," I grumbled. "See you in nine months."

She laughed, rolling her eyes. "Go and have a sleep. I'm sure you'll feel better."

I drove home to have a nap before I had to go back out to pick up the boys. Logan would do it if I asked, but I didn't want to inconvenience him while he was working. At the very least, I could get a couple of hours sleep before I collected them.

Pulling into the car park, I looked up at our apartment and grimaced at the thought of climbing the stairs. Right now they were like a mountain that I was not looking forward to struggling up.

And then I saw her: blonde with big hair and big sunglasses that hid her face, not that I could see much at the distance I was from the apartment. She came out of *my* front door, with *my* boyfriend in tow, and they hugged before she came down the stairs and jumped into what looked like a late-model BMW.

My nausea grew with my anger as I watched her drive off, before getting out of the car. Determined to get up those stairs and confront Logan, I almost ran, tired and exhausted, nearly tripping over my own feet, and then flinging open the door.

Logan sat on the couch, looking up in surprise as I came in.

"Liv? What are you doing here?"

"I could ask you the same thing." I dropped my handbag just inside the door, resisting the urge to take a seat on the couch next to him. Standing was a struggle, but I would deal with this first.

"I just had some stuff to take care of."

"Some blonde stuff?"

He stood, walking slowly towards me with his hands up. "Liv, there's some things I have to explain."

Explain? *Crap.* That meant there was something going on.

"Too right you do. I'm not going to put up with any bullshit, Logan. I've been through way too much for that."

My heart was pounding and the ache in my stomach moved to my head. The tears were forming as we looked at each other. My legs wobbled underneath me, and Logan moved closer.

"Are you okay?" he asked, concern evident in his voice. "Liv? Are you okay?"

"No, I'm not okay. What are you keeping from me?" I couldn't help it. I thought I'd gotten through all this doubt and fear. Maybe I would have handled it better if I hadn't felt so awful, but I couldn't face being alone with another child.

My legs went out from under me before I could stop them. Somehow Logan grabbed me before I fell, and he lifted me, carrying me through to the bedroom, laying me on the bed.

"Baby," he said, stroking my cheek with his finger.

"Don't *baby* me," I said, battling tears. "No secrets."

"Liv, I—"

"The blonde. I saw her, Logan. Why are you at home in the middle of the day with another woman?"

He smirked.

"What's so funny? You are such a pig."

"Olivia," he said, shaking his head. "Didn't you recognise your own mother?"

I sat in stunned silence, the words rolling through my mind as I tried to process what he'd just said. Last time I'd seen my mother, she was cleaning motels, her dirty-blonde hair tied up in a ponytail as she struggled from room to room.

"I tracked her down because with the new baby coming, and the new house, I thought I might be able to give you the gift of reconciliation. What happened between you was a long time ago. I had planned to take you guys over to the house to see the last of the work that's been done and meet her there. She wants to see you and the boys."

My head was swimming, and I reached out to him to squeeze his hand.

"I'm sorry I thought the worst. I should have known that you weren't up to anything bad."

"You hormonal, hotter-than-hell woman. Do you really think I'm going to run around on you after what you went through? I waited my whole life for your special brand of craziness. I'm not about to put that at risk." He grinned, lifting my hand to his lips and kissing me gently

I laughed. "Sorry, you're just not where you're supposed to be, and hanging out with blondes. I didn't recognise her; she had those big sunglasses on, and she wasn't driving a BMW when I last saw her."

"The owner of the motel was widowed, and she's jumped right on in there. They were married a year ago." He laughed.

"That'd be right." I shook my head at the memory of the men in her life. They were usually as useless as Evan had turned out to be. I didn't know what her intentions were in getting married, maybe she loved him, maybe she was using him. Either way, at least she'd found someone who obviously cherished her. Just as I had.

"What are you doing home?" he asked, smoothing my forehead with his other hand.

"I just felt awful. I thought I'd have a sleep and then pick up the boys."

"Sounds like a very good idea to me. Can't have anything happen to you, or my baby." Pulling his hand from mine, he rested it on my belly. "I can't wait to feel our baby kick."

Hot tears spilled down my face, everything piling on top of me at once.

"Shhh." He stroked my cheek, his gentle touch calming me. My body ached, tired from the stresses put on it, and I cried at the idea of having months more of this feeling, even though I knew it would get better.

Logan bent over, kissing me on the forehead. "Sleep. I'll pick up the boys. You'll feel better with some rest, and I'll run you a bath after dinner so you can have a soak. Love you, Liv."

"Love you too," I whispered hoarsely, wiping the tears from my eyes.

I sank into a deep sleep, and by the time I woke the apartment was filled with the delicious smell of cheese. I bet anything that Logan had cooked the boys their favourite mac and cheese. My stomach grumbled in recognition of the aroma. At least it was something solid.

"Hey," he said as I emerged from the bedroom. Jack and Thomas sat in the middle of the living room floor, their heads buried in books. "I made mac and cheese. I know the boys love it, and I remember Maddy saying something about how she craved it when she was pregnant because it helped settle her stomach. Wasn't sure if it would help or not, but I thought you could give it a go."

Overwhelmed with emotion, I moved towards him, flinging my arms around his neck and holding him close.

"Are you okay?"

"Thank you," I whispered.

"What for?"

"Everything?"

He rubbed my back, kissing my hair. "I'd do anything for you, Olivia. You should know that by now."

"I know. I'm sorry. I'm just feeling so up and down right now. You have to forgive me if I'm a little nuts."

He laughed, and I snuggled in closer. "You're going through a lot at the moment. I know you still love me."

I looked up, and we swayed as we gazed at each other. He bent his head, giving me a peck on my nose.

I felt safer than ever.

30

THE HOUSE WAS ALL but finished. I stood at the gate, my heart pounding as I looked at it. After a very long wait, this was about to become our family home.

Logan had been over earlier, mowing the lawn, and I couldn't wait to get stuck in and weed out the garden. The boys wanted to plant flowers and they'd asked for an orange tree. I had no idea how long the tree would take to produce fruit, but Logan had stood with them, as they planted the tree together.

I loved him more and more each day.

I squealed as Logan threw me over his shoulder awkwardly to carry me inside the house. The boys were running around the tree as he showed me the final touches to the interior. The boys' rooms had been painted the colours they wanted. This was beautiful.

"It's all ours, Liv," Logan whispered as if reading my mind. He'd gotten good like that, able to anticipate what I was thinking. There was something wonderful about being so in sync with someone. I'd never had anything like that before.

"It's beautiful."

The thick carpet in the living room that felt soft and fluffy under my toes, the brand new stove and other kitchen appliances ... I'd never felt so spoiled my whole life.

We could spend the rest of our lives here. Logan had even set up a small room as an office for me, where I could sit in peace to write, and where he could muddle through the accounts for the workshop. It was our own little piece of perfection.

"Happy?" he asked me, his eyes smiling. He didn't need to say just how happy he was, and I felt it too. We'd grow old together here.

Before I could answer, there was a rap on the door and I stiffened, knowing who it was.

"Relax, baby," Logan murmured, "I'll get it."

That was easier said than done. I was about to confront the woman who had kicked me out, without any regard for what was to happen to me. My boys were only young, but I knew damn well that whatever happened, I could never do that to them.

I closed my eyes and took a deep breath. My past was about to walk in the door and I had to deal with it. I hadn't spoken to my mother in nearly nine years.

"Olivia?"

Her voice was, soft and gentle. Not the harsh tones that came the last time we spoke.

I turned. She stood there, motionless, with tears in her eyes and Logan beside her. He nodded reassuringly as I took a step forward. This was not the mother I remembered; this lady looked well taken care of. *Loved.*

"Mum."

Tears were welling in her eyes as she looked at me, and I fought them back myself. Maybe it was the pregnancy hormones—I thought I'd cried all the tears I'd had for her years ago.

"Logan contacted me. He thought it was about time we buried the hatchet, and I agree. I'm sorry for everything that happened, sweetheart. I just loved you so much, and I was so disappointed that my baby got involved with that useless piece of crap."

I laughed through the tears, in this kind of half-sob, half-laugh that must have sounded demented.

"I didn't want to let you down, but my baby …" I kind of flapped my arms, unable to finish the sentence. Back then she would have been happy if I'd terminated my pregnancy and broken up with Evan, but that would have left me without my babies, and they'd been my world for so long. I couldn't imagine doing anything any other way.

She took a step forward, reaching for me, and I went into her arms, leaning on her shoulder, the tears flowing readily now.

"You did what you thought was best, and so did I. You know, when I got married, the only person I wanted to share it with was you. But I was too stubborn to find you and reach out. You've got a really good man there."

I looked up over her shoulder at Logan. He winked at me, and the strength of our love flowed through me, the tears easing up. I didn't need my mother's approval, but having her love back would be a start.

"He's wonderful," I whispered.

"Mum?" Jack stood in the doorway, Thomas just a little behind him.

"Come in and meet Grandma, baby," I said.

"Grandma?" Jack looked at Mum in awe.

"Mum, this is Jack, and that's Thomas behind him."

She let go of me, turning back toward them. Logan moved to my side, pulling me into his arms as we watched my mother meet her grandchildren.

"Hi boys. I've heard a lot about you. Logan and your mother are so very proud of you."

Thomas retreated further behind Jack, and I smiled at his reticence. My little shy boy.

"They look so much like you, Olivia." She tilted her head to look at Thomas. "Especially the younger one. What sweethearts."

That you never wanted to know. Stop it. If you're going to reunite with her, you need to stop it.

"They're the best things that ever happened to me. Apart from Logan."

She frowned, knowing the underlying meaning to my words.

If I'd done what you wanted me to do, they wouldn't be here.

"If I had to re-do things, I'd handle everything a lot differently." She took my hands in hers. "I'm sorry I missed them as babies, and I'm sorry I missed holding your hand when you needed me. I'm sorry I wasn't there when Evan left. But I can be here for you now, and for this new baby. If you let me."

Logan nuzzled my ear as I closed my eyes.

"Just one thing at a time, Mum," I said, hoarsely, struggling to find my voice.

"I've got everything ready for a family dinner," Logan said. "I thought we might start with that."

"Can we have bacon?" Jack shrieked.

I laughed, leaning harder against Logan.

"I thought we might have a barbecue. You two haven't seen the surprise in the back yard yet," he said, laughing.

Both boys took off, running through the dining room and out onto the deck. I smiled, shaking my head at the gasps and screeches fading into the distance as they found what Logan was talking about.

"I would say they've discovered the trampoline," he said.

Mum let go of my hands. "Let's go watch them play," she said.

"You two go out. There's a swing seat out there for you to relax on, and I'll bring you out some juice. You packed some with the barbecue stuff, right babe?"

I nodded, and led Mum out the back of the house, and we watched as the boys ran around and around in circles, laughing and whooping.

"They're beautiful. You've done well," Mum said.

"I had to."

I moved to the swing seat. Logan had arranged the furniture so I could sit and watch the boys. He was always so thoughtful and considerate. I still wasn't sure what I'd done to deserve him.

Mum sat beside me. The silence wasn't awkward, but it was weird. I hadn't spoken to her in so many years, and had so much I wanted to say, but the words wouldn't come. They hid, and I was scared, as if I were eighteen all over again, terrified to tell her I was pregnant.

"Logan's great," she said, breaking the heavy silence.

"He's amazing."

"I wasn't sure where you'd moved to. He came and found me. I was so grateful just to know where you were."

I turned my head to look at her, and found my own eyes looking back at me. I'd never noticed just how much like her I was.

"We had to move. When Evan left it just got too hard with childcare, and I couldn't afford to keep living there."

"I saw your apartment. I wish things had been different. It's all my fault."

I said nothing. There was nothing that I could say.

31

AS MY PREGNANCY ADVANCED, the yucky feeling went away and I felt more like myself. In fact, it became enjoyable being able to put my feet up when I got home, and be cared for by Logan and the boys.

With Jack, I'd worked all the way through, unable to stop as I'd just moved in with Evan and away from Mum. Dealing with the loss of my relationship with her had hit me hard, and every day became a struggle, especially when I was in the advanced stages of pregnancy.

Thomas was a new challenge. We were more settled by then, but I was dealing with Evan not completely convinced the baby was his, although that seemed to have been an excuse for his more frequent absences. I'd had a toddler, that I was raising practically by myself, growing bigger by the minute. It was hard, but the days they were born had been the best days of my life.

Now I was pampered and loved, doing nothing by myself. Logan was always there, by my side, ready to take over when things did get too much.

I had a real partner.

And when Logan wasn't fussing, Rebecca was, knowing that at

some point she'd lose me. Not for good to start with, but with the pending house move and the baby's arrival, it was more and more likely. I loved my job, but the opportunity to spend more time with all my children and make up for some of the time I had lost with the first two was far too tempting.

I could be there for my baby, and take the boys to school and pick them up again. I'd carried all the responsibility for so long, and finally I had the support to ease back a little and not overwork myself. I couldn't wait.

At the halfway point, we went to have the anatomy scan, and maybe find out what the baby was. I didn't care; I had two healthy, happy boys, and another one would be welcome. But then a girl would help balance things out, and I got the feeling that Logan liked the idea of a girl, a little me he could cherish just as much as he cherished *big* me.

He held my hand the whole way, squeezing it as the cold gel was squirted onto my baby bump. I closed my eyes as the wand glided over me, warming the gel, and I could have quite easily gone to sleep, I was so comfortable.

"There's the heart," the technician said. I looked up, watching it thumping on the monitor. There was my beautiful baby, alive and strong.

Now Logan gasped beside me as he noticed every little thing about our baby, and I watched as he cast his eyes across the screen.

"That's our baby," I whispered.

"It's going to sound weird, but it's real, Liv. It's really real."

We looked into each other's eyes while the scan went on, the technician accounting for all the organs, taking measurements, and we looked back at the screen to watch the baby kicking like crazy.

"Soccer player," Logan said.

"Footballer." I laughed and the baby rolled slightly, reacting to me. It was just so amazing to watch.

"Did you want to find out the sex?"

The question hung in the air for a moment, even though I knew

Logan was keen to know, and I gave him a small nod and raised my eyebrows as if to ask if that was what he wanted. He grinned. "Yes, please," he said.

I nodded, and the technician moved the wand back and forward until she had it in just the right place.

"Do you see this? The bone goes down here on either side, and there's a little gap. You're having a girl."

I let out the breath I didn't even realise I was holding, and Logan squeezed my hand so tight I squeaked.

"Thank you so much," he said to the technician.

"Was that what you wanted?" she asked.

"Yes," he said, just as I said, "I wasn't worried either way."

We laughed, and he leaned over to kiss me as I snuggled into his chest.

"The boys aren't going to take this well," I said with a sigh.

"What? What do you mean?"

"Another girl to boss them around? I'm bad enough."

Logan chuckled. "Well, I'm going to love having another girl around the place. And it didn't really matter to me. Any child we have will be a freaking rock star."

WE STOOD at the front entrance of the house. A beautiful home for our family.

The moving truck sat outside with all of our things in, the moving men ready to bring the furniture and boxes from the apartments and Logan's storage unit. The bedrooms were already done—we'd bought new beds and made sure they were all ready for us to spend our first night here.

I loved this house, and not just because we'd spent time working on it together. It made up for so much that I'd lost, and being so happy was the icing on the cake. There was nothing that could stop us now.

"Where do you want these?" Logan asked as he brought in box after box. It was all so overwhelming not having to squish things into corners; the simple joy of having cupboard space for everything in the kitchen, among other places, filled my heart. Anyone not part of my family might just think I had gone crazy. I couldn't wait to find a place for everything, his and mine together.

Ten minutes into it, I wanted to lie down. I patted my bump. I'd not long ago started feeling kicks, and she was really going for it today. I still had half a pregnancy left, and I'd forgotten just how wonderful this was, and then how annoying.

"Settle, baby," I whispered.

Logan stood up from the box he'd just placed on the floor. "You okay, Liv?"

"Just a bit tired and being used as a trampoline."

He walked to me with a smile and placed his hand on my belly, closing his eyes. Another kick got him laughing. "Whoa, that was a big one. Pretty sure she's dancing in there. Go and lie down. I got this."

That made me feel weird sometimes. 'I got this' was a phrase I was still getting used to.

"I might just do that."

Slowly, I mounted the stairs. Giggling came from the boys' bedrooms, and I grinned as I drew closer. Logan had gone all out for their rooms.

Jack had wanted a plane theme while Thomas wanted cars. Jack's room had been painted blue, and he had blue curtains with pictures of planes all over them. Thomas's room was green with car curtains. I'd even gotten them linen to go with it, their beds covered in blankets that matched the theme. They had never had anything so new and just for them. I couldn't blame them for being so excited.

"Hey you two, how are your rooms?"

"Awesome, Mum!" Jack said, Thomas nodding in agreement.

"Keep the noise down if you can. I need to have a nap."

"Okay," they chorused quietly. I knew it wouldn't last for long.

The fourth bedroom had become the nursery. Logan had erected the cot, but I had yet to make the bed up with the pastel yellow linen I'd bought. I'd figured I'd keep it neutral, just in case we decided to do something crazy and make even more babies.

I took a breath as I got to our bedroom. I loved the sight of it. Cream and pale blue, we'd combined what we both wanted to make something beautiful. I ran my hand across the floral duvet, pulling it back at the top and exposing the mauve sheets. A splash of colour that just looked so pretty.

Sinking into the bed, I closed my eyes and drifted off.

We were home.

32

"ARE YOU OKAY?"

What a *stupid* question. I was about to push a small person the size of a watermelon out of a very small hole in my body. It might have already let two of them out, but this one was proving to be just as stubborn about leaving. And I hadn't even gotten to the pushing stage.

"Do you want some ice chips?"

No. I want you to have the baby. I gritted my teeth and nodded.

Logan rubbed my lips with ice and I opened my mouth for him to drop it in. I'd forgotten just how much giving birth hurt. It was funny how your body blocked you from remembering, trapping you into a false memory of it being all unicorns and rainbows. Okay, maybe not quite.

"Does it hurt?"

It took everything in me not to smack him, but this was his first, and he'd been with me the whole time. Mum was staying at our place with the boys, so at least I didn't have to worry about them. We were building our relationship slowly, and this was a big step for me to trust her with them, but I knew she was sincere in her efforts to grow closer to us.

"It really hurts. If I kick you in the balls, you might have a tiny bit of an idea of how much this hurts."

He grimaced. "Shit. I hope it's over soon."

You and me both.

The midwife checked one more time and smiled so sweetly, I switched my yearning to hit someone to her.

"It's time to push."

"Oh thank freaking heavens," I groaned.

Logan grabbed hold of my hand, and I gripped tightly as the next contraction hit, bearing down to get this baby out. Sooner the better.

"I don't think it'll take many pushes to get this baby out." Either I was hallucinating, or she sang the words. I'd had gas, but not that much, surely.

Logan fed me some more ice, and I looked into his sad gaze. He hated I was in pain; I could see that. I closed my eyes, lying back on the pillow when it hit me again, this time with an intense burning sensation that made me want to chop the bottom half of my body off.

"That's it, Olivia. The head is crowning."

Oh. That'll be it.

"Not long to go, babe." I opened my eyes to see his sad expression replaced with a hopeful one, his eyebrows not as lost as they had been, a tiny smile on his face.

I felt euphoric at being so close to the pain being over, remembering just how good it felt when the boys had finally made their way out. Soon, I'd hold our little girl, and there would be nothing stabbing me in the guts or anywhere else.

When the next contraction came, I closed my eyes again and pushed hard.

Damn it. Get out of me.

And just like that it was over, as I felt her slip out and into the hands of the midwife. The next few minutes were a blur as she was placed on my chest to meet me, and Logan kissed my temple, lingering on my skin as we met our daughter for the first time.

She was beautiful, her head covered in dark hair. Grey eyes stared at us as her little head rested against my heart, her tiny hands waving.

Logan and I fell in love.

WE NAMED HER CHLOE. I had no idea where the name came from, other than it being a name on the huge list we made that we both liked. And it suited her. She was a delicate little thing. The boys had both been big and demanding right from the start, but Chloe was more lady-like, not crying very much and feeding gently, not gulping, as Jack and Thomas had done.

We came home the day after the birth, and the boys homed in on their sister as soon as I walked in the door. I sat on the couch and they sat either side, just staring at her, laughing when she moved a hand, gasping when she turned her head to look in their direction.

"So boys, what do you think?" Logan asked them.

"She's so little," said Thomas.

"You were that little once too," Logan said, chucking him under the chin. Thomas pushed his hand away.

"Stop it." He giggled. I loved the sound of the boys laughing. It happened so much these days.

"She doesn't look like us," Jack said.

"That's because you've had time to grow. I can show you photos where she looks just like you."

He leaned on my arm. "We missed you."

I held Chloe out for Logan to take, and he scooped her up, winking at me. Holding open my arms for the boys, I hugged them both, one on each side. "I missed you too. Did you have fun with Grandma?"

Thomas nodded.

"She made us go to bed," Jack said.

"I should hope so. You guys need to get lots of sleep and grow to be big boys."

He pouted. "I wanted to see the baby."

"Well, you can see her all you like now. Just wait a few months and she'll be crawling around and trying to keep up with you two."

Jack wrapped his arms around my waist, burying his face in my side. "What if she doesn't like me?"

I glanced at Logan. He stood over us, rocking Chloe in his arms, that faraway smile on his face a semi-permanent fixture. It'd take a while for that to disappear.

"You know what? I think she'll love both of you. She's so lucky. She has two older brothers to take care of her, and play with her. I bet she'll think you're superheroes."

"If we are, can I be Batman?" Thomas asked.

I laughed. "If you want to be."

I squeezed them until they protested, giggling and trying to squeeze me back.

It was good to be home.

33

WITH THE CHILDREN ALL ASLEEP, the house was quiet. Logan was working late; he had a deadline to get a bike finished and tonight was the night. I'd covered his dinner, placing it in the fridge for him to heat when he got home. Him working late didn't make me anxious, not like the old days with Evan.

Now, I stood in front of the mirror, frowning as my jeans refused to button. This wasn't the first time. I'd been here before, and my mind wandered to the days I'd confronted this issue after Jack and Thomas were born. I hadn't expected them to button up, I'd just been hopeful.

I was so lost in thought that I didn't hear Logan come up behind me. The scent of him overwhelmed me as he wrapped his arms around my waist, kissing my neck. I loved that all he smelled of was himself—no alcohol, no perfume, just Logan. And I had no doubt that home was the first place he'd come after finishing work.

"Kids all asleep?"

"They sure are. Couldn't believe my luck." I laughed as he nuzzled my ear.

"It's been a while, baby," he murmured.

"Four long weeks," I said.

He moved around, falling to his knees in front of me.

"What on earth are you doing?" I laughed.

Logan pulled at my jeans, sliding them down my legs. His hands on either thigh, he leaned in to kiss the patch of fabric between us.

"Oh baby, Daddy's missed you," he said, looking straight at my panties.

I shook my head. "You are crazy."

"Is it time to come out and play?" He looked up at me hopefully.

I screwed up my face. "I'm sure the doctor said six weeks. Maybe it was six months."

He leaned in, rubbing his nose against the delicate fabric. "You're not playing fair, Olivia."

"Neither are you with your nose right near my happy place."

His lips brushed against my thigh. I was sure I could hear the blood rushing in my ears trying to get to him.

"Okay, you win."

His face lit up, as if he'd just gotten the best Christmas present ever. He buried his nose between my legs, taking a deep breath as I shook with laughter.

"Logan."

He slid a finger inside my panties, pulling them to one side. "I think we need to go get in to bed and get to know each other again." His brown eyes twinkled with mischief, and I stroked his head as he wiggled his finger inside me.

"Sounds good to me," I whispered and he stood, taking my hand in his and leading me to the bed.

"Are you sure you're ready?" he asked.

"I'm fine. I want to be with you."

He tugged at my shirt, pulling it over my head, and I reached for the button on his jeans, unzipping them.

"I love you," I whispered, watching him slip his shirt off. He was beautiful, his tanned skin the colour of bronze, his muscles flexing with the movement. Perfection. Then I saw the bandage wrapped around his right bicep.

"What happened?" I asked, resting my hand below it, concerned he had hurt himself while working. At least it wasn't covered in dirty oil.

"Can I tell you after I've had my way?" he asked, pulling me into his arms for another kiss. He was hard against me and growing by the second.

I wasn't about to be distracted. "No. I want to know about this."

"Did you know you have a one-track mind? We have other priorities."

He let go, running his fingers through his hair, exasperated by my questioning.

"I'm not the only one," I said, reaching for the bulge in his underwear I had yet to remove.

"You don't make this easy, Olivia."

I shook my head.

He sighed. "I got another tattoo this afternoon. I managed to get ahead on the bike, so I took a couple of hours off to get some more ink. Nothing too big, and you can see it soon."

Picking at the bandage, I wriggled against him. "So, what is it?"

"Can we look at this later? You are seriously busting my balls, woman. In fact, I think they might literally explode from lack of use."

I laughed, kissing his chest. "Fine. You can show me later."

"Finally." He rolled his eyes, and bent, scooping me up and into his arms as I squealed with delight. "Now I've got you."

"You always did," I whispered. His lips crashed into mine as he claimed my mouth, carrying me the rest of the way to the bed and placing me down gently, unhooking my bra as he stood.

"Multi-talented, huh?" I asked, laughing.

"You'd better believe it." He grinned, leaping onto the bed and nearly landing on top of me.

"Gentle, baby," I murmured.

"Always," he said, stroking my breast, his thumb grazing my nipple.

"You be careful with those. You might get a surprise if you squeeze too hard."

Logan laughed, leaning over to gently tongue the nipple. "I won't squeeze at all."

His hand landed on my panties, and he slid them down my legs slowly, growling at the sight of me naked.

"Logan," I whispered.

"Do you remember, Olivia?" I had no idea what he was talking about, but I shivered at the sound of my name. It rolled off his tongue like an aphrodisiac, making my body tingle in anticipation.

"Remember what?" I managed to find the words.

"Remember that day in your kitchen? When you asked me what I do when I go down on a woman?"

Oh dear God, the words alone nearly undid me, the ache I felt for him growing as I met his eyes. He looked at me with an intensity I hadn't seen since our first time together, and I guess it was like that all over again. A month without sex seemed like an eternity, given the constant need we both had to be together.

"Yes," I whispered.

Satisfied, he leaned over me, kissing my thighs, slowly, tenderly, taking his time while every part of me throbbed, needing his touch.

"I've missed you so much, baby," he said, and ran his tongue up towards my clit. I pushed forwards, willing him to lick me, play with me with his tongue, but he chuckled, shaking his head as he propped himself up.

"Aren't you impatient?"

"I thought you were too." I was gasping, begging my body to find the air it needed. The anticipation cramped within me, straining to break out. I remembered his words about his balls exploding and laughed out loud, feeling the same need within me.

"Are you okay?" His forehead wrinkled in concern.

"More than okay. I just need to be with you."

He said nothing more as he bent his head again, attacking my clit with his tongue in a frenzy. There was no way he was going to play fair tonight.

I exploded, crying out his name, stroking his hair as he slowed down. And then I did one of the worst possible thing when the love of your life is making love to you for the first time in a long time. I started crying.

"Liv? Are you okay? Did I hurt you?"

I shook my head as he moved beside me, pulling me into his arms. Tears rolled down my cheeks and he kissed them away, stroking my face with his thumb.

"I just love being with you," I whispered. "I'm so hormonal and stupid right now."

"Never stupid," he said. I looked into his eyes and all I could see was concern.

"I'm sorry."

"You never have to say you're sorry for feeling. Hell, the day you don't feel anything, then I'll be worried. You just had a baby, and you finally feel settled, and you settled me, Liv, more than I ever thought possible. What keeps me going during the day is the thought of coming home to you at night. And I plan on doing that for the rest of my life."

I tried to find the air to fill my lungs, and struggled as the tears flowed. His embrace tightened around me and I closed my eyes, inhaling deeply as his scent overwhelmed me. I felt safe—loved.

"Here, take a look." He sat up, unwrapping the bandage that covered his bicep. I saw my name first, and then my children's names listed on his arm, one under another. Olivia, Jack, Thomas, Chloe. "This. This is what you mean to me. You've been under my skin since I met you, and I wanted to show the world. Nothing else matters but you and our children. I know I'm not the boys' father, but I might as well be, for all the attention *he* pays to them. I don't consider them to be any different than Chloe in that regard."

I traced around the tattoo with my finger, still fighting the tears that just kept coming. "I never really loved until I found you, and I never felt loved until I found you," I said.

"That's because your ex is a fucking idiot. He threw away the warmest, most gentle, sexy woman I know. I know you went through a lot of heartache before me, but I'm kind of glad that you did. It gave me the chance to find you, and to love you."

"Logan ..."

He kissed me with a hunger that I recognised. I felt it too—the desperate need to have him, to be one with him. I wanted him deep inside me, connected to me in a way no one else ever would be. He was it.

"We're forever, baby."

Trailing kisses across my face, down my cheek, until he gently sucked on my neck, he moved over me, thrusting against me so I could feel how hard he was, pressing against me when all I wanted was him inside.

"Now," I whispered.

"Anything my beautiful girl wants." He grinned, sliding his underpants down his legs, and repositioning himself to push into me.

I closed my eyes, him filling me, his groan in my ear telling me he felt the same way I did. We were one again, and nothing had ever felt sweeter.

"Better?" he asked. He ran his tongue from my shoulder up my neck as I nodded, closing my eyes, my heart racing at the joy I felt at being his again.

"I love you, Olivia."

I opened my eyes to see him looking at me, running his gaze across my features, taking all of me in.

"I love you too," I whispered. He bent his head, brushing my lips with his. His pace slowed, and we gazed at each other, lost in the moment.

Running my finger around his tattoo, I smiled. We were so important to him that this was his offering to show how much he loved all of us.

"My heart," he whispered.

He tensed, and his eyes glazed over as the moment overtook him. He groaned, thrusting hard one last time, and I lifted my hand to his face, tracing down his cheek and round to his chin.

Kissing my nose, he grinned, rolling onto his side and pulling me in to his arms. I closed my eyes, settling in his embrace.

"Tired?" he asked.

"Always." I laughed. "But, I'll always have time for this."

"What were you doing when I came in? Standing in front of the mirror with your pants open like that?"

"I was trying to do them up, but I'm still too fat."

He sighed. "You had a baby four weeks ago. The last thing you should be thinking about is your weight. Besides, you're beautiful just the way you are."

Logan ran his hand down my body until it rested on my belly. "This was where my child grew. I don't care if you can't get back into your jeans yet, or if you ever do. You're beautiful, Liv."

"How did I ever find someone so perfect?" I asked.

"I ask myself that question every single day," he said, leaning in to kiss me, his soft lips telling a story he didn't need words for.

I turned, hugging him tight. "I love how you make me feel."

"How do I make you feel?"

"Like I'm the most special woman in the world."

Gently, he pushed me away, lifting my chin with his index finger. "Because you are."

34

THE LAST PERSON I ever expected to see on my doorstep was Evan. I'd started the divorce proceedings a while ago, so that Logan and I could get on with our lives, but I guess in typical Evan fashion, he'd just gotten around to doing something.

I let him in to the living room to talk and he sat on the couch, looking around.

"Nice place you have here."

"Better than the shitty little apartment we'd been living in."

He nodded. "You look good, Olivia. Put on a bit of weight, but otherwise you look good."

I couldn't say the same for him. The dark marks under his eyes showed lack of sleep, and his shirt was baggier than he used to wear them, hiding the beginnings of a paunch at a guess.

"Uh thanks. You haven't really changed."

"How are things?"

I shook my head. "Seriously? What are you actually here for, Evan?"

"I want to see my kids."

"The ones you walked out on?"

The silence was awkward as we looked at each other, before a gurgle came through the baby monitor, followed by a loud squawk.

"Excuse me, Evan. There's the reason why I've put on a bit of weight," I said, putting on a fake smile to show my annoyance.

I carried Chloe back to the living room, clucking at her as I went. She calmed in my arms and I sat down, not sure if I felt comfortable feeding her in front of Evan. Then I realised I didn't care; this was my house.

She fed hungrily, and I rocked her as the door opened. Logan came in, rubbing his eyes, clad in shorts and a singlet. His muscular arms looked huge when he dressed like that, and the tattoos down them were enough to intimidate most people.

"Morning, babe. This little one up already?"

"Did she wake you?"

He leaned over, tickling Chloe under the chin.

"I was lying there wondering when you were coming back to bed." He grinned, and noticed Evan sitting on the couch. "Aren't you ..."

"Logan, you remember Evan?"

"Oh." He just stood, looking at Evan. Jack and Thomas came running in from the yard. Logan had been out there most of the day before building them a playhouse. They were in the midst of setting it up, having raided the linen closet and stripping all the spare pillows from the beds.

"Logan! Are you coming out to see the house? We made it awesome," Jack said, grabbing at his hand.

"Not just yet, mate. I just got out of bed. I've got to have coffee and wake up first."

"Awww," said Thomas.

"Is this Thomas?" Evan asked. "Thomas, do you remember me?"

Thomas just looked at him blankly. As far as he was concerned, Logan was his dad.

"Jack?" Evan smiled at him.

Jack looked at Logan. "Can you come out?"

"In a little while, bud. Want to say hi to your dad?" Logan asked.

Jack looked back at Evan before turning away and running out the back door.

"Jack," I called. Thomas followed behind.

"Should have expected that, I guess." Evan said, the forlorn look in his eyes telling me just how much that had pained him.

"If you want to go out the back and try again, you're more than welcome," said Logan. I looked at him, surprised he was being so pleasant. "I mean, you are their dad."

Evan shook his head. "Maybe another day. I don't want to push them."

"To be honest, I'm surprised that you're even here," I said.

He shrugged. "I got the divorce papers, then got kicked out of the house when I didn't want to sign them straight away. Donna thought I was clinging onto the past, but I wanted to make sure you were okay."

"What if I wasn't?" The words hung in the air as he looked between Logan and I.

"I don't know to be honest." He laughed nervously. "I just felt like I should check on you."

I stared at him. "When did you get a conscience as far as I was concerned?"

"Olivia, don't make this any worse, please. It made me think of you and the boys and I had to see for myself." He looked up at Logan. "I can see you're well looked after, and with the little one ... I'll go back home and sign the papers."

"Thank you," I said.

"We appreciate it," said Logan, sitting on the couch beside me. He placed his hand on my knee and I smiled at him. We were showing a united front against the man who had deserted me.

Evan didn't stay long, just long enough to see we were okay, apparently. I wondered how bad his relationship with Donna was if he'd taken the time to seek me out. But then again, I didn't really care. He'd made his choice.

"I'll walk you out," I said as he made a move to go. I just wanted to see him leave, but Logan reached over, taking Chloe into his arms and smiling at me reassuringly.

I trailed behind him. A beat up old Toyota sat in the driveway, and he walked to it, turning as he reached the door.

"It was good to see you again. I know we made a lot of mistakes, but I'm glad to see you happy."

We made mistakes? I was not about to pick a fight with him if he was about to sign the divorce papers.

"I think you'll be fine, Liv. That Logan really loves all of you."

I smiled. "Very much so."

"I saw what he had tattooed on his arm. A man doesn't just tattoo people's names on himself if he doesn't care. He had everyone. You, Jack, Thomas, the little one ..."

I nodded, and watched as he got in the car, backing down the driveway and waving before driving away.

I knew who got the better deal.

"PFFT." Carly ran across the backyard, her arms stretched out as she pretended to be a plane. Thomas was right behind her, a bigger plane, but making just as much noise.

I loved how he doted on the two-year-old, and just knew he'd be the same with his sister as she grew older. Andrew and Maddy were over for dinner, and despite the age difference between our children, they all got along famously.

Logan and Andrew struggled to put up a tent for the kids to play in, and I idly wondered if they'd ever notice what they'd done wrong.

"Think we should tell them?" Maddy nudged my arm.

I turned, grinning at her. "You noticed it too?"

"Yeah. They might have more luck if they turn it up the other way."

We giggled, and Logan looked back at me, one eyebrow raised.

"Should I go and put them out of their misery?" Maddy asked.

"Go on. We'll be here all night otherwise. I'll check on dinner."

I walked back into the house and opened the oven door. Taking a deep breath, I smiled at the sight of the roast beef, browned to perfection, and the potatoes roasted in beef fat nearly done. It was nice to be able to take the time to feed my family, not rush as I used to do.

Standing, I looked back out the window. The tent was already up and Andrew was talking to Maddy, with no sign of Logan. She had her hands on her hips as if telling him off, and I couldn't help but smile at the look on his face. The adoration he had for his wife was clear from his grin.

Warm hands landed on my waist, and I tilted my head while Logan nuzzled my neck.

"I bet you knew that tent part was upside-down."

I laughed. "Might have done."

"You and Maddy could have saved us about half an hour putting the damn thing up."

He wrapped his arms tight around me, pressing his body against mine. "I know it's the kids that want to play in the tent, but do you want to play in it with me later?"

I leaned back against him, chuckling. "Maybe."

"After our guests are gone, and the children are in bed, it's a date," he whispered.

A chill ran up my spine as he kissed my neck and let me go. I turned toward him. He walked to the doorway before turning around.

"Love you," I said.

"Love you too." His lips were turned up slightly, his eyes so full of affection that my heart swelled to look at him.

"Dinner's nearly ready. Give me ten and we'll be ready to eat."

"I'd rather eat you," he said, waggling his eyebrows at me before disappearing out the door. I rolled my eyes and returned to the counter to finish getting the meal ready. Even so, I grinned to myself as I took out the dinner plates.

"Need a hand?" Maddy stood in the doorway, a smirk on her face.

"I'm just setting the table. The food is nearly ready if you want to help me here."

She took the plates from me while I gathered the cutlery.

"I figured the kids could just sit at the table with us. I'll just grab some cushions from the living room."

She laughed. "My Little Miss Independent will like that."

I followed her as she walked around the table, setting the cutlery beside the plates.

Logan appeared in the doorway, Chloe in his arms.

"This little one just woke up. Want me to change her nappy?"

"Yes please." I walked over to him, chucking her under the chin as she grinned at me.

"Aww little baby, I can do it if you want. Then I get to have a snuggle." Maddy had Chloe off Logan in a moment and I laughed as he stood there, his hands held as if she were still in them.

I bit down on my bottom lip, trying not to laugh at the look of utter disbelief on his face. "That's *my* daughter, Maddy. Don't you have one of your own to snuggle?" He looked at me, gaping and shaking his head. "Liv?"

"Don't look at me. I'm going to serve up dinner."

I laughed, looking over at Maddy, standing over the change table as she changed Chloe's nappy. Shaking my head, I walked back into the kitchen, retrieving the roast from the oven and placing it on the chopping block to carve.

Logan came up behind me, wrapping his arms around my waist. "Aren't you going to defend my honour? I didn't wake Chloe up to play with Maddy."

"You woke Chloe? I thought she was already awake." I turned my head back towards him, looking at him with one eyebrow raised.

"Caught me," he whispered, leaning closer.

"You're so naughty." I laughed as he nuzzled my neck.

"You two should get a room," Maddy said from the doorway, rocking my baby on her hip and looking right at home.

"Excuse me," said Logan, "we've got a whole house. Just gotta get rid of the interlopers."

She laughed, shaking her head as Andrew walked in.

"Who do you have there?" he asked, tickling Chloe. She grinned, waving her arms excitedly. It wouldn't be long until those two had another child from the way they clucked over her.

"Isn't she gorgeous? We should have another one."

I had a silent chuckle. Maddy never was one for holding back, and I had to give Andrew credit for not really being all that surprised. He nodded at her, looking at her in that way that spoke volumes.

"How on earth do you put up with it, Andrew?" Logan asked.

I flicked him with the tea towel, laughing as he slid out of my way, looking at me in the same way Andrew looked at Maddy. My heart fluttered and other parts of me burned for him to be near me.

Later.

THE HOUSE WAS silent with all the children asleep and our guests gone.

"Meet you in the tent," Logan whispered as I went up to check one more time.

I came back down the stairs and looked out the back, spotting the torchlight flickering through the tent door. Shaking my head, I laughed, going out the back door to the deck and poking my head inside, waving a small white box at him.

"What are you doing?" he asked.

"I brought the baby monitor so we could listen out for the kids. I know we're only on the deck, but it's safer."

Logan grabbed my hand, pulling me down on the makeshift bed of sleeping bags.

"You're so responsible," he said.

"Someone has to be."

I put the monitor at the edge of the tent, and he pushed me gently onto my back, leaning over me on his elbow.

"Why are we out here?"

He shrugged. "I just thought it might be fun. Quick camping holiday by ourselves."

Tracing down my face with his hand, he drew his thumb across my lips. A bolt of electricity passed between us, and that familiar ache between my legs began as I closed my eyes and kissed his hand.

"I'll never stop wanting you," he whispered. He leaned over, kissing my cheek, trailing his lips down to my neck while his hand moved to my breasts.

Tears gathered in my eyes as he raised his head to kiss my lips, pressing his to mine so softly and tenderly. He loved me more than anyone had loved me, except for my children. This man made me complete, was the other half of me.

"Olivia," he said.

Just the way he said it sent shivers through me. Whatever had brought me to this moment, all the good times and the bad, they had all been worth it to find him.

His mouth claimed mine and I kissed him back with all that I had. He needed to see how much I loved him, how much I loved being with him.

He tugged at my dress, and I sat as he lifted it over my head, reaching behind me to unhook my bra.

I lay down, and he kissed each breast. "I love you more than anything," he whispered. He ran his tongue over my skin and I closed my eyes. Logan pulled at my panties, and I helped pull them down my legs, lying naked beside him.

"You're just so damn beautiful. I spend all day thinking about doing this with you."

I ran my fingers down his shirt, lifting the hem and he grinned, sitting up to pull it off. I ran my hand over his chest, feeling his soft skin, the patch of light hair across the middle. He was perfection.

"I don't know if I can wait," he said.

"Hurry up then," I whispered, pulling him back down to kiss me. I wanted to taste his kiss, feel his tongue press into my mouth with the urgency that was him needing to be inside me. Just as I needed it too.

He pressed fingers into me, and I gasped as he thrust them in and out until he was happy I was ready. Discarding his pants, he moved on top, pressing himself to me as he slid inside. Each movement filled me with a new sensation of joy, and I raked the ground, the groundsheet crinkling in my hands, pushing my hips to meet him.

Logan kissed my throat, taking gentle nips as we moved as one.

"I never thought life could be so perfect," he whispered. "In a million years, I never dreamed I'd find anyone who loved me, believed in me, wanted everything I did."

"Don't. You'll make me cry."

"Olivia Grant, you cry all you want. I know it's because I make you happy. And I'll go on making you happy for the rest of my life if you want me to."

He linked fingers with me above my head, kissing my lips, grinding himself against me and I struggled to keep my eyes open.

Our eyes met and I watched as his face contorted, never taking my gaze off him as he groaned, releasing inside me.

"Damn it. I swore I'd always make you come first." He laughed, rolling over.

"I think I can excuse you." I snuggled into him, and he ran his fingers down my back.

"Let's get married, Liv. I want you to be my wife. There's nothing stopping us now."

Tears rolled down my cheeks and he kissed them away, the way he always did. "I think, Mr Mitchell, that I would very much like to be your wife."

And then he kissed my lips, selling the deal we'd just made.

This was perfection.

I woke with a start as the sound of Chloe crying came wailing over the baby monitor.

Logan laughed softly beside me. "Give you a fright?"

"I didn't know I'd fallen asleep."

We were spooned together, his warm body pressed against mine, and reluctantly I pulled myself away, slipping my clothes back on before heading back inside. She'd be looking for her 3am feed. I glanced at the clock in the hall. Yep, bang on 3am. That kid had a built-in alarm clock.

She let out a scream as I entered the room. If I didn't get to her fast enough she'd be inconsolable, and I gathered her into my arms, rocking her until she quietened.

A small sniffle and bleat let me know she was still waiting, and I settled into the rocking chair to feed her, closing my eyes as she latched on and began to drink.

"Love watching you guys," Logan said from the doorway.

We were surrounded by stars and moons, projected from the nightlight he'd installed. In the soft glow, he came toward us, kneeling at my feet as I gently rocked our daughter. I thought I'd felt all the love I could, but every time we were together it grew.

Chloe snorted and snuffled, gulping down the milk as if it were the last time she'd ever be fed, and Logan stroked her head, grinning up at me.

"You get to bed. I'll be there soon," I whispered.

"I'm in no hurry," he replied, gazing down at our daughter with all the love he had for her.

I leaned back, closing my eyes again.

Bliss.

35

MY HANDS SHOOK as I read it. 'Dissolution of Marriage' it read. This was it. I was free of the past and I could move on with my future. Our future. Our family's future.

Evan hadn't made contact again. He'd just signed the papers and now I got the notification I'd been waiting for. Maybe one day he could have a relationship with his children again. He'd shown some regret, but hadn't reached out to Jack and Thomas a second time.

I wouldn't stop him. He was their father.

Logan sat in the living room, Chloe on his knee, and a boy on either side. Thomas and Jack were both reading, and Chloe was all grins and dribble, her father tickling her under the chin while chattering away to her in baby-talk.

Every time I saw them together like this I was pretty sure my ovaries would explode, and I just knew another baby would be on the way in the not-too-distant future.

"Guess what I've got?" I said, swooping down to grab Chloe from his arms and handing him the piece of paper.

Logan scanned the text. "Liv, this is awesome. When do you want to get married?"

I grinned. "I should have known you didn't want to wait."

He smirked. "I know you don't want to wait either."

Chloe dribbled on my hand, and I laughed, wiping it with her bib. She smiled up at me, and I kissed her cheek. "Hey, baby. How would you like to be my bridesmaid?"

"Jack and Thomas will have to be my groomsman." Logan looked at me with so much love. A love that grew every day, never stagnating or growing old.

"Just us, your mother and my mother," I said. "Does she still have Kat living at her place? She won't want to come too, will she?" I grimaced at the thought.

Logan shook his head. "I haven't asked and Kat hasn't contacted me. No one is going to be at the wedding we both don't want. I do think we need to invite Andrew and Maddy, though. She'd never forgive us."

I laughed. "I think you're right there. Then I want to invite Rebecca."

Logan rolled his eyes. "You know this is where it starts."

"Where what starts?"

He put his hand up, as if to shield his face. "Bridezilla."

"Ha ha. As if. I'd marry you in jeans if I had to."

"I have been thinking about venue. What about the park across the road? There are some lovely trees and that pond with all the flowers around it. Close and easy to get you back home." He waggled his eyebrows at me, and I grinned, knowing what was behind that.

"Naughty."

"Always." His eyes darkened with desire as we gazed at each other, lost in the look that no one could break into.

Except for Chloe.

Her little foot poked my side, and I grinned at her. "I'm sorry, sweetie. Is Mummy not paying enough attention?"

Little arms and legs waving excitedly told me just how happy she was, or hungry. Even after having three, it was still hard to tell what babies wanted. But, having recently discovered food, I was pretty sure that was what she was after.

"Is it time for dinner?" I asked.

She kicked and waved some more, and I carried her to the dining table, placing her in her high chair. It was a beautiful thing, watching her grow so fast, even though I wanted her to stay a baby for as long as possible.

I went into the kitchen to get her food, already prepared and waiting. By the time I got back, Logan sat next to her at the table, tickling her under the chin again.

"She's going to start giggling any day, aren't you, Chloe?" he said, nodding at her.

She chortled, kicking her legs as she chatted at him.

"You'll look so pretty for the wedding, won't you, miss?" He took the bowl of vegetables from me, and started spooning them to our delighted daughter.

A snorting noise came from her, as if she thought it were the funniest thing in the world. Laughing with Daddy.

I BEGAN MAKING plans at the start of the week.

We knew the venue and who to invite. Kat proved to be a non-issue as she'd found a job and moved out of Beth's place. By all accounts she was safe and sober and Logan's relief was obvious.

Neither of us wanted anything too fussy, so it would be a quick wedding across the road and then back here for a meal with the people we loved. The sooner the better as far as we were concerned.

On Wednesday, the latest car Logan had been working on had been a tough fix, and he called me to let me know he'd be late.

"Sorry, babe. I'll be home as soon as I've finished. It's being picked up first thing, so best to get it done tonight."

"It's okay. You let me know. That's all that matters."

He growled down the phone. "I'll make it up to you, Mrs Soon-To-Be Mitchell."

A warm glow built in me as his words made my heart beat faster.

"Love you," I said.

"Love you too. I'll be as quick as I can. Promise."

A promise I knew he would keep.

With the boys in bed and Chloe fast asleep, I sat in front of the television for a while. I hated the house being so quiet, but it would give me a chance to start working on my wedding present for Logan. An idea that had been brewing for a while.

I went to the table, opened the laptop and started to write. The words flowed faster and easier than I had thought they would, and I got lost in the story that was us. Me and him. The man who gave my life meaning again, who slotted into my family as if he'd been there the whole time. The man who had given me the world and asked for nothing but my love in return.

That was my Logan.

I was in tears when he found me, and he knelt beside my chair, all frowny and worried.

"What's wrong?"

"Nothing," I sniffed.

He ran his fingers down the side of my face, tilting my chin until I met his eye.

"I'm writing."

A smile snaked across his face, growing in intensity as he studied me "Glad to hear it. Not so glad you're upset."

"I'll be fine. I just get emotional sometimes."

He kissed my forehead, my nose, and leaned in to kiss my lips. "Let's go to bed. I'll make up for being late."

I threw my arms around his neck. "Just hold me."

"Hey, hey, hey," he whispered as I clung to him, the tears starting again. "Olivia. What's wrong?"

"I just love you so much."

"I love you too. More than anything else in the whole world. I never thought I'd find my soul mate, and there she was. I knew it as soon as I spent time with you. Something felt so right. More right than anything else."

That just made me cry harder, and he grasped my arms, releasing himself from my grip.

"Come on. I'll hold you until you stop crying, and then I'll make up for being late."

I nodded, unable to say anything else, and he helped me up.

And then he kept his promise about making it up to me.

36

WE LAY NAKED IN BED, *his body pressed against mine as he kissed my lips, my neck, every part of me that responded to him. I curled my leg around his, pulling him as close as he could be.*

"Olivia," he whispered. I was putty in his hands, melting into him as he possessed me, and we tried our best to quench the thirst we had for one another. But that would never happen. The more we were together, the more we wanted.

It was the never-ending need for one another that kept us so close. It fed our love, the love that will last for the rest of our lives. Of that I'm sure.

With Logan, I will never have to worry about whether he's coming home or not. Every morning he's in bed with me, and I lie in his arms knowing that I am the only woman who does. Every night he was the most amazing father, showing his love to all our children without favour.

And then he was mine, all mine. There was no one to take him away from me, and his heart was far too entangled with mine for there ever to be.

This was it.

We were forever.

I took a deep breath as the tears rolled down my face, threatening my makeup. Today I would give him this book as a wedding gift. The story of our love—the story of our life together.

Taking one last look in the mirror, I patted down my curls and stroked the foundation back in place to cover the streaks the tears had left behind.

My last wedding had been a rushed registry service thing with just Evan's mother in attendance. In the park were people who cared about us, loved us. Everything was perfect.

I turned around when the knock on the door came. "Come in."

Andrew poked his head around the door as he opened it. "You ready?"

"I guess so."

"You know, it's never too late to make a break for it." He gave me that cheeky grin that Maddy adored, and I was struck by just how many good people I was surrounded by now. As difficult as it had been, I still maintained a wary distance with Maddy. Maybe I'd give in and be closer friends with her, let Logan win that one.

"As if that's going to happen."

I stood and he crossed the room, coming toward me. "You look gorgeous. Logan is one lucky man."

"I like to think so."

"Well, you can't get any better than him either. Except for me, of course."

I laughed. "Oh, of course."

"Let's get you married, then."

"Thank you, Andrew. Thanks for helping me out today."

He nodded. "It's no problem at all. I wasn't too sure about Logan at first, given how close he'd been with Maddy once upon a time, but he's a good guy. And you two seem really happy."

I smoothed down my dress with my palms, making any final adjustments. This was it.

"We are. You know, he told me he knew it was love when he realised he looked at me the same way Maddy looks at you."

He held out his arm for me to take, and I looped mine around his.

"Maddy is rather hard to miss. She did kind of stand in my way when I first met her."

I cocked my head. "Do I want to know?"

Andrew laughed. "As I once told Logan, I never stood a chance. She has been all I see since I met her."

The tears were creeping back and he shook his head. "Don't you start crying now. At least, not until your husband is there to wipe your tears for you. Me doing it would be weird."

Laughing so hard I snorted wasn't part of the plan, but that just got Andrew laughing too. Hopefully everyone was too far away to hear us laughing over something so silly.

"Come on," he said gently.

Arm in arm, he led me down the stairs and out across the road. Under a tree near the pond, Logan stood, Jack and Thomas at his side.

Maddy was right up the front with Carly beside her, my mother next to her, Chloe in her arms. Logan's mother stood there too, beaming at me as I walked toward them. The only person who hadn't made it was Logan's brother. He was overseas and had already booked his return later in the year. We hadn't wanted to wait.

I met Logan's gaze, and his eyes told me how he was feeling. Andrew stayed with me all the way to Logan's side before patting my hand and letting me go.

"You look beautiful," Logan said, taking hold of my hand and squeezing it tight. I looked down at my dress. Cream in colour and flowing to my ankles, it clasped in at my reclaimed waist and swept up into a halter neck covered in lace. I felt amazing in it.

"Thank you." I squeezed back, and snuggled up to his side as we exchanged our vows.

Everything was perfect.

OUR HONEYMOON WOULD WAIT a few weeks until the school holidays when we could all go away together. Nothing seemed more perfect than a family trip for us.

After photos in the park, we all walked back across the road to the house, our big, extended family on our way to celebrate with a barbecue dinner in the back yard. It seemed the perfect end to a perfect day.

I'd taken Chloe from Mum, and Logan walked across the road hand in hand with the boys. Seeing him warmed my heart the same way it had all that time ago when we'd crossed a different road.

Andrew had already lit up the barbecue, and the smell of steak and lamb chops hit us as we walked in the door.

"I'm hungry," Jack moaned.

"From the smell of that, dinner's not far away," Logan said, ruffling his hair.

Jack took off toward the backyard, Thomas close behind him. Chloe was nearly asleep, her head flopping onto my shoulder.

"I'll take her upstairs and feed her. I think she's out for the count," I said.

Logan leaned over and kissed me. "I think once these boys have something to eat, they'll be the same. Then we can get on with our night."

"The best part," I murmured.

"Night, night, sweetheart," Logan said, stroking Chloe's hair. Her eyes fluttered as if saying goodnight, and I stole one last kiss before ascending the stairs.

I placed Chloe on the change mat, fussing over her as I changed her nappy and pulled her pyjamas on. She yawned, her cherubic little face screwing up, and her hands flapped as she grumped. She was so tired.

"Time for sleep, little one," I whispered.

I nestled into the rocking chair, lifting her to my breast to feed and closing my eyes as she suckled hungrily.

"Did you know, today was one of the best days of my life?" I whispered. "Right up there with you being born, and your brothers. We're all going to live happily ever after, Chloe. You, me, your father, the boys ... I never thought I'd ever be this happy."

Her body slumped in my arms as sleep took over, and I rocked, nearly falling asleep myself. This was my bliss.

After tucking her into her cot, I went back downstairs and looked out onto the deck. Andrew and Logan stood by the barbecue, drinking beer and flipping the food. My mother sat at the table with Logan's mother, deep in conversation.

And Maddy? Maddy was lying out on the grass getting tickled by Carly and my boys, their laughter a joy to listen to. She was giving as good as she was getting, and I watched as she grabbed Thomas, pulling him into a bear hug.

"She's so good with the kids." Logan walked towards me, wrapping his arm around my waist and pulling me in to kiss my temple.

"They are just going to crash tonight."

"I believe that's why she's playing with them. Wearing them out so we get zero disturbance. Not that Chloe will care."

I snuggled into him. "Maybe I should spend some more time getting to know her. It's always just been a bit weird, with her being your ex."

His chest vibrated with laughter. "I understand. But I think you know now more than ever how much I love you, Mrs Mitchell."

As I met his gaze, I couldn't help but grin. "Love you calling me that."

"Mrs Olivia Mitchell."

I giggled, and Maddy looked over at me with one eyebrow raised, a grin on her face a mile wide and a look in her eye that told me just how happy she was for us.

Someone was missing, and I looked around, counting everyone. "Where's Rebecca?"

"She said she was going to leave us in peace. I pointed out everyone else was staying for dinner, but she said she didn't want to get in the way of ..." Logan paused, leaning in to murmur in my ear. "... your sexy times."

I let out a loud laugh, and Mum looked back over her shoulder at me. It was still unusual to have her in my life again, but we were slowly adjusting and getting to know one another again. It took time to rebuild a collapsed bridge.

Here we were though, surrounded by the people who loved us the most, and this was the best wedding present of all. To know we had their support felt better than I ever could have described. My heart was fulfilled. And the best thing of all?

The love of my life, my soul mate, my every-other-descriptive-word-I-could-come-up with stood by my side, and I knew that he'd be with me for the rest of our lives.

WE HAD SAT at the table, feeding each other, completely oblivious to everyone around us and when dinner was over, I tucked my tired boys into bed with hugs and kisses.

"Today was awesome, Mum," Jack said.

"It sure was, baby."

"Now Logan really is our dad."

I took a deep breath. "You guys are really lucky. You have two dads."

"Other dad doesn't visit us, though."

I smiled. "You didn't want to see him. Remember? But if one day you want to, that's fine too." I kissed him goodnight and went next door to Thomas's room.

Logan sat on the bed, pulling the blankets over him and leaning over to give him a kiss.

"Night, night, Thomas. Love you." He straightened up, and reached to brush the hair off Thomas's face.

"I love you too, Dad."

I watched as my husband's eyes filled with tears, and Thomas pushed off the blankets to sit up and hug him. His arms wrapped around Logan's neck, and Logan rubbed his back as Thomas squeezed him tight.

"Hey, got any of those hugs for me?" I asked.

Logan looked up at me, and held out an arm for me to go to. I leaned over and kissed Thomas's forehead.

"Love you, buddy. Night, night."

"Love you, Mum." Thomas let go of Logan, and laid back in the bed, pulling the blankets back up, his eyes so tired. Logan left the room first, and after another kiss I followed.

Logan stood outside the bedroom, leaning against the wall.

"Liv, I didn't tell him to call me that."

I rubbed his arm, pulling him into my embrace. "I know. He just loves you so much. So does Jack. If that's what he wants to call you, I don't have a problem with it. The door is always open for them to see Evan."

He nodded, hugging me tight. "I guess. Let's go get rid of our guests now so we can have some sexy newlywed times."

"I've got a present for you."

His jaw dropped. "I thought we decided no presents."

"I know. But I had this awesome idea, and I think you'll love it."

His mouth twisted into a sly smile. "Does it involve lots of lace and frilly things?"

"No."

Now his eyes narrowed. "Getting naked?"

"Eventually, but no." I grinned, feeling his body against mine and realising that our little cuddle was having an effect on him.

He growled, waggling his eyebrows. "Whatever it is, let's go empty the house."

By the time we returned to the living room, our guests had anticipated our wishes and were on the verge of leaving. Andrew had

Carly falling asleep on his shoulder, and he and Maddy stood as we walked into the room.

"We are going to go and get her to bed. Besides, we figure now the kids are asleep, you'll be wanting to be alone," Andrew said.

Logan nodded. "Thank you so much for coming, you two."

Maddy flung her arms around his neck, hugging him tight. "I'm so proud of you. Who ever thought we'd end up with the right people and still be friends?"

Logan laughed, kissing her hair. "Thanks, Maddy."

She stepped back, a knowing look on her face, and I wondered what was coming as she hugged me. "You best get your mothers out of here." She gave me the thumbs up, and I didn't even have to ask what she was referring to. Only Maddy could come out with that.

"Roger that," I whispered, chuckling as she let go.

Andrew led Maddy out, waving as he went, and Logan and I went in search of our mothers. They were in the kitchen, one washing dishes, the other drying, still talking.

"Hey you two," Logan said.

"We thought we'd get these done before we went. So you don't have to do them in the morning," Mum said.

I went over to her and kissed her cheek. "Thanks, Mum, but we were just going to stick them in the dishwasher."

"There's a dishwasher?" Beth said.

Logan and I looked at each other, laughing as I hugged my mother. "Oh well, we're nearly finished," she said.

"Don't worry about drying the last ones. Just leave them to drain," I said.

"Someone's anxious to start their wedding night," Beth said.

"Yeah. I am. So hurry up." Logan leaned in and kissed his mother on the temple. "Thank you for being here today. Both of you. We really loved that you were part of it."

"I'm very proud to be here," Mum said, and Beth nodded in agreement.

When we got to the door, Mum hugged me. "I love you, Olivia. I'm sorry I didn't say that enough when you were younger."

"I know, Mum. I love you too. I'm glad we worked things out."

"You've got a good man there. One who'll stay with you for a lifetime. I can't ask for anything more for you than that." I teared up as she gave me one last kiss.

"Have a good night," she whispered.

Oh, I will.

LOGAN WAITED for me while I was in the bathroom, taking off my dress and slipping on my nightgown. Nothing too over the top, but it was frilly and lacy, even though I knew I'd only be in it for about five seconds once he got his hands on me.

I picked up the parcel I'd taken in with me hidden among my other things. Hugging it tight, I kissed the ribbon around it.

"Our story," I whispered.

I'd sold stories to total strangers, had praise and not so good feedback. But there was only one person whose opinion mattered. One person who would ever read this.

Taking a deep breath, I opened the door. Logan sat in bed, and seeing him made my heart beat faster, the way it always did.

"Wow. You ... you always did take my breath away, Olivia."

Don't. You'll make me cry.

"Come here. Let me get that nightgown off you."

The urge to cry vanished as I laughed and I approached the bed, holding the gift out in front of me.

Logan cocked his head. "What's that?"

"I made you a thing."

"What kind of thing?"

"Open it and see."

I handed it over, slipping between the sheets beside him as he pulled at the bow, tearing open the wrapping paper.

When the paper came off, he turned it over in his hands. "You wrote another book? It's got your new name on it. Babe, that's awesome. Something Real by Olivia Mitchell."

"I wrote you a book," I said gently. "A one-off, never-to-be-repeated deal. Just like us."

He started to flick through the pages. "What is this?"

"Us. Our story. From the day we met through to now."

I watched his Adam's apple move as he swallowed hard. "Thank you. I love it," he whispered.

"I love you, Logan," I bent over to kiss his cheek.

He turned his head, dropping the book on the bed and pressing his lips to mine. "I love you too," he said.

His lips burned a trail down my neck as he pulled me close. "Why the hell did you wear that damn nightgown?"

I laughed. "Well, we are married now. We're not supposed to do the naughty stuff anymore."

Logan sat up, his eyes wide in mock horror. "What? No one told me that."

And he kissed me again, harder this time, stroking my body, bringing me the joy I always felt when I was with him.

And now I make the vow to love him for the rest of my life. The man who will always love me, will never desert me, will never leave me feeling stranded and wondering what to do.

With all my heart, I know that forever, we have something real.

REBECCA'S STORY IS NEXT.

After a nasty break up, Rebecca vowed no more serious relationships. Becoming friends with benefits with neighbour Elliot wasn't supposed to be anything other than fun. But Elliot revealing the secret he's keeping will change both their lives forever.

The Right One is Rebecca's story, and is available here

ALSO BY WENDY SMITH

Coming Home

Doctor's Orders

Baker's Dozen

Hunter's Mark

Teacher's Pet

A Very Campbell Christmas

Fall and Rise Duet

Falling

Rising

Fall and Rise - The Complete Duet

The Aeon Series

Game On

Build a Nerd

Bar None

Hollywood Kiwis Series

Common Ground

Even Ground

Under Ground

Rocky Ground

Coming soon Solid Ground

Stand alones

For the Love of Chloe

Only Ever You

The Friends Duet
Loving Rowan
Three Days

The Forever Series
Something Real
The Right One
Unexpected

Chances Series
Another Chance
Taking Chances

Lifetime Series
In a Lifetime
In an Instant
In a Heartbeat
In the End
At the Start

ABOUT THE AUTHOR

Wendy Smith is a multi-platform bestselling author, whose book In the End, written as Ariadne Wayne, was named one of Apple's best books of 2017. She lives with her two children and two cats in New Zealand where she bases her books because she loves living there. All her stories come with a quirky sense of humour, and she cries over everything.

Find me online
www.wendysmith.co.nz
wendy@wendysmith.co.nz

Milton Keynes UK
Ingram Content Group UK Ltd.
UKHW042144031224
452078UK00004B/443